nightplay

And Other Stories from the 1980s

Ed Molloy

OUTRUN PRESS

contents

ISBN: 978-0-9965996-4-1

Library of Congress Control Number: 2025937280

For Susan

a note to the reader

All stories were written and take place during the 1980s.

one
nightplay

July, 1983

MY WIFE ROLLED onto her side and faced the half-lit bookshelves on our bedroom wall. She stayed put for a moment, but it was only for a moment, and soon she was rolling onto her back once again, propping her pillow and then herself against the headboard of our bed. "Are you getting any sleep out there?"

"Not a chance." Her friend, Lisa, was sacked out on the living room couch, about a dozen feet from our open bedroom door. She wore only her underwear: a flesh-toned bra and a pair of matching panties. Our oscillating fan, set on the coffee table to the left of her, blew at the light-brown wings of her hairdo. She sipped from a tall glass of vodka and tonic. "It's almost midnight," she let us know. "How long do they go on down there?"

"Till Sunday," my wife said. "Unless they beat the crap out of each other first."

"That's what it sounds like now."

"No, listen. It sounds more like dancing." My wife tilted her head and considered it seriously. "It makes you wish they did beat each other up."

"I know." Lisa saluted us with her glass of liquor. "Let's hope, huh?"

My wife laughed and, to be sociable, so did I. Tonight would not be the first night, however, that one of the parties downstairs ended in a brawl. I could recall more than a few times the sounds of glass breaking against a wall, of a kitchen table being overturned or of a body being hurled across the room and tripping angrily to the floor. Those were the party fights my neighbor had with his friends. The fights with his wife were simpler, if somewhat sadder: the quick slurred voices of a young couple arguing, a face being slapped; a woman's frightened scream; another slap; another; and then a cry; and then there would be silence.

Tonight, though, was party night for my neighbor and silence was not a possibility. It was difficult to make out how many people were down there; judging by the sound of it, anywhere from eight to a dozen would be a good guess, most of them male and in their twenties and most of them feeling rather good about themselves. They made no effort to keep down their voices, nor did they hold back on the volume of the stereo. From our apartment above, over the half-drunk banter and rowdy laughter, we could hear the crisp bold brag of a rap tune they were playing, loud and funky: "Like that, y'all / Rap-a-dap, y'all / I'll rock your minds, y'all / Freak, freak."

It was enough to roll my wife over one more time. Again, she stayed put for a moment and then she propped herself back up, heaving an exhausted and painful sigh as she leaned her shoulders against our head-board. She held the pose, giving me a good long shot of her profile: the finely balanced nose, the serious gray eyes and the dark layered hair. She brushed a handful of it from her cheek and, beneath her breath, muttered a soft yet audible, "This stinks. . . ." The face that she displayed to me was an attractive one but it was a sad one, too, as if it had been sculpted by a man with a broken heart. She lifted her arm and placed the backs of her fingertips onto her forehead, sort of Blanche-Du Bois fash-ion, as she stared lifelessly, without hope, into my eyes.

I had to laugh. It was quite a show that she offered but, if she was dramatizing for my sake, her theatrics were wasted. I had no intention of stomping down the staircase to apartment 4E, cast-iron frying pan in hand, and ordering a roomful of boozed-up losers to *Pipe down*. I'd had my looks at our neighbor, Nicky Beale, and his tough-guy friends before and I knew what my chances with them would be. My pan and I would be sent packing back up the staircase in a minute, a barrage of beer cans and barbecued potato chips whizzing behind us.

Instead of making such a suggestion, however, my wife simply wiped the perspiration from her brow. "It's hot in here," she told me. She pulled at the top of her pink nightie. "And Lisa, somehow, managed to finagle the fan. Where is she anyway?" My wife peered into the living room but her friend was gone from the couch. The fan remained where it had been: on the coffee table, blowing its gentle breeze at an unappreciative wall. "She's probably in the kitchen, fixing herself another drink."

"Or downstairs," I said, "doing the Freak."

"Be nice. She might have gotten sick . . . Lisa? Are you alright?"

From the kitchen: "What?"

"Are you okay?"

"*Denise*," Lisa called out, over the voices, the music from the floor below, "you want me?"

"Is everything okay?"

"I could use some ice. Where do you keep it?"

"In the . . . where do you think I keep it? In the freezer, Dummy." My wife let out a quick laugh. "No. Wait. Check the kitty litter box. We usually keep a few extra cubes in there."

"What? No, I didn't. . . ." But, from the kitchen, Lisa, too, was laughing. "You must think I'm a jerk."

"A little tipsy, that's all. Anyway, come in here. We've got business to discuss."

Lisa hollered an answer, an amusing retort judging by the inflection of her voice, but her words were hard to decipher; the crowd from 4E had her drowned out. There was an argument going on. Someone named Theresa was warning someone named Carmine not to change the record. Carmine told Theresa, "Shut your hole" and changed it anyway. . . . "Young Ladies, if you're so inclined," the stereo blared, "I'd like you all to wiggle your behinds."

It was hopeless, I realized, any thought of sleep. There was the arguing, the horseplay, the wisecracking and the music; on top of it there was the clip-clopping of their dancing heels. This past April, for my wife's twenty-seventh birthday, her parents offered her a choice of gifts: a color

TV set or a heavy shag carpet similar to the one that had covered her bedroom floor when she was a teenager growing up in Ridgefield, Connecticut. My wife chose the carpet, hoping that it would insulate some of the racket from the weekend parties below. It didn't help, however; not on this particular night. From our bed, it seemed that I could hear every voice down there as loudly as I could hear my own. I could hear every belly laugh, every coarse, unfunny insult, every "Hump your mutha" and every "I'll bust your sister"; every bit of every dull, repetitive argument and, of course, every word, every bass note and every guitar pluck of every record that they played. They had been at it now for hours. Earlier this evening it was tolerable, just a few guys popping a few beers, swapping a few stories. But, every so often, the party would grow just a little louder and a little larger and by the time my wife had returned home from dinner with Lisa, the party, as it is, had shifted into overdrive.

That was at ten o'clock. It was midnight now and it was only getting louder. We were starting to feel the strain, too. My wife crossed the bedroom to our dresser and pulled the next-to-last Marlboro from a pack I had opened only that afternoon. She looked me over sideways as she lit the cigarette, then tossed back her head and blew a stream of smoke toward the ceiling. Her mood was different, soured. When she returned to bed, she sat upright, straight and stiff, and gave me her coldest, most somber look (what she and I often referred to as her "no-nonsense look"). She had an announcement for me: enough was enough, unless I had a better suggestion, she was going to call the police. "It's as simple as that," she said.

Her tone surprised me. She had been so chipper with Lisa just minutes before. "Denise," I said. I touched her shoulder and then gave her hand a paternal pat. "Police won't do any good."

"It'll shut them up."

"But they're our neighbors."

"You think they care about us?" She gave her cigarette a flick and stuck it back into her mouth, Bogart-style, letting its filter dangle from her lower lip. "I don't think they care about us. I don't think they care about anyone but themselves." She crossed her ankles and folded her arms beneath her breasts. She took another drag from the cigarette and stabbed it out in the ashtray, smoke exuding from both nostrils as she wiped the back of her neck.

If she was trying to intimidate me with her gun-moll routine she was missing the mark. Stretched alongside me in her baby doll nightgown and pink fluff ball slippers, she looked more like a model for Sealy Posturepedic than a hardened thug. "Maybe you're right," I said, "but we can't go calling the police on them."

"Then you suggest something."

"Alright, I suggest that we call the Swat Team." This was from Lisa. She stood at the bedroom doorway, her tanned, slender body swaying just slightly. There was a soft, pleasant glow to her face and a look of mischief in her cheerful brown eyes. "We'll tell them to bring grenades." She held two glasses of vodka and tonic; one, I assumed, was for my wife. "Good idea, no?" She walked cautiously towards our bed, careful not to spill a drop from either of the king-sized drinks she had prepared. She still wore only her underwear, the flesh-toned bra and matching panties.

"I wish that we could," my wife said, "but he won't even let me call the police." She jabbed a disgusted thumb in my direction, then took one of the drinks from Lisa, "Thanks," and stirred it with her finger. "I see you found the ice."

"Right where you said it'd be."

"In the cat box, huh?"

"I was going to scrape the litter off but then decided, *What the hell* . . . cheers." She clinked glasses with my wife. "Actually, it looks yummy." She sucked a cube between her lips and then played it around in her mouth. She had a face, it occurred to me, perfect for a television sitcom. She could play the naïve roommate or the secretary who's been around. "You know, I think we've really got something here."

My wife faked a shudder. "Yuck. You're terrible." She turned to me and gave a happy nudge. She was feeling better now; no hard feelings. "You want a beer or something, Michael? Join the party."

"Maybe later."

"It's no problem," Lisa said. "I'll get you one."

"Thanks. In a while."

"Okey doke. Tell me when." Lisa walked to the dresser. She made no bones about swiping the last cigarette from the pack of Marlboros and made no bones, either, about plopping herself down on the edge of the bed next to my bare feet. She lifted her heels onto the mattress and shimmied around to face my wife and me. "This is sort of cozy, huh?" An erect brown nipple, her left one, poked at the flimsy nylon of her bra. I felt sleazy spotting it, but I spotted it nonetheless.

"Can I get you a shirt?" I said. "A pajama top or something?" The thought of my wife or Lisa noticing the nipple bothered me.

"Are you serious?" Lisa asked. "It must be ninety degrees in here. Look at me. I'm sweating as it is." She started to reveal her underarms for my inspection but, with her hands raised halfway into the air, she remembered her etiquette and pulled them back down. "Sorry."

My wife laughed, but not at Lisa. She took a gulp from her drink and then gave me a squeeze beneath the bed sheet. "Don't tell me you're embarrassed, Michael. When did you ever mind seeing a pretty girl in underwear?"

"Leave him alone," Lisa said. "I think it's cute."

"So are your tits. That's why it surprises me."

Lisa crossed her arms in front of her. "Let's leave my tits out of this, okay? Before *I* start getting embarrassed." She turned to me then. "Is Denise like this all the time?"

"I'm worse," my wife butted in. "You should see me sometimes. I'm baaaad!"

This was hardly the case, however. She was out of character right now; they both were. They rarely drank together but, on the occasions that they did, they could become silly very quickly; they could also become crude, sentimental, sexy, childish—you name it. "I think I'll have that beer now," I said.

Lisa shot me a look. "Well, get it yourself!" Then she busted into a laugh. "I'm sorry. Kidding. Just kidding."

"I'll get it for him," my wife said. She took another swig of her drink. "I have to pee anyway."

Lisa's eyes brightened, appearing ready to flash onto another joke (some *let's pee in his beer* joke) but nothing seemed to come to her. "Are you sure," she asked my wife. "Really, I was just kidding."

"No, I've got to go to the bathroom anyway. You want to come for the ride?"

Lisa rose from the bed with my wife. It was no surprise that she chose to go with her. She and I got along decently but, without my wife nearby, our dynamics changed. "I just want to keep an eye on her," Lisa explained. "So she doesn't slither downstairs and crash the party."

"Yeah, right," my wife said. "Can you imagine? Crashing their party in my pink nightie. And you in your underwear. Trying to act all nonchalant and everything. We'd blend in just . . ."

. . . and they went sauntering off into the living room, Lisa splashing a bit of her drink as she and my wife bumped shoulders. "Watch it."

"You watch it."

I let out a chuckle loud enough for them to hear me if they cared to and then rolled over and waved goodbye to the backs of their heads as they separated for opposite corners of the apartment. I slid an arm beneath my pillow and, with nothing, really, better to do, I listened once again to the sounds from apartment 4E.

The music down there hadn't changed much; if anything, it had slipped a decibel or two louder. The conversation, though, had quieted some; there wasn't as much shouting as before, nor as much laughter. Someone was rattling on about an early model Thunderbird he wanted to sell: the body was in "mint condition" and the engine, he said, was "friggin' primo." A smooth-talking dude named Junior was trying to "procure an adequate sum of currency" for a beer run to the local delicatessen; no one, however, trusted him to return with either the beer or the money. There was a card game of sorts going on in the corner of the apartment just below my bed: a few guys teaching the rules of poker to a loud, uninteresting girl named Valerie. "This is stuuuuppid" was one of Valerie's frequent expressions. "Would'ja get off me?" and "You pig!" were a couple more. She sounded to me as though her looks were on the unpleasant side, and I pictured her, in my mind, to be wearing too much makeup and an overkill of some bargain brand perfume. Just the type, I figured, for Nicky Beale and his T-shirted friends.

I reached to the nightstand for a Kleenex and wiped the sweat from my face. A warm, faint wind was wheezing its way through the open bedroom window: it blew at me with all the lung power of an asthmatic kitten. It was too hot to stay in bed. I got up and stretched my arms toward the ceiling. Out of modesty for Lisa, I was wearing a pajama top and a pair of gym shorts. I doubted now if Lisa cared one way or the other about seeing my bare chest. I pulled off the top and tossed it into the hamper by the dresser and went to the closet for the "emergency pack of cigarettes" that my wife always kept stashed there.

She had a few peculiarities, my wife: hiding cigarettes from herself was one of them. I didn't know where to look first. The closet was a small one, six feet across by two feet deep, holding mostly my wife's things, but the cigarettes could have been hidden anywhere inside of it. Aligned neatly across the top shelf were a bunch of oddball hats that my wife had never worn and never would wear. Her old, boxed wedding dress was standing upright against the corner wall. I checked there first but without any luck. Another box (her box of "important papers") was jammed against the opposite wall. Again, there were no cigarettes. A pile of sneakers, loose sandals, shoes and boots filled the rest of the closet floor, and a mixed wardrobe of sweaters, jeans and jackets hung from wire hangers, all packed in tightly against one another. I frisked down a few of the jacket pockets and peaked inside a couple of the shoes. I shuffled the hats around and then went back to the jackets. Before I had the chance to search any further, however, my wife appeared at the bedroom doorway. She held a bottle of Budweiser in one hand, a glass of vodka and tonic in the other. "Caught you," she said.

"Trying to steal Denise's emergency pack, huh? Let's spank him." Lisa stood behind her. She, too, was holding a drink.

"It's his first offense. We'll let him go this time." My wife handed me the beer and then made herself comfortable on the bed. She sat against the headboard; her long firm legs stretched lengthwise across the mattress.

I opened the beer and took a swallow. "So, what took so long?"

"It wasn't my fault," Lisa said. She bit a fingernail and thought it over. "It was Denise's. I caught her hanging out the bathroom window, trying to kiss one of the guys downstairs. I had to grab her by the ankles and haul her back in. She was about to slip him the tongue." Lisa sat on the bed, too, choosing the far end. "That means you and me can fool around for a while, Michael." This time she sat sort of cross-legged, so that the soles of her bare feet touched against the backs of her bare thighs. She looked at my wife and then at me. "What are you waiting for, Handsome . . . Christmas?" She patted the mattress, inviting me to sit down next to her.

Actually, I was waiting to find out where the cigarettes were stashed. Lisa was in rare form tonight, on her way to a good, long drunk. I shut the closet door and kept the observation to myself.

"He looks different," she said to my wife. "I think he lost his pajama top."

"Hey Muscles," my wife called out, "what's with the no-shirt business?" She clucked her tongue and gave my body a quick once over with her eyes, insinuating, perhaps, that the reason for my bare chest was to impress Lisa. She glanced at Lisa in bra and panties and then looked back to me wearing nothing but my gym shorts. "What is this? Exhibitionist Night?"

"I got hot," I said. "So, I took off my shirt." The question had been addressed to me but I had the feeling that it was aimed as much, if not more, towards Lisa than to myself. The topic was an old one for them. It dated back to their last semester in college together when Lisa, nude except for a pair of Keds, had streaked across the full length of campus. Since then, it didn't take much for my wife to accuse her of being an exhibitionist: a low-cut blouse, a pair of sassy looking jeans or, like tonight, for Lisa to be strolling around in nothing but Maidenforms.

"Oh," my wife said. "Michael *got hot*. I see. So, he took off his shirt."

"Leave him alone," Lisa said. "What's wrong with a little beefcake?"

"Nothing. Except it's a little more cake than beef."

"I think he looks good," Lisa said. She squeezed my upper arm as I joined her on the bed and feigned a sexy swoon. "Ooooh, Michael, you're so strong."

"He lifts weights now and then," my wife told her. "He's got a pretty neat system." She curled her arms, showing us a pair of feeble looking muscles. "He lifts the weights for a minute or two and then spends the rest of the night posing in front of the mirror."

"What are you talking about?" She surprised me with that one. I hadn't lifted weights in months and I never once posed in front of a mirror (not that she knew about, anyway). "That's untrue," I said.

She reached across the bed and tousled my hair. "Just teasing."

Lisa gave my hair a rub, too. "Now, Michael. Don't get all embarrassed."

"I'm not all embarrassed. It's just that it's not true."

There was, of course, a little truth to it but not as much as my wife had suggested: a bicep shot here, a check of the abdomen there; that was all; no more than your average guy.

"Even if it is true," Lisa said, hushing me with a raised forefinger, "there's nothing wrong with it. One of my boyfriends . . . well, one of my ex-boyfriends, used to lift weights. You remember him. The cop?"

"Gary," I said. "Sure. I remember him." He was a difficult character to forget. I met him only once although he and Lisa had been going together for a couple of years. Their romance, by all accounts, had been a stormy one.

"Well, he used to lift weights all the time. Did the posing. Entered contests. It was all he ever talked about, too. Except for his cop-on-the-beat stories."

"I got the same impression," I said. "He cared about weights. Being a cop. And nothing else."

Lisa smiled, happy with the idea of a former boyfriend and I knowing one another; especially if my memory of him was as poor as hers. "He's not a cop anymore. They kicked him off the force a year ago."

I popped my eyes a bit, as if I was surprised to hear it. The information, however, wasn't new to me. My wife had told me about it when it first happened.

"He still lifts weights, though. He told me he invited you to his gym for a workout once. You turned him down, huh?"

"I couldn't get into something like that. Dead-lifting four-hundred pounds with a bunch of jocks looking over my shoulders. I've got to do it alone."

"You never know," Lisa said. "You might have liked it."

"No. I can't concentrate that way. Benching three hundred next to some juiced up gorilla working on his leg squats."

My wife laughed. "Would you listen to this guy? Tell me, Michael, when did you ever bench press three hundred pounds?"

"He could do it," Lisa said.

"Yeah. In three lifts, maybe. A hundred pounds a crack."

"You can do it, Michael. Can't you?"

My wife was right. Three hundred pounds was out of line. I have a tendency to exaggerate where numbers are concerned. "What was it, Denise? My best lift. Two forty?"

"You're getting closer," she said. "Two hundred, maybe. Two ten."

"It was more than that."

"We've got it written down someplace. It was a long time ago." She shook her head and grinned at Lisa. "You should have seen him in those days. This was a year or so before we were married. When he was lifting every day."

"I knew him then."

"When he had all those funny looking muscles? What he called his V-shaped torso and his cobblestone stomach?"

"I was kidding around," I said.

"And those veiny forearms," my wife added, "and the tight little knots in his biceps?"

Lisa chuckled, encouraging the subject. "I thought he looked cute. The way Popeye looks before eating his spinach."

"You think so?" My wife took another swallow of her drink. "How about his pectos, though? Pecals? The chest gadgets?"

"Pectorals," Lisa said.

"Yes. Pec-tor-als. You should have seen those things. He loved to show them off. Making them plip up and down without using his hands. Wiggling them around every chance he got."

"I never wiggled—"

"You should have seen him. At the beach. Ball games. Parties. He didn't care. My company picnic. He even whipped them out at my cousin, Marcie's wedding. At the hors d'oeuvres table. Right in front of her poor old mother."

Lisa laughed. "That was the night he asked you to marry him."

"I know. He thought he was the hit of the wedding. Him and his writhing muscles. And this eighty dollar blender he gave my cousin as a present. It was like, *If Denise won't marry me after tonight, she never will*. That's what a smashing success he thought he was." She tipped her glass to Lisa. "I was drunk. I told him I'd think about it."

Lisa snickered into her drink. "I'll bet that swelled his pectos with pride."

I had heard my wife tell variations of this story before. Little, if any of it, was true. I never *whipped them out*. For the record, Marcie's mother had asked me if she could feel them and I said okay and I let her poke them a few times and that was it, nothing more.

"I was young," my wife continued. "In those days, I wanted someone like him, a creep with an eighty dollar blender and a bunch of funny looking muscles. I was a creep, too, I guess." She took another sip from her glass and then placed it carefully on the nightstand beside her, affording me the opportunity to deny either all or part of what she had just said.

I didn't bother. She was having a good time, getting drunk with her girlfriend, turning what was left of the night into a sort of slumber party for herself and Lisa. They'd be heading to Long Island in the morning. My wife was looking forward to it; it would be her first time on the sand this year. There was no point in begrudging her a few laughs.

"I think he was going through a stage," she continued. "He was twenty-two or -three at the time. Two, I think. But it was like he was going through his adolescence all over again. I read an article on it once. It explained the whole thing."

"Alright," I said. "Let's drop it, Denise."

She waved me away with her hand. "No, let me finish." She held her gaze on Lisa. "Because sometimes I think he's still going through it, his adolescence. In some ways he acts more like a child these days than before we were married."

"Careful," Lisa said. "It looks like he's getting embarrassed again."

I wasn't embarrassed. I was bored. I inched up the bed away from her and stretched out alongside my wife. More from habit than any real desire to get comfortable, I rolled onto my side and slid an arm beneath the pillow, still holding onto the bottle of beer. I was getting tired. The clock on top of the dresser said a quarter to one. I shut my eyes for a moment and let my mind drift back to the sounds coming from the floor below.

The party, if it was possible, had grown even more raucous, the voices drunker and louder than before. Off to the kitchen, several cans of beer were being popped open. There was a brief round of applause then for the fellow who had brought the cans with him. "My man . . . My Boss man . . . My Number One man . . ." It seemed that the smooth talking, Junior, had finally "procured the currency" for his beer run to the delicatessen. From the sound of it, he had procured enough for a few cases of the stuff. In the corner of the apartment, just below my bed, the card game with Valerie was still going on. Other than the exchange of a new player or two, the game hadn't changed a bit. "Would you leave me alone?" I heard her shout. "I already got a boyfriend. . . ." A dispute of a different sort was taking place in another corner of the apartment, this one involving Beale's wife, Rosanne, and someone named, of all things, The Professor. Rosanne wanted to play an Elvis Presley record; The Professor wanted to keep the rap albums going; he thought they were "more fun." Rosanne called The Professor a kook and said she'd put the record on herself. An old Elvis tune, "Blue Suede Shoes," was placed on the turntable. She hiked up the volume and started to clap her hands in rhythm. The record sounded like a newly bought one, almost fresh out of the package. It didn't have the usual skips or crackles I associated with Elvis's earlier records, nor the worn-out grooves. It was probably a Ronco edition, sold directly through television on one of those advertisements broadcasted mostly after midnight. The offer would have been a limited one; good only while supplies lasted: a bargain, to be sure, at any price.

"Wonderful," my wife said. "Just what I was hoping for . . . Rockabilly." I felt her stirring beside me, fidgeting with the top sheet of the bed. She forced a dry, painful cough from her throat and then crossed and uncrossed her legs, allowing a knee to brush against my spine. Even with my eyes shut, I could tell that her mood was changing. She wasn't much of an Elvis fan to begin with; at this hour, she probably found him even harder to tolerate. She had another taste of her drink and muttered something to Lisa about coming down with a headache.

"Maybe it's the booze," Lisa said. "You want some more?"

My wife didn't answer. It wasn't the booze; it was the party. Every time that I had listened to Beale and his pals, she had done the same.

Her patience, I knew, was going to give out soon. And, when it did, she'd either call the police station and put in a complaint or she would try to shame me into going down there by myself.

I didn't look forward to either prospect. I'd met Nicky Beale before and I'd heard more than my share of stories about him. Indeed, the rumors of his foul deeds were countless. I'd heard that the last neighbor to complain about one of his parties found a concrete brick through the windshield of his car the following morning, his tires slashed and his Sears Diehard battery stolen. It was said that Beale had vandalized a bar named Chimneys last October, evacuating its patrons with a smoke bomb and then blowing out its front windows with a twenty-gauge shotgun. There were rumors that Beale was the one responsible for a string of local robberies last summer. He was supposed to have been a mugger, too, a mugger who was as fond of brutalizing his female victims as he was of stealing their purses. In all but one of these cases, detectives dropped by, asked questions, made their reports and never filed charges. The one exception, I'd been told, was when Beale had vandalized that bar, Chimneys. There, the police had arrested him on the spot. They detained him overnight and, with a district attorney, brought him before a judge. But, for reasons unknown, they were forced to release him the next morning: to "let him walk," as my source had put it.

The most bizarre story I'd heard about Beale, and maybe the most difficult to believe, had to do with his wife's puppy named Ruffles. Supposedly Beale stabbed the dog to death last winter—stabbed it with his wife's own carving knife. He carried its bloodied, lifeless body through a snowstorm and stuffed it down the slot of a Salvation Army bin, more than a half mile from home. All because the dog couldn't hold its pee until the snow stopped falling. No one that I was aware of, actually, saw or heard this happen but, like me, they all knew the story by heart.

There were other stories, too, most of them originating from Beale's neighbors on the fourth floor (angry, intimidated people, to say the least). There were stories that he had spent time in prison, that he was psychotic and that he nearly killed his wife by setting her hair on fire. I didn't know how many of these stories were true. Not one of them, in any event, suggested a reasonable solution to our problem.

I opened my eyes slowly, feeling as though I'd just woken from a long sleep. Something hurt. I tensed my legs and stretched them toward the foot of the bed, trying to ease the kinks from my muscles. A dull, stabbing pain worked at the top part of my ass, a pencil point or a blunt tool jabbing its flesh. The pain wasn't necessarily uncomfortable; just an odd sensation. I lifted my head from the pillow and took a look over my shoulder. It was Lisa. She was poking a fingernail into my right buttock. When she caught my eye, she gave a cheerful wink and then went back to what she was doing. "Michael's got nice buns," she announced.

My wife looked at us both. Her eyes showed little interest. "They're okay. You get used to them after a while."

"I'd never get used to *these*," Lisa said. "They're round, you know? But hard, too. I like that." She gave my ass a pinch and then lifted the waistband of my gym shorts. "Mind if I peek . . . ?" She didn't go so far, however, as to actually pull it down. She released her finger from the waistband and snapped it back onto my hips. "Only kidding. I'd never look."

"Knock yourself out," my wife said. "He doesn't care."

"Oh, yeah? You don't care if I check out your ass, Michael?"

My wife shrugged. "Why should he? He's been checking out yours."

"Really? That's cute. I never noticed."

"You've been too busy shaking it around to notice. I've seen him, though. He's been checking it out. Discreetly."

"No," Lisa said. "I don't believe it."

"Go ahead. Ask him."

Lisa lowered her eyes and relaxed the corners of her mouth, showing a thoughtful pout. "Michael," she said, "is it true that you've been checking out my ass?"

"Don't ask him like that. Ask him casually."

"Like this?" She took a shot of her drink and tossed back a wing of her hair. "By the way, Michael, there's something I'd like to know. Have you been ogling my bottom?'"

I didn't answer. I finished what was left of my Budweiser and then sat up against the headboard, hitching the shorts back to my hips as I went. What was there to say? If I denied it, or, for that matter, if I admitted to anything less than "ogling" Lisa's bottom, my wife was likely to take off on another of her trumped-up, only half true stories. If I challenged her at her own game—"Damn right I've been checking it out . . . best butt I've seen in months"—then she was likely to accuse me of coming onto her best friend. It was a no-win situation. I put my empty bottle on the nightstand and then fussed a bit with my pillow, hoping to let the subject simply drop.

"Look," Lisa said. "I knew it. He's getting embarrassed again." She waved a long, manicured finger before my face. "Let's do something to really embarrass him. You know? Like mooning him. Just to see what he does."

"Mooning him?" My wife shook her head. "I said you could look at *his* ass, Lisa. No one said anything about putting *yours* on display."

"We'll flash him together. A split-second's worth. Like a test."

"What are you talking about?"

"To see whose he looks at. Mine or yours. We won't give him time for both."

"Forget it," my wife said. "I know what you're up to."

Lisa was grinning. "Oh, yeah?"

"I can see right through you." My wife turned to me. "She got a tattoo in Jersey last week. That's all. She wants to show it to you."

"So?" Lisa asked. "Wouldn't you? If you just got one?"

"No, not if it was on my ass I wouldn't. Not to someone else's husband."

"C'mon, Denise. Don't be such a prig. Michael doesn't care."

"It's me that cares."

"What tattoo?" I asked.

My wife looked at me through the corner of her eye. "A yellow rose," she answered. "It's not bad. She showed it to me in the kitchen. It's cute. Bright yellow. A standard tattoo. Nothing to get excited about."

"Oh, yeah?" Lisa straightened her posture. "Why not let Michael be the judge of that?'"

"Because I don't want him looking at your ass. He's my husband, okay?"

Lisa nodded patiently, eyes closed, as if she was dealing with an imbecile. "I want to show him my *tattoo*, Denise. Not *marry* him."

"Well, forget about it," my wife said. "What is it with you, anyway? You seem to have this great problem just keeping on your—"

"Oh boy . . ." Lisa let out a soft whistle. "Here we go again."

"No, I'm not talking about college days, Lisa. I'm talking about tonight. Since we got home from dinner, you've been parading around in nothing but your underwear. You got half your tits hanging out. Your nipples have been poking through that bra for over an hour. And now you want to pull down your underpants so you can show my husband your ass. You're an exhibitionist, Lisa. You really are."

She was unfazed. "If I showed him my other parts, Denise, then I'd be an exhibitionist."

"Well, you're not going to. So don't even think about it."

Lisa polished off the rest of her drink. She gave a lazy shrug and raised the palms of her hands overhead as if in surrender. "Alright, party poop. Forget I even mentioned it." She pointed towards my wife's empty glass. "You want a refill?" And then she rose from the bed, seemingly happy to leave the issue at that. There was, however, a prankish look to her eyes. I had little doubt about what she was going to do next. As she headed towards the doorway, she reached around and hooked her thumbs into the waistband of her panties. She pulled the fabric tight, giving it a good, firm yank, until it was wedged snugly between both cheeks, creating a sort of G-string effect. She looked over her shoulder, examining first her bare ass and then me. "Well?" she asked. "What do you think, Michael? You like it?"

There it was: a short stemmed rose, yellow and slightly moist, centered on the lower half of her right buttock. As a matter of fact, I did like it. It was saucy but it suggested a certain femininity, too: the way the right makeup can make a woman appear both sexy and innocent, or the way the proper piece of lingerie can make her appear both wanton and pure. I didn't mention this to Lisa, however. In deference to my wife, I remained silent.

Lisa kept her eye on me, attempting, perhaps, to cause me a little more embarrassment. She rolled her hips to one side, then to the other. With or without the tattoo, her ass was one of her better features and she seemed to know it. When she was satisfied that I had seen enough, she readjusted her panties and walked towards the living room. "All I said, Denise, was that I wouldn't show him my other parts. . . ." Then she closed the door behind her.

My wife said nothing, just held her position on the bed: shoulders against the headboard, legs stretched along the mattress, parallel to my own. If she was upset, she wasn't saying. There was no telling from the expression on her face. A vague, lifeless stare was all that she offered. She might have been planning tomorrow night's dinner menu, for all that it appeared, or contemplating the works of Plato.

I nudged her elbow and hovered above her face and lowered my chest onto hers, brushing the tip of my nose against the tip of hers, trying to cheer her mood. Sometimes this sort of thing did the trick. Just to make sure, I kissed her mouth and told her that I loved her.

"Do you love me more than Lisa?"

"More than the Earth and Mars and Jupiter put together."

She touched me behind the neck. "You'd still give her a tumble . . . provided I didn't find out."

I traced a finger along the curve of her shoulder, saying nothing.

"You would," she said. "If no one knew about it? You'd screw her. I've been watching you. You haven't taken your eyes off her for a minute."

"She hasn't shut her mouth for a minute. Neither have you."

"So what? We're having a good time. And don't change the subject. I've seen the way you've been looking at her. You haven't stopped panting since she broke into her underwear."

"I wasn't panting."

My wife removed her hands from my neck. "And then drooling over that tattoo of hers. Flirting with her like you're at some singles-pick-up bar."

"Flirting?" I said. "Get out of here."

"All that macho talk about workouts and muscles, about twirling five hundred pounds over your head when you're lucky if you can handle my groceries for me."

"It was you and Lisa who brought up the muscles. Not me."

"No, no. All Lisa said was that her old boyfriend used to lift weights. Then, out of nowhere, you start coming on like Arnold Schwarzenegger, making up these poundages a gorilla couldn't lift."

"That's not true," I said. "And I wasn't *drooling* over her tattoo. I thought it added a little flair. So I looked. Big deal."

"A little flair, huh? You thought so?"

"Yes. It looked cute."

My wife coughed rather ladylike into her hand. "Personally, I think she made a mistake. It's not going to look so cute when she hits sixty."

"Where'd she get it, exactly?"

"Atlantic City. Tattoo parlors are legal in Jersey. Why? Do you want one, too?"

"I was hoping you'd get one."

"Something to break up the monotony of my ass?"

"You're offended," I said.

"Don't be foolish. What would you like? A topless mermaid? Or something raunchier? Something like 'Prime Beef'?"

"The mermaid sounds naughty," I said. "It'd be sexier than Lisa's."

My wife sucked the inside of her cheek. Her look was a bitter one; I'd said the wrong thing. "What do you mean, 'Sexier than Lisa's'?"

"Just what I said. Sexier than Lisa's."

"A minute ago, you said her tattoo looked 'cute'. And that it 'added a flair.' Now it's 'sexy' too?"

I had to think for a moment. Did I say all that? "The tattoo is sexy. I didn't say Lisa is sexy."

"It's the same thing. If the cleaning lady had one, you wouldn't call it sexy."

"What cleaning lady? We don't have a cleaning lady."

"You know what I mean. If your Aunt Marge had a tattoo, let's say, on her ass, you wouldn't call it sexy. Because you don't think Marge is sexy."

I had to agree with her on that one. I didn't see the point, though, in dragging Marge into it. Or, for that matter, an imaginary cleaning lady.

"But you call Lisa's tattoo sexy," she went on, "because you think Lisa is sexy. Do you get my drift?"

"Yeah. So?"

"So, you think she's sexy. That's all. Why can't you admit it?"

I stifled a yawn and then bobbed my head to show that I was listening. Downstairs, a scuffle had broken out between Beale and one of the card players. They were shoving one another back and forth, each one warning the other to "fugg off." I ignored them, turning back to my wife, hoping that she would ignore them as well. "I can admit it," I said. "Lisa's sexy. She's got a pretty face. One of those bubbly personalities. She stays fit. Keeps an attractive figure. What's wrong with that?"

"Nothing's wrong with that. I'm glad to hear you admit it. Lisa will be, too." My wife smoothed the bottom of her nightie. "Who knows? Maybe I'll let you two have the bed for the night. I'll sleep on the couch."

"C'mon," I said. "Let's not start again."

"Is her figure bubblier than mine?"

"I didn't say her figure was bubbly."

"No, that's right. You said her figure was attractive. Is it more attractive than mine?"

"It's different," I said. "That's all."

"Don't give me that. You must like one better than the other."

"No, I mustn't."

"Of course you must. Our bodies are completely different. You said so yourself. I've got big tits, Lisa's got mediums. I'm tall, Lisa's average. You have to prefer one over the other."

"Why do I have to?"

"Because that's the way men are. You're always comparing women's bodies."

"Not our wives' bodies."

"Just tell me, okay? And I'll shut up."

I kept silent. This was an aspect of their friendship that I never liked; while my wife and Lisa shared a certain love for one another, they also shared a certain rivalry; a rivalry that ran the gamut from "who had the better body" to "who could slurp an ice cream soda the loudest." To tell the truth, though, I didn't know who had the better body. My wife, as she said, was on the tall side, as tall as me when she wore heels, most of the height being in her legs. Her figure was balanced and nicely rounded: full hips, a hint of a belly, and large breasts that she tended to play down with her wardrobe rather than accent. Lisa was half a head shorter than my wife, her body thin and tight, but—as she, herself, once described it to us on a Friday night similar to this one—she was "Okay in the places that count. . . ." It was hard to say whose figure I liked better. Maybe Lisa's.

"Look," I said, "we've already been through this."

"No, we haven't. We never have."

"I'm not going to answer. It's your game, not mine."

"No. Let me try it this way," she said. "If there was no way that I'd find out about it, would you screw Lisa?"

"If there were no attachments," I asked. "And no one would be hurt by it? I don't think so. May—No, I doubt it."

"You're lying. I can tell."

"Why am I lying?"

"Because," my wife said, "you are. You're trying to tell me that there's absolutely no one in this world except for me that you'd want to make love to?"

"I didn't say 'no one'. You asked me about Lisa."

"Fine. Who then? Who else would you spend a night with?"

"I don't know. The obvious, I guess. TV stars. Movie stars. Charlie's Angels. Raquel Welch, probably."

"No, no. Girls in real life."

"You didn't say anything about real life."

"Well, I am now." She folded her arms and slouched into the pillow.

"There's this woman on the train to work," I said. "Stylish. Pretty face."

"C'mon. Someone I know, too."

"You're changing the rules. But okay. Do you remember that sales girl from last week? At Sears. With all the makeup? And the pants that were too tight? You made some comment about her crotch."

"With the camel toe? Get out of here. You'd screw anything, wouldn't you?" My wife shook her head, laughing. "No, she doesn't count, either. We've got to know her personally. Like one of our own friends. Close friends."

"I don't have any," I said.

"One of my friends then. If you had to make it with—"

"If I *had* to?"

"Yes. No more nonsense. If you had to make it with any one of my friends, who would you pick?"

She was really narrowing it down for me, almost rigging it so that I'd have no choice other than Lisa. Except for the several girls she introduced me to at our wedding reception, my wife had, precisely, three friends that I'd had an acquaintance with. Lisa was one of them. The other two, Diane and Gertrude, l barely knew. Neither one, at any rate, offered much pizzazz. Her friend, Diane, wasn't bad to look at—thick red hair, green eyes and a toothy smile—but there was something in her voice and the way she delivered a sentence that made me uneasy, She seemed to have two separate voices: one was frail, almost little-girl soft, without the slightest trace of an accent; her other voice, however, was as harsh and as masculine as a carnival barker's—somewhere down the road, Diane was headed for a neurosis or two. My wife's other friend, Gertrude, had a few quirks of her own; the most obvious being her fondness for arctic clothing. No matter what time of year it was, Gertrude was dressed for a blizzard: long overcoats and ski caps in the springtime, wool sweaters and fur lined boots well into the summer months, hardly the glamour girl that my wife and I were talking about right now. Physically, she was as drab as they came: pasty blonde hair, a pear-shaped figure and zits the size of M&M's. What my wife saw in Gertrude, I could never figure out. I found her about as appealing as last night's potatoes. "Alright," I said, "if I had to make it with one of your friends, I'd pick Gertrude."

My wife laughed, expecting as much. "Her name is Gretchen. And you're full of crap. Last time she was over, you called her homely."

"Not to her face."

"So what? That's not the point. Good. Don't admit it. I know you want to screw Lisa. You know it. But I'm glad I found out what a hot-pants you are . . . Charlie's Angels. Girls you ride trains with. That one in the slutty pants. I'm sure there's no way that you wouldn't fit Lisa into this little schedule of yours."

"*Little schedule*," I said. "What are you talking about? Okay, Denise, who would you pick?"

"I thought you said you didn't have any friends."

"I don't. Who would you pick from your friends? Assuming, of course, that you had to."

She gave me one of her go-to-hell looks. "What are you suggesting?

That I want to make it with Lisa?" She doodled with a clump of hair and tucked it delicately behind an ear. "Let's not get dirty, okay? She's going to be back soon." My wife gazed at the ceiling and then toward the door. "What's keeping her, anyway? Lisa," she called out, "is everything alright?"

"Denise?" There was a knock at the bedroom door and then a jiggling of the knob. A few soft kicks were placed at the door's bottom edge before it slowly swung open, revealing Lisa. "Look what I found," she said. "I think I'm in love . . ." With one arm, she held two glasses of liquor and a bottle of beer. With the other arm, she held what appeared to be our kitten, Lester. "Say Hi to your mommy," she said. Engulfed in the crook of her arm the way he was, all that could be seen of Lester was one of his tiny gray ears and the whole of his thin gray tail. "What a pipsqueak," she said. "He's so skimpy. Like a furry french fry."

My wife reached across the bed and took the two glasses from Lisa's arm. "Where'd you find the little stinker?"

"In Michael's sneaker. I think he was stuck." Lisa squinted her eyes and regarded me sternly, a reprimand for leaving my sneakers in the kitten's play area. "You've got to be more careful, Michael. Lester's been very sick."

She handed me the beer and dropped down alongside my knee, still clutching Lester close to her chest. A fresh pack of cigarettes was tucked into the waistband of her panties.

"So, you like our kitten," my wife said.

"He's a sweetie. I'm going to kidnap him, okay?"

My wife reached over and brushed Lester across the cheek. "Your landlord would kick him out. I thought you said he didn't allow pets?"

"He'll change his mind," Lisa said, "once he meets Lester." She placed him onto the center of the bed. His soft blue eyes were confused, his legs unsteady. Between the music and the arguing from the party below and then the fuss being made up here, he must have been more than a little frightened. He opened his mouth to meow but, due to a throat problem, only the slightest rasp came out. He crossed the bed slowly, awkwardly, then nestled himself onto my wife's lap and started to make dough with the nylon of her nightie. "He likes you better than me," Lisa said. "I'm hurt."

"Well, I'm the one who feeds him and takes him to the doctors. I give him his medicine, too." My wife stroked Lester around the neck, looking idly into his eyes. She worried a great deal for the cat. He was five months old yet still weighed just over two pounds. He'd been the runt of the litter, according to the woman that gave him to us, and almost died at birth. Since then we'd had him back and forth to the animal hospital several times: worms, anemia, digestive and throat problems, an upper-respiratory infection that caused him fits of sneezing and sapped what little energy was left from his already weakened body. Last month, when we were told that he had only a short while longer to live, my wife cried until the following morning. Unable to sleep, she sat out on the living room couch, looking over snapshots and watching some old movie on the TV, while Lester and I slept in the bedroom. Since that night, with a new veterinarian and a change of prescriptions, Lester had been given a reprieve.

"You feed him," Lisa said, "take him to the vet and you give him his medicine. What does Michael do for him?"

"Good question." My wife shifted to me. "What do you do for . . . oh, that's right." She looked back at Lisa. "Michael's teaching him to read. They're starting with the Bible."

Lisa reached around and pulled the cigarette pack from her panties. She searched around back there until she fished out a book of matches and then tossed them both onto my chest. "If you're going to teach him the Bible," she said to me, signaling for one of the smokes, "I hope you start off on The New Testament. I read some of the Old parts once. It was scary." She took a cigarette from me and held it between her lips as I lit it for her. "I don't remember much of it except that God had to come down to Earth because there was a huge war going on and everybody started circumcising everybody else. It gave me the creeps."

I smiled, lighting a cigarette of my own. "I must have missed that part."

"Lucky for you," she said and then addressed my wife. "I keep forgetting to ask you. Is Michael circumcised?"

My wife broke into a laugh. "Ask him yourself."

"Are you circum—? Wait! Forget it. Don't answer. You'll get embarrassed again." She took a swallow of her drink and smacked her lips loudly. Her eyes were glazed. "C'mon. Drink up. You've finished one beer while me and Denise have been drinking since dinner."

My wife shook her head. "Lisa's been drinking since dinner. I didn't start until we got home."

"You had wine. And half a joint."

"I had a few puffs. You finished the rest."

Lisa tugged my leg. "Don't listen to her. She's high. She smoked as much as me. And she had plenty of wine, too. I made sure of it."

My wife tugged my other leg. "Smell my breath. I had one glass of Chardonnay and three puffs of the joint. I barely had a thing."

I put out my cigarette and passed the ashtray to Lisa. She accepted it without looking at me, still watching my wife. "You kill me," she said. "You had as much to drink as me and just as much to smoke. Now you're trying . . . *Jesus! What was that?*"

Lester leapt from my wife's lap and darted into the living room. My wife rose from the bed and went after him. "That's it," she said. "We're calling the cops." She followed Lester into the living room and coaxed him out from beneath the coffee table. She scooped him into her arms and carried him towards the kitchen. "I mean it this time, Michael. We're calling the police."

It was a crash from the apartment below that had scared Lester off. Down there, the scuffle between Beale and the card player had turned worse. There'd been some shoving earlier and an exchange of threats; then it had quieted down. Now the two of them were at it again, this time using their fists. I could hear a chair being overturned, people scuffling to get out of the way. A girl screamed as a plate broke against the floor. It sounded as though the partiers were knocking into one another, trying to move away from the fight. One of them fell against the stereo. Another fell against a wall. The card player was trying to reason with Beale but he wasn't getting anywhere. "I didn't mean nothing, goddammit. Ask her yourself." A lamp tipped over. The card table, with its poker chips and beer bottles, came crashing after it. Someone, either the card player or Beale, was losing the fight badly, taking a series of loud, fast blows to the face and body. I didn't figure it to be Beale getting hurt; if Beale was losing the fight someone would have jumped in to stop it. No, it sounded as if he was in complete control. They had wrestled themselves to the floor and Beale, it seemed, had come out on top. "You're a wise prick," I heard him saying, "ain't ya?" I pictured him, at the moment, to be sitting on the card player's chest, punching his face at will. There were a few murmurs of protest from the others; most of it pretty routine. "Cut it, man." "Cool out." Other than that, no one made an effort to stop it.

No one, as it turned out, had to stop it. The fight was over in a minute. The card player was escorted from the apartment, there was a brief cleanup, and then the partiers moved into the kitchen area for fresh bottles of beer as they recounted the fight blow by blow.

"They're so weird," Lisa said. "They sound like they liked it." Someone down there was putting on a record; it was Beale's wife, Rosanne; she cranked up the volume. "I hate them," Lisa said. "They're a bunch of jerks. And they scared your poor kitty."

"Lester'll be okay. Denise is with him."

"I hope she's giving him something to eat." Lisa took a sip of her drink. "Do you think she's pissed?"

I nodded my head.

"Me, too. Do you think she'll call the cops?"

"She'll have me call."

"Are you going to?"

I lifted my shoulders; I wasn't sure.

"Maybe I should put on some clothes then. Just in case."

"Wait a while," I said. "See what happens."

Lisa crawled across the bed and stretched herself out alongside me, taking my wife's old spot on the mattress. She leaned into the pillow. "So, you don't want to call the police," she said.

"There're other ways of handling it."

"Not with that guy. He sounds crazy."

"He probably is," I said.

"Why can't we call the police then? Because you don't want to look like a wimp?"

I didn't offer a response.

"How about if I called up my old boyfriend? The cop?"

"Ex-cop," I reminded her.

"He might be able to help. This was part of his territory. He knows a lot of people."

"How's he been?"

"He's alright. Guess what he's doing now? For a living?"

I shook my head. I had no idea.

"He's a professional bouncer. For some bar in the Bronx."

"That's a rough job," I said.

"He likes it, though. Just the sound of it. Professional bouncer. He likes the authority, too. Checking I.D.'s. Keeping drunks in line. I think he gets a kick out of bossing people around."

"You stay in touch?"

"Not really. He calls me when he's upset. To complain about the police board and how they screwed him over. He tells me how he's going to even up the score someday. Then he starts whining that his life sucks, that he wants me to come back to him and start all over again. It's strange. If I call him tonight it'll be the first time in months."

"You won't have to call," I said. That was all we needed right now: a *professional bouncer* with a chip on his shoulder. Downstairs, the party had moved back into the living room. Beale and a couple of his pals were singing along to a record by Queen: "We Are The Champions." Beale was singing the song's verse by himself; two of his pals were accompanying him during the chorus. In addition to vocals, all three were doubling on rhythm instruments; one of them was shaking a pair of plastic maracas, another was whacking a tambourine, while the last one, probably Beale, was trying to keep rhythm on a set of cheap sounding bongos. From the sound of it, they didn't know much about percussion. They kept losing the beat, accenting the wrong notes and throwing all sense of rhythm to hell whenever they sang along to the song. This was the type of thing, I realized, that could go for hours: three drunks banging away on a set of instruments they knew nothing about. Conceivably, one of them might get bored after a while and decide to lay his maracas down for the night but, without a doubt, there would be another drunk right behind him, waiting his turn to pick those maracas right back up. And then there would be another drunk and then one more, until, finally, it was Beale alone, half out of his head, beating the maracas like drumsticks against his cheap sounding bongos. "Check me out here. I'm a one-man band. I'm a frigging maniac. . . ." Somewhere along the line there would be talk about getting another jam session together. They could schedule it for next Tuesday maybe. Or better still, they could schedule it for tomorrow. They could get all the guys together and really rip loose. It wouldn't be anything formal. Just a bring your own instrument type gig. Guitars. Amplifiers. Drums. Whatever they could get a hold of. Who knew? If it sounded good, maybe they'd start a band. It'd be cool. People respect guys in bands. Guys in bands get laid a lot, too. They might even become a bunch of fuggin' rock stars. Stranger things have happened. And even if they didn't turn into stars, it'd still give them something to do. Everyone could chip in for beers and pizzas and they could hold their practices right here at Beale's place. It'd be one continuous party. Seven nights a week. Midnight till whenever. . . . The hell with the neighbors.

I took a sip of Budweiser and scratched at the bottle's label. "I'm going down there," I told Lisa, "and see if I can quiet them down."

"Alone?" she asked,

"I'll be okay."

"Denise won't like it."

"She won't mind," I said and rested back against the headboard, adjusting the pillow as I went.

My wife was standing at the doorway. "What won't I mind?"

"Michael's going downstairs," Lisa said. "Alone."

My wife sat down next to us. "No, he's not. We're going to call the police. Remember?"

"I don't think he wants to."

"Tough. No one's going down there tonight. They're drunk. They'll hurt him."

"Beale's not going to hurt me," I said.

"You don't know that. He's crazy. You should hear the stories I've heard."

"That's all they are, Denise. Stories."

"Did you hear what he did to his wife's puppy? Or how he went berserk in that bar?"

"I didn't hear," Lisa said. "What happened?"

"He practically destroyed the place," my wife told her. "He went in there with a shotgun and started . . ."

"No," Lisa said, "what happened with the puppy?"

"There was a blizzard outside and the dog had to pee. So, instead of . . ."

"Denise," I said. "Let's not get carried away. I'm going to go down there and speak to him. That's all. I should have done it an hour ago."

"You should have called the police an hour ago."

Lisa sat up. "Michael doesn't want to."

"The reason Michael doesn't want to call the police is that he doesn't want a long, drawn out feud with this guy. Beale's got a reputation for it."

Lisa took her drink from the nightstand. "That's why I wanted to call my old boyfriend, Gary. He's not a cop anymore but he might know how to handle it."

My wife frowned. "Gary scares me more than Beale does."

"Gary's fine," Lisa said. "He acts like a jerk sometimes but he's okay."

"You don't mind calling him?"

"I don't care. If he gives me a hard time, I'll just hang up."

My wife thought it over. "And he'd come over? It's kind of late."

"He'll come over. He loves stuff like this."

My wife gave it some more thought. Her mind, however, seemed to be made up. "Good," she said. "Let's call him. If it's alright with Michael."

I finished the rest of my beer. It wasn't alright with me. Not at all. "There's no point bringing him into this. It's my problem. I'll take care of it, myself."

"Why your problem? I live here, too," my wife said. "It bugs me just as much as you. Besides, Gary is an ex-cop. And he's a bouncer. That's what he does now. He knows how to deal with this kind of thing."

"That's right," Lisa said. "And he doesn't mind being brought into it. He'd rather help out than have you go down there alone."

"He barely knows me. Why would he care?"

"Me and Denise care. You're going to need someone with you.

Someone strong. And Gary's the strongest guy I know. And he took boxing lessons, too, and he knows karate."

I put the bottle to my lips but it was empty. "I know a little karate," I told Lisa. "Enough to . . ."

My wife looked at me as though I was nuts. "Since when have you known karate?"

"Since a long time ago," I told her. "Since I was a kid."

"C'mon, be serious, Michael. All kids think they know karate. How old were you? Seven?"

"Older than that."

"Seven and a quarter?" Lisa asked.

My wife smiled. "We've been married three years, right? And he never bothers to mention that he's a karate expert?"

"I didn't say I was an expert. I said I knew a little."

Lisa handed my wife her drink. "How many bricks can he bust?"

"I don't know but he must be busting them with his head. It's starting to affect his brain." She took a sip of her drink, pleased with her little joke. "Next he'll be telling us he was a Green Beret in Vietnam. Or a Rough Rider at San Juan Hill."

I straightened my posture. "Look," I said, "have it your way. Call Gary. Call the cops. Call whoever you want. But I'm going down there."

"Good," my wife said. "I will call. And I'll call an ambulance, too. You'll need one."

"Do what you want. I'm getting dressed." I stretched my arms a bit and reached down to touch my toes. For the first time tonight, I felt wide awake. I went to the dresser and pulled open the bottom drawer and began to look for a suitable shirt to wear. From the looks of it, I didn't have many to choose from. The drawer held less than a dozen, most of them long-sleeved and of one solid color. I scanned them all quickly and then went through them one by one.

My wife was watching me, somewhat amused. "I was only teasing," she said. "Come back to bed. Let's be friends."

"I have to find a shirt."

"Come on," Lisa said. "Talk to us. Don't be a baby."

My wife smiled, "He is a baby. Remember what I told you about that adolescent stage he's been going through? I think it's starting to regress."

I didn't react. I searched through the shirts, instead. I did feel like a baby, like an adolescent, but I wasn't going to let it stop me. I went through the shirts carefully and picked up a bright yellow one that I hadn't worn in years. The last time I had worn it, in fact, was the last time I had painted the apartment.

"Pretty snazzy," Lisa said.

I held it to my chest and tried to picture myself wearing it. Its color clashed with everything in the room. Like most of my old shirts, it was also too large for me, most of its looseness being in the shoulders and waist. Still, it was the color that bothered me most. It struck me, somehow, as being a sad-man's shirt. With its flashy yellow hue and its two top pockets and its extra wide collar and cuffs, it was the type of shirt a newly-divorced man might buy in order to "spruce up" his wardrobe.

"I don't like it," Lisa said. "And it doesn't match your gym shorts."

She and my wife were sitting side by side against the bed's headboard. My wife was smiling. "And it's too loud," she told me. "It's making me nauseous just looking at it."

"Maybe it'll make the guys downstairs nauseous," Lisa said, "and Michael can beat 'em up while they're puking."

They were right. The shirt was too flashy. I needed something more conservative, something less distracting. I wanted Beale and his friends to be concentrating on my face, on the menace in my eyes and the violence in my sneer, not on the color of my shirt. I went back to the drawer and looked for one in a darker shade. I had a choice of two: one was brown, the other was maroon. I preferred the brown one (it was one of my favorites, actually) but if things down there were to turn rough, I didn't want to risk the chance of ruining it; I didn't have that many favorite shirts to ruin. I took the maroon instead. It still looked better than the yellow. Its material was soft and light and its color, on the whole, was inconspicuous. My only argument was with its size; it must have been another old shirt from my weightlifting days and it was even larger than the yellow shirt I'd considered before. I put it on anyway, much to the enjoyment of Lisa, and stood before my wife's makeup mirror. Maybe I was making too much of this but I wanted everything to be just right. I didn't want to offer Beale any distractions, nor the opportunity to go wisecracking about my clothes. When I looked down at my shirt, however, I saw that I might be doing just that. It was way too large. The cuffs fell past my knuckles and the tails hovered just above my knees. I flexed my arms a bit. It was too loose in the chest and much too loose in the shoulders. Even the pockets appeared big. I felt as though I was wearing a larger man's overcoat. I took a look in the mirror . . . Jackie Gleason couldn't have filled this shirt. Come to think of it, this wasn't my shirt. I couldn't recall wearing it before, nor having ever come across it. I turned to my wife for an explanation.

She was laughing. "I found it mixed in with the laundry," she said. "It doesn't fit good, huh?"

Lisa was laughing, too. "I think he looks cute. Like a little boy playing dress up."

"Have your fun," I said. "I'm still going down there." I returned to the mirror. It was difficult now to judge the shirt objectively. It didn't look that bad. An artist roaming his loft could get away with it. So could a retired suburbanite puttering around his garden. On occasion, even my wife wore shirts as ill-fitting as this one . . . I didn't want to go downstairs looking like my wife, however, nor like a retired suburbanite. It was hard to say what I wanted to look like. I wanted to look mean, but not blatantly so. I wanted a look that suggested a quiet sort of violence; a look Clint Eastwood might have on one of his moodier days.

"I think he's stalling," my wife said. "I don't think he wants to go down there."

"I'm going," I said. "Don't worry about that. I have to find a decent shirt is all."

"How about your green one?"

"It's too formal."

"How about one of your tank tops, then? Show off your pectos."

I shook my head. "Too obvious."

Lisa raised a hand in the air, as if requesting permission to speak. "How about your light blue one?"

"It's in the hamper," my wife told her. She got up from the bed and Lisa followed. They carried their drinks with them. "Let me and Lisa look. We'll find one."

I moved out of their way as they bent over the drawer to search through my collection. "I was thinking of wearing the brown one," I said. "But it's one of my favorites. I didn't want to risk ruining it."

"No, don't wear it," my wife said. "It's one of my favorites, too."

"Mine, too," Lisa said.

I took off the maroon shirt and sat on the bed. Downstairs, Beale and his friends were still making their music. In fact, they'd added a new instrument to their band. Someone was sitting in on spoons, smacking them against table tops, snack trays and anything else that made noise.

"Try this," my wife said. She tossed me a plaid shirt and went back to the drawer.

Lisa was holding a faded gray one. She turned to give it to me but decided against it. She put it back in with the others. "Michael needs new shirts," she said to my wife. "These are pathetic."

"So? What do you want me to do about it?"

"Take him shopping. That's what I'd do."

"Michael's a big fella. He can shop for himself."

Lisa shut the dresser drawer. "But he doesn't care about things like shirts. Some guys are like that."

"Well, he sure cares about them tonight," my wife told her. "What's taking so long, Michael? Try it on."

The plaid shirt was in my lap. "It looks stupid," I said. "I hate plaids."

"Yeah," Lisa said. She took it from me and held it in the air. "Plaids are too cheerful. They'll think he wants to join the party or something."

"Well, I'm not going to spend all night," my wife said, "picking out shirts for him to get beat up in." She reopened the dresser drawer and handed me the brown one. "Take it," she said, "or leave it."

I decided to take it. So what if it got ruined? The thought was secondary now. I put it on and went to the closet for a pair of jeans.

"He's looking for pants now," my wife said. "Watch him. He'll make a bigger production of this than the shirts."

"Well, he should," Lisa said. "Pants are important."

"Oh? What's so important about them?"

"I don't know. They're just important. Anyone will tell you that."

My wife shook her head. "You know, Lisa, you say some odd things when you drink."

"So? You're supposed to. That's half the fun of drinking."

I turned from the closet and tapped my wife on the arm. "Where are my new jeans?"

Her expression was one of curiosity. "Why do you want your new jeans? You don't have to get all dolled up for Beale."

"I'm not getting all dolled up for him. I just want to wear something that fits."

"Wear what you have on then. Don't go ruining brand new—"

I took her hand into my own and gave it a squeeze. Her mood, it seemed, was headed for another plunge. She was like that sometimes: pleasant one moment, hostile the next. There wasn't much that could be done about it, however, not right now. I turned back to the closet to see what pants there were to choose from. My selection was limited: a tight-fitting pair of designer jeans or a scuffed-up pair of Levi's. I chose the Levi's and pulled them on over my gym shorts. Wearing them over the shorts made for an uncomfortable fit but I didn't want to start another flirtation with Lisa by asking her to close her eyes while I removed the shorts. I didn't want to open myself up to Lisa's or my wife's ridicule, either, by ducking into the bathroom to take the shorts off. I sucked my stomach in an inch or two and zipped up the jeans. "How do I look?"

"Sort of doofy," my wife said. "You should tuck in the shirt, don't you think? And put on a belt or something. You look like a hick."

"No," Lisa said, "he looks okay. But he should roll his sleeves up and fix his collar. It'll make him look more like he means business." She stood before me and raised her hands to my shoulders and straightened the collar by snapping it upright against her thumbs and then folding it back down with her forefingers. She undid the top button and brushed a strand of lint from my shoulders. There was something authoritative in her touch and something gentle, too. "Good," she said. "That's better." Then she moved to the shirtsleeves and rolled each cuff back twice. The palms of her hands were moist with perspiration. "Now he looks like someone to be reckoned with. Nobody's going to give him trouble when he looks like this."

"Are you serious?" my wife said. "He looks about as scary as a chipmunk." She took another taste of her drink. "I don't know why we're helping him get dressed in the first place. We should be calling the cops. Period."

"No, we shouldn't." I moved a step toward her and tucked in my shirt. "I'm going to go downstairs and tell them to knock it off. I'm going to tell them to lower the stereo and quit playing the bongos. That's all. They can't argue with that."

My wife appeared skeptical. "They're drunk and they're in a nasty mood."

"That's too bad," I said, "because I'm in a nasty mood, too."

"Oh, really?" She turned to Lisa. "Are you listening to this guy?"

Lisa shook her head. She was not listening to this guy. She was going through the top shelf of the closet, playing with my wife's collection of hats. She exchanged a look with my wife and then returned to the hats, pointing to a bright red one with a floppy brim. "You never showed me this. Where'd you get it?"

"Macy's. Why?"

"Just wondering."

My wife looked at the hat and then at Lisa. "I bought it on sale. You don't like it?"

"I didn't say that."

"Try it on. It'll look good on you."

Lisa shook her head again. "*No thank you.*" She was standing on tiptoes, examining the closet's top shelf. Her balance was not steady. She looked over a few more of the hats and then moved down to the rod that held my wife's blouses. "You've got a lot of stuff."

"Most of it's old."

"It doesn't look old," Lisa said. Then, as an afterthought, added, "Some of it doesn't." She turned back to the closet and began to browse again. She picked through the blouses first, passing through them quickly, gathering speed as she went. She flicked past the sweaters and then moved on to the pants and then onto the skirts, skimming through them as quickly as she might have thumbed through the discount racks at Woolworth's. She scanned half of them before zeroing in on a tiger striped miniskirt that my wife had bought years ago. She bit her lower lip when she saw the skirt and popped her eyes in disbelief. "A miniskirt. I don't believe it." She lifted it into the air. "Oh, Denise, this is so you!"

The skirt, indeed, was a sight. Its fabric looked like velvet and it had several black tiger stripes zigzagging from top to bottom. It came with its own vinyl belt and had two oversized zippers that ran diagonally, front and back. "I like this, "Lisa said. "I like this a lot." She laughed with delight as she held the skirt to her waist. The hem barely touched mid-thigh on her. "This is my favorite. It's so punk."

"Leave me alone," my wife said, revealing the beginnings of a smile. "It was a gift."

"Right. Tell me about it." Lisa turned to me. "It wasn't a gift, was it Michael?"

"It might have been but it was so long . . ."

Before I could finish, she was back at the closet, poking into the long cardboard box that held my wife's old wedding gown. She pulled a piece of its fabric through the box's top flap, examined it, then tucked it back inside. "Your gown was white," she said. "You're lucky. I could never wear white to my wedding. They'd make me wear scarlet."

My wife waved her glass of liquor. "Don't say that. You're not that much of a slut."

But Lisa wasn't listening. She was checking out the closet once again, this time searching through the shoes that covered its floor. She picked up a pair of sandals and held them at a distance from her body. "Where'd you get these things?"

"Sears." My wife laughed and shook her head. "God, you're nosey."

"I can't help it," Lisa said. "I love snooping through other people's closets." She returned to the footwear and held up a pair of argyle socks. "Whose are these?" She held up the socks and dropped them back onto the floor.

"They're Michael's. He thinks argyle is cool." My wife turned to me and flashed a smile. "Don't you think argyle is cool, Michael?"

"Argyle is my favorite color," I answered on cue.

The joke was an old one but my wife laughed just the same. Her mood was improving and I was happy to see it. There was an attractive gleam to her eye and her face showed a degree of energy I hadn't observed since earlier in the evening.

This was as good a time as any, I figured, to make my exit. Downstairs, someone was bouncing a large air-filled ball against Beal's living room wall. Someone else, maybe Beale himself, was telling the ball bouncer to "Knock it off. You're scuffing the wall."

I touched my wife's hand and headed for the doorway. "I'll be back," I said.

Lisa looked up from the shoes. "You're going now?"

I nodded.

"How long should we wait before calling the police?"

I gave a mirthless laugh. "Don't call the police. I'll be back in a while."

"You better be," my wife said. And then she kissed me goodbye.

The remainder of that night is not so clear to me. I've played it over in my mind again and again and each time I've remembered it differently. It's not the events that I have trouble recalling; it's the details: the inflection of a voice, the look in an eye, the exact words and the order in which they were spoken.

My wife and I separated after that night. She moved back with her parents in Ridgefield, Connecticut, while I continue to live at the apartment. Maybe that's why I find it important to remember everything exactly as it happened: if it wasn't for that night, my wife and I would still be together.

There was no way I could have foreseen it at the time. My thoughts were focused strictly on Beale and how to turn down the volume of his party. A few more hours and it would be daylight. I hollered goodbye to my wife and Lisa and then I headed for the front door.

Lester was in the entryway to see me off. His eyes looked wide awake, ready to play. I reached down and brushed him along the cheek. He'd been tagging behind me, on and off, since I'd left the bedroom. He followed me into the bathroom when I'd gone to take a leak and then followed me around the rest of the apartment, keeping me company as I hunted down the sneakers that Lisa had hidden "for his protection." She had stashed them, it turned out, in the linen closet, bottom shelf, behind the family pack of "Charmin." Now, as I opened the front door and took a step into the fifth floor hallway, he was making circles around my ankles, curling his skinny tail against the lower parts of my calves. I nudged him back inside and pointed him towards the bedroom where my wife and Lisa were still browsing through clothes. Then I shut the front door behind me.

Outside, in the hallway, the air was cooler and less stagnant than inside the apartment. A soft breeze was blowing from the hall's far window. It felt almost refreshing. I took in a full breath, then filled my lungs twice more. It helped clear some of the sluggishness the two bottles of beer had induced. Alcohol perks me up, it seems, only as long as I continue to drink it. Once I've stopped my mind and body tire quickly. I walked past the elevator and descended the staircase to Beale's floor, taking it slowly, pausing briefly at each step. I was in no hurry to get to his apartment. Despite the self-assurance I had displayed to my wife, I wasn't that confident about settling this thing so easily. I was never good with people I didn't know well and I knew Beale barely at all. Our relationship, in the year and a half that we'd been neighbors, was based on little more than a nod of the head if we passed one another in the hallway and a less than cordial grunt if we crossed one another's path outdoors. It would surprise me now if he even recognized who I was.

I continued my descent down the staircase nevertheless, and, when I reached the fourth floor landing, I squared my shoulders and sucked in my gut. I was uneasy but determined, too. Clearing all thoughts from my mind, I walked the length of the hall and stopped within two feet of Beale's partially opened door. From there I was able to hear it all: the laughter coming from inside the apartment, the music, the horseplay and the quarreling. I could hear parts of an argument going on between someone named "Glass Eye Dick" and the one they called "The Professor." Glass Eye Dick wanted to put the Elvis record back on the stereo. The Professor wanted to listen to something more sophisticated and wondered aloud if there wasn't a jazz album somewhere in Nicky's collection, something with a bit more swing. Off in the distance, the fellow who, for twenty minutes, had been bouncing a ball against the living room wall was now bouncing it against an uncarpeted floor. Toward the center of the apartment, a couple of the percussionists were still banging on their instruments, playing them no better now than they had been before. And above all of this noise, above the bickering and the music and the ball bouncing, someone was shouting for "Smooth Albert" to get out of the bathroom: there was a phone call waiting for him.

I slid back a pace and moved to the side of the door to get a glimpse of what things looked like inside. A few feet into the entryway, a drunk in a Hawaiian shirt was lying alongside a pair of snack tables. He was barefooted, curled into the fetal position, sound asleep. His presence on the floor didn't seem to inconvenience anyone; they appeared happy to simply step over him. In the kitchen a food fight was going on: a couple of guys flinging sauerkraut and hot dog buns at one another. ("Quit messing with the kraut," I heard a woman yell.) I pulled a cigarette from the pack in my shirt pocket and lit it up. The movements alone—drawing it from its pack, sticking it between my lips, putting the flame from my lighter against its tip—relaxed me as much as the cigarette itself. I took a drag and then one more and then I moved towards the front door and jabbed the buzzer twice.

Beale's wife was the one to answer. She wore cutoff jeans, a man's T-shirt and, on her feet, a pair of plastic thongs. Her face was tired and her eyes were dull, offering me neither interest nor courtesy. "S'up?" she said.

I made a gesture towards the staircase at the end of the hall. "I'm from upstairs. Five E."

"Uh, huh," she said, deadpan. "Nice to meet you."

"I'd like to talk to your husband."

She stuck her thumbs into the front pockets of her jeans and leaned against the door. "Talk to me instead. I'm his secretary."

"I'd rather talk to him personally."

She shook her head. "He's busy with his bongos. Hear him?" She stared me in the eye and shifted her weight from one foot to the other, checking me out as I checked out her. She was somewhere in her early thirties, medium height, with athletic shoulders and a head of curly brown hair. Her legs were firm and well-tanned. She had long polished nails and her stance at the doorway suggested an air of quiet confidence. On the downside, her face was not very pretty: she was a stern looking

39

woman, almost masculine, with a particular hardness around the mouth and the eyes. I wasn't used to seeing such hardness in a woman.

"I'll wait till he's done. It's not a problem."

"You might have yourself a long wait. Once he gets started on the bongos it's hard to get him to stop."

"He has a gift," I told her.

She examined me quizzically. "What do you want him for? I'll bet it's about—Hey, are you and that lady really married?"

"What lady? Denise?"

"The tall one. Kind of snooty. You help her with the wash."

"Three years. Why?"

"No reason. I was wondering. Some guy told me she was single."

"The same guy that told you she was snooty?'"

"No," she said. "That I figured out for myself."

I took a drag on my cigarette and flicked an ash behind me. "Denise isn't snooty. Just reserved."

"Whatever," Rosanne said. She looked over her shoulder and lowered her voice confidentially. "I gave her my phone number one time and she never called me. . . . Not that I'm choked up about it or anything. You guys have no children, right?"

"Right," I said. "None."

"I hang out on the bench sometimes. By the playground. Watching the kids sliding down the board, playing on the swings. It gives me a kick."

"They're fun to watch," I agreed, attempting to create a bond between us.

"That's a nice shirt by the way. Where'd you get it?"

"This?" I touched my breast pocket. "It was a present."

"I like the color . . . Hey! You got any pot?"

I shook my head that I didn't.

"How about papers? Rolling p—"

"Who you?" A guy about my height with black hair and a bulky chest had joined her at the door. He was a year or so older than me and I guessed his weight to be close to two hundred pounds. He wore a sleeveless sweat shirt that showed off his biceps. "What's going on?" he said to Rosanne. "Trouble?"

She pointed her chin towards the living room, indicating that I was here about the party.

"Is that right?" he said to us both. He turned to face me and edged Rosanne out of the way. "You got a problem?" he said to me. "Something I can help you with?" In his hand he had a can of Schlitz and, in his mouth, he had a stick of gum. He pushed the gum around with his tongue and snapped it a couple of times for my benefit, slow and sassy, showing me how tough he was. "You got a problem?" he said again. "May I assist you in some way?"

"No problem. I want to talk to Nicky Beale."

"Nicky's busy," he said and ran a finger under his nose, giving the right nostril a swipe with his knuckle. "Matter of fact, we're all busy. We're having a party. Can't you hear?" He took a chug from his can. "Is there something else I can do for you?"

"You could shut off the stereo," I said.

He nodded, disinterested, looking past me.

"And you could tell them all to stop playing the bongos."

"Right," he said, low and dry. "Cut bongos. Shut off stereo. Anything else?"

"You could ask the guy bouncing the ball to knock it off."

He narrowed his eyes and screwed some of his face into a scowl. "Is that all?"

I dropped my cigarette behind me, rubbed it out with the heel of my sneaker. I wasn't getting anywhere. "What I'm asking you to do is to keep down your voices and lower the . . ."

He wasn't listening. He was facing Rosanne, popping his eyes in exasperation. "We can't talk, too? That's what he's telling us now?"

"I'm not telling you that."

"It's what it sounds like to me." He rolled his shoulders a bit and took a new stance at the doorway: arms at his sides, legs spread apart.

"It's late," I told him. "People are trying to sleep."

"So, we're supposed to have ourselves a silent party. No music, no talking, no laughing. We just sit down and shut the hell up. Play solitaire or have a nap contest."

"If you're not going to . . ."

But he was giving Rosanne another of his looks: head cocked to the side, eyes bugged out, his mouth a large "*O*," expressing disgust, confusion. "What's with this guy? He thinks we're his slaves?" He turned back to me. "What do you think we are? *Your slaves*? Like we got nothing better to do than take orders from you all day?" He glanced at Rosanne's hand on his shoulder and gave it a tap. Then he took another chug of beer and, through his nose, let out a soft belch. You could tell he was enjoying himself, coming on loud and uncouth, playing the role of a bad-ass.

"Don't get excited," Rosanne said from behind his arm. "Let's all just play nice."

And then, from behind Rosanne: "Que pasa, people?" A guy in a checkered vest worked himself into the doorway. He was carrying a plastic cup filled with a beverage I couldn't identify. Around his neck he wore a thin gold chain. His face was more friendly than it was hostile. He smiled and put his free hand out for a shake. "I'm Junior. You a friend or a foe?"

"A neighbor," I said, shaking the hand he offered. "I want to speak to Beale."

Junior nodded slowly, sympathetically. "I'll bet you can't sleep," he said. He stuck a forefinger into his ear and smiled again. "It's the noise, right? We're making a racket."

I shrugged. A racket was putting it too gently. Since I'd arrived, someone had turned the volume of the stereo all the way up, probably to taunt me. In the kitchen, the food fight had come to an end but one of the kraut flingers had found the inspiration to fill a water pistol with cold beer; he displayed a nice talent for squirting it at whoever would squeal the loudest.

Junior showed me his grin again. He saw some humor, apparently, in all of this. "Don't look so sad, man. They'll lighten up."

I studied him for a moment. He seemed like a decent type but I doubted if he could really be of much help. Half drunk and decked out in his snazzy vest, it was hard to imagine him carrying much clout down here. Indeed, it was hard to imagine anyone but Beale, himself, exerting any influence on this gang.

Junior lowered his gaze at the floor and made a sucking noise with his mouth. "They're not bad, these boys. Most of them are just wasted.

We don't need no cops, you hear me? Some of us are in enough trouble already."

"I'm not calling anyone," I said, "unless I have to."

Junior stepped back into the apartment. "Lower that thing," he called into the living room. "There's people trying to sleep."

The guy with the beer pistol, kneeling in a sharpshooter position, regarded Junior irritably. Someone from the living room told him to "Buzz off" and another told him to "Lower *this*." Other than that, no one showed him much interest. Nor much respect. No one, certainly, was about to lower the stereo for him.

"The hell with it," he said. "I'll lower it myself."

It was just the two of us at the door now. Somewhere along the line Rosanne and her companion had wandered off.

"I don't want to cause any trouble between you and Beale. Let me talk to him alone."

Junior took a chug from his cup. "That's not something you want to do," he said, "until you really have to."

"I feel that I have to."

He smiled slowly, his mouth growing into a broad, gentle grin. "Gimme a chance, okay? If I don't fix it, I'll hand it over to you."

I watched him head toward the living room then and, a moment later, I heard the volume of the stereo lowered from, say, Ten on the dial to somewhere around Four. A definite improvement.

Seconds later, Junior returned to me at the door. There was someone with him: a tall sinewy guy carrying a tambourine and a can of beer. "My apologies," he said. "Junior told me we've been messing up your sleep."

I shrugged: no big deal. To Junior I said, "Thanks for helping me out."

He showed me his smile again. "You want me to shut up the marimba band, too?"

The guy with him laughed. "Yeah," he said. "They're starting to give me a headache." He shook his tambourine to punctuate the point and then turned to Junior. "Yeah. Tell them to shut up, huh? They're making everybody nervous."

Junior nodded and disappeared again, leaving me alone with the new fellow. He raised the beer can he was holding and offered me a sip from it.

When I told him "No thank you", he held out his tambourine as if offering me the opportunity to shake it. Then he laughed again. "Only kidding you, man. Goofing with you. My name's Lenny if you're interested."

"How are you, Lenny? I'm Michael."

"I like your shirt," he said, pointing his tambourine at my chest. "Brown . . . it's nice."

"Thanks."

"Looks new. Is it?"

"It doesn't get worn much."

"Uh, huh. Just special occasions. I know what you mean."

I pulled the pack of Marlboro from my pocket and offered him one of the cigarettes. He wasn't a bad sort.

"I don't know why," he said as he took one, "but I only smoke when I drink."

"Your resistance is lower," I said and returned the pack to my pocket.

"Nah, that's not it. I think I do it just because I want to look cool."

I smiled with him and lit the cigarette with a flick of my lighter. "Have you known Beale for long?"

"Just tonight," he said. "I'm here with Junior. Me and him are like this . . ." He stuck his tambourine under his armpit and crossed his fingers together, demonstrating just how close he and Junior were. "Junior's got a good heart, you know? Not like the rest of these numb-nuts. Junior's one of those guys that wants to keep everybody out of trouble—not put them in it. He hates to see somebody mess up and go to jail. . . . Hey, check it out. He got them to stop."

I put the lighter away and listened along with Lenny. The percussion playing had, indeed, come to an end. An argument between Junior and Beale, however, had taken its place. From the doorway, I could hear Beale arguing the loudest. Apparently, he was having a difficult time understanding what the trouble was. He paid his rent like everybody else; he paid his taxes. "If they don't like it," I heard him say, "let them buy their own frickin' bongos."

I heard Junior laugh; it was a hard, disparaging laugh. "Be real, man. Nobody wants to go buying bongos."

"Good," Beale said, "cause I'll ram them down their throats."

There was another exchange and then I heard Beale tell his wife to turn the stereo back up.

"Somebody's going to call the cops," Junior told him. "You want that?"

"I got as much right as anybody," Beale said. "Let them call the cops. I'll ram the phone down their throats, too."

The argument grew quieter after that. Occasionally, I'd hear Junior mention the word *police* or *arrest* or *jail*, and then I'd hear Beale say something like "Oh, yeah? Well, screw jail. . . . Oh, yeah? Screw that, too."

Rosanne joined the argument. She, surprisingly, was siding with Junior: she wanted the stereo kept low and she wanted no more bongo playing. Beale called her a Communist: he paid his rent like everybody else; he paid his taxes, too; he and his friends had a right, he argued, to play the bongos: it was written, he told her, in The Constitution.

The argument went on in this vein a while longer. Most of it was being kept between Beale and his wife. Now and then, Junior would put in a word on my behalf but his voice was constantly drowned out by Beale's. My fate, oddly enough, rested with his wife, Rosanne.

Lenny smiled and pointed his tambourine toward the living room. "You still want to talk to him yourself?"

"It couldn't hurt," I said.

He moved away from the door. "Don't be so sure." Then he motioned me inside.

I stepped into the front hallway and shut the door behind me. An odor heavy with alcohol and cigarette smoke lined the air. To the right of me, in the kitchen, a large green bin was filled to the top with empty beer cans and bottles. Several more empties littered the floor beside it. "Quite the party," I said, stepping over the drunk in the Hawaiian shirt.

Lenny laughed. "We certainly enjoy the brew."

"What's his story?" I gestured to the drunk below me.

"That's Harold. He isn't feeling so hot. He got his lights punched out by Nicky."

"Are you serious?" We had come to a stop in the hallway. I could hear Beale around the corner, holding court in the living room.

"Yeah, I'm serious," Lenny said. "Harold's not that bright. He's only got about eighteen brain cells—ten of which are misinformed."

"So?"

"So, nothing. When he drinks, he gets demented. After a couple of sixes he started grabbing our girl, Valerie. Kept grabbing the fat around her thighs—her saddlebags and whatnot—kept trying to rub his face against them, calling them his Love Bumpers. It was sick, man. He wouldn't let up. So Nicky stepped in. Messed him up good, too."

"When did this happen?"

"Forty minutes ago. An hour ago. Something around there. You hear it?"

"Parts."

"It livened things up, I'll tell you that much." Lenny drank the rest of his beer and placed the empty can carefully on the floor next to the other empties.

"Did anyone try to stop him?"

"Nicky did. I just told you that."

"No, I mean did anyone try to stop Beale? From beating up Harold?"

"The dude was asking for it, man. Everyone was in on it. We rushed him down the stairs and threw him on the street. Then we had to drag him all the way back up . . . Valerie, we found out, was looking to get even, so she stole his shoes. Bright, huh? She said the cops'll pick him up quicker that way . . . What the hell do we want the cops for?" Lenny shook his head. "She's not that bright, herself, Valerie. She lost all her beer money playing poker and then tried begging for it back. Tried pretending nobody explained the rules."

"That's a shame," I said, starting to lose interest. We had resumed our walking. I was now in the center of the Beale's living room, standing behind a bare-backed guy with hairy shoulders. Like most of the partiers here tonight, he was holding a container of beer: a Schlitz "Tall Boy." Sticking out of his rear pocket was a pair of plastic maracas. To the left of him, a thick-waisted girl in white stretch pants was smoking a long skinny cigarette, freshly lit. Their attention, like everyone else's in the room, was focused on the argument between the two Beales.

"When I want to do something neighborly," Nicky was telling his wife, "I'll sweep out the lobby. Right now, I don't care about the neighbors. I care about the music. Turn it back up."

"No way," Rosanne said. "That's it for tonight. The cops are—"

"Screw the cops."

"You won't be saying that when they come."

"Let them come. Let them come in their pants for all I care."

"Oh, that's clever," Rosanne said. "Real witty."

"Yeah, ain't it?"

"They teach you that in prison?"

"Go to hell."

"You go to hell."

Neither of them were aware of my presence in the room. Rosanne was standing a couple of feet ahead with her back facing me. Beale was on the couch, middle cushion, legs crossed at the knee, with a set of bongos on his lap. A chrome plated cow bell occupied the cushion next to him. "I don't see," he was saying, "why you've got to stick your nose into all of this."

"Our neighbors are trying to sleep," she told him. "I feel bad for them, okay? And I feel bad for myself, too. I'm tired of getting their dirty looks every morning. None of them ever talk to me. I know what they think of us and I hate it. I'm tired of being an outcast. I want to be normal."

Beale stood up, letting the bongos fall to the floor. A small bruise was visible on his upper cheek. "Go ahead and be normal. Just don't go screwing up my party because of it." He wiped a line of sweat from his forehead and made an adjustment on the cap he was wearing, a red and white cap that bore an advertisement for a spark plug company. "Be normal all you want," he went on, "but that music is getting turned back up. Understand? I want it louder."

I looked him over as he spoke. He wasn't the most reasonable-looking man I'd ever seen; nor was he the most debonair. He was about my age and height but that was where his resemblance to me ended. He was broader than I was and he carried several more inches around the gut. He had a wide unshaven jaw and a nose that looked as though it had been broken once or twice. His eyes were small and they moved slowly. You didn't see eyes like his very often. They were dark and lacked humor and had a flatness you were more likely to associate with a shark than with a human. I didn't envy him those eyes.

"The music is not getting turned back up," Rosanne was saying. "It's getting shut off."

"I'll shut your mouth off," Beale told her. "How'd you like that?"

I took a sidestep to the right and moved around the bare-backed guy that was blocking me out. I cleared my throat and stepped towards the couch. Beale noticed me instantly. "I'm from upstairs," I said. "Five E."

Rosanne did a little spin on her heels, wagging a finger at me. "This is the person I've been telling you about."

"I know who he is," Beale said, "I've seen him around. In the hallways. In the laundry room with his stuck-up girlfriend that don't say 'Hi' to nobody." Beale looked toward a few of the partiers sitting on the floor and gave them a wink. Then he sat back down on the couch and picked up the bongos. "What do you want, Five E? I already told my wife, if you're here about the music, forget it."

"I *am* here about the music," I told him. "I want you to turn it off. And I want you to quit making noise. It's after two."

"I know what time it is. I got clocks." He raised his forearm and pointed to his wrist. "And a watch, too."

"Then you know it's time to end the party."

"No, I don't know that. I don't know anything like it."

"I'll call the police."

"Go ahead. No one's stopping you."

"Nicky," Rosanne said, "he means it."

"Let the man do what he's got to do," Beale told her. "I'd hate to see him or his snobby girlfriend get themselves in trouble is all."

One of the guys on the floor snapped his fingers at me. "Hey, Five E? You know what happened to the last dipshit that called the cops on Nicky?"

Beale laughed aloud, clapping his hands together. "Go ahead. Tell him."

"He found a brick through his window."

"Through his car window," Beale clarified.

"Driver's side," the guy on the floor said. "And his battery ripped out."

Beale raised his hands in the air, palms up, grinning slyly. "Maybe I did," he said, "and maybe I didn't." He lowered his voice to a whisper. "Only the night knows for sure."

"That's real poetic," Rosanne told him. "Now how about shutting off the stereo? Our neighbor is trying to be decent with us. He doesn't want trouble. *I* don't want trouble. And *you*, if you want it or not, can't afford any trouble. So why don't you do like we say?"

"Because," Beale told her, "you're both full of crap, that's why."

"She's right," I said. "There'll be trouble."

"I'm shaking," he said, holding out his arm, making it tremble. "Look at me. I'm petrified."

"You're making a mistake, Beale. I'll call the cops."

"Call the cops," he said. "No sweat off my ass."

"That's what I'll do then. You give me no choice."

"I give you *choice*!"

"Do you?"

"You could leave us alone. Ever think of that? The music isn't that loud."

"Not right now. But as soon as I go back to my apart—"

"It never was to begin with. Not so you could hear it all the way up there."

"Of course I could hear it. Why else would I be down here?"

He shrugged. "Beats me. Maybe you like ruining other people's parties. How do I know why you're down here? I'm not a detective." He turned to the partiers sitting on the floor. "Who does this guy think I am? Kojak?"

I pulled the front of my shirt from my chest. It was warmer down here than upstairs. "Look, Beale, I'm not an expert on—"

"Yeah, I know you're not."

"But I know a little about law. I know you're—"

"What do you have to bring up law for? First, you're going to call the cops and now you're talking about law. Why can't we just discuss this like gentlemen?"

"Gentlemen?"

"You got a problem with that? Why can't we settle it ourselves? Come to some agreement?" A quart-size bottle of Miller, half empty, was by his feet. He took a swig, then wiped his mouth with the back of his hand. "My suggestion is that we leave the stereo as is, okay? We don't put it louder and we don't shut it off. We let it stay as is. Nice and quiet. We compromise." A few of the partiers hooted at the word. Beale, however, ignored them and turned to his wife. "That okay with you, Ro?"

She frowned, not really sure. "It might be okay. If we don't let it get any louder. And we keep our voices down." She was talking to both of us. "Is that alright with you?" she asked me.

I looked at the cowbell on the couch, then at the bongos in Beale's lap. I examined the faces of the partiers on the floor. It was hard knowing what to say.

"Good enough?" Beale asked me.

"We're sorry about the inconvenience," Rosanne said. "We really are. No hard feelings.?"

"You'll cut out the bongos?" I asked. "All the banging and the maracas?"

"Sure," Beale said. "Not a problem."

"And the ball bouncing?"

He looked confused. "What ball bouncing?"

"Someone was bouncing a ball. Against the wall. Scuffing the wall. You told him to quit it."

"Sure. Whatever. He'll stop, too."

I paused for a moment, wondering if there was anything I'd left out: bongos, stereo, voices, the ball. I couldn't think of anything else. "Alright," I said. "If you're telling the truth. I'm not out to spoil your night." I felt two hands fall onto my back. Junior and Lenny were on either side of me, both pleased with the solution.

"It'll be okay," Lenny told me. "Not to worry."

"As long as we all understand one another," I said.

"We got carried away," Rosanne told me. "It won't happen again."

The guys on the floor were rising slowly to their feet, grunting, stretching, making a production of the effort.

"Me and Rosie will keep them in line," Junior said. "Extend our apologies to your lady, huh? She must hate our guts."

"Yeah," Rosanne agreed, "tell her I'm as sick of this as you are. I'm sicker. When the party's over, you two get to have some sleep. I've got to clean up this mess."

I let go of a chuckle, trying to appear sympathetic. We were halfway out of the living room. There was movement all around us. A few of the guys were heading back to the card game in the bedroom. Some were in the kitchen grabbing fresh beers. Beale was about the only one who wasn't in motion. He was lying on the couch now with a cushion beneath his head, the bongos and cow bell no longer in sight. He was waving goodbye to me. "So long, Five E. Sorry if we bothered you."

I parted my lips into something like a smile. I didn't know how straight everyone was being with me. Junior and Rosanne impressed me as sincere; the others left me uncertain, particularly Beale. There wasn't much else I could do, however. To pursue the argument would be fruitless. I imagined the potential conversation: "You better not be playing games, Beale." "I ain't playing games," he'd reply. "I already told you I'd be quiet. What more do you want?" "I want a promise," I'd tell him. "You want a what?" "I want you to promise me you'll be quiet." "Alright, I promise." "Not like that. Say it with sincerity. Like you mean it." "I promise." "Now swear to it." "I swear." "Say I swear I'll be quiet." "Okay. I swear I'll be quiet." "Now swear with one hand on your heart and the other raised in the air." No, persuing the argument would get me nowhere. I'd have to show some trust.

Lenny and Junior motioned for me to leave and led the way back through the hall to the front door. Junior offered his hand. "Appreciate you're not calling the police," he said.

Lenny stood a few feet behind us, his head turned slightly. Out in the kitchen, Rosanne was telling someone to keep the refrigerator door closed "super-tight. The milk'll sour."

I shook Junior's hand and then Lenny's and thanked them both for their help.

"Be good," Junior said, beginning to shut the door behind me.

"See ya, Five E," I heard Rosanne call from the kitchen.

I started back across the fourth-floor hallway. I took a few slow steps, glancing down, watching my feet as I went. I lifted my arms into a position for jogging and broke into a semi-trot, half running/half walking towards the staircase. I felt suddenly anxious to get back to my wife and Lisa, wanting to let them know how I had made out. I took the stairs two at a time to the fifth floor and then I loped down the hallway, rolling my shoulders, taking short quick jabs at the air, trading off my punches, jabbing with the left hand and following through with the right. They weren't so bad, the Beales; neither were their friends. Everyone could have been a lot more difficult than I'd anticipated. I wasn't about to sponsor any of them for a Humanitarian of the Year Award, but, under the circumstances, they hadn't behaved that indecently either.

I reached my front door and pulled the key from my pocket. I felt exhilarated but winded. My breathing was heavy and my face felt flushed. I unlocked the door and went to the kitchen for something to drink. Lester chased after me from the living room, his little paws sprinting almost silently across the floor. He scooted past me and put on the brakes as we approached the refrigerator. After a good long stretch, he began weaving through my legs, making figure eights around them.

I grabbed a bottle of Budweiser and drank half of it down in one straight chug. My breathing was starting to even off but I still felt flushed. I held the bottle against my forehead and then drank the remainder a little slower. I was out of shape; badly so. A year ago, I'd have run up that staircase twice as quickly and still felt better than I did at the moment. The late hour had something to do with my condition; the previous bottles of beer had taken their toll as well. Still, I was not as fit as I'd been a year ago and, barring some lifestyle changes, I'd be even less fit next year.

The thought depressed me. As impulsive as it was, I put the bottle on the counter and dropped to the floor for a round of pushups. Sixty, I told myself. It was asking for a lot but, winded as I was, I felt like doing something physical. Something macho. I assumed the position, pushed myself cleanly off the linoleum and locked my arms at the top of the movement. I was under way. Taking a deep breath, I lowered myself to the floor and pushed myself up once again.

The first ten repetitions I knocked off without a problem. The next passed just as easily. Lester came up to my face, examined me, then stepped back to a safe distance and watched as I worked on the following twenty. At forty reps I felt myself beginning to tire. I was losing rhythm, my breathing starting to slip. I squeezed out another five and felt my lungs begin to heave. I slowed the pace a tad. Maybe this wasn't such a great idea. I did one more set of five, let out a groan and rested at fifty. I pushed myself back up for one more and then another and then I called it quits: Fifty-two.

I lowered my chest onto the linoleum, sucking for air, and rested my chin on top of my fist. Then, for what seemed like the thousandth time tonight, I listened to the party downstairs. Surprisingly the noise was tolerable. There was some conversation going on, but none of it particularly loud. Beale and his wife were arguing about something that I wasn't able to make out. I could hear Junior's voice, too, and a few that were unfamiliar to me. Other than that, the party appeared to be as peaceful now as when I had left it. There was no more percussion playing. There was no more quarreling about what record to put on or what show to watch on TV. None of the card players were grabbing at Valerie's body. Even the guy with the water pistol seemed to be behaving himself. If there was any problem, it was with the stereo: its volume was beginning to creep back up.

I got off the floor, grabbed another bottle of beer and went to join my wife and Lisa in the bedroom. Lester followed my first few paces. When he was certain of my destination, he cut in front of me and led the rest of the way to the bedroom. He scooted across the carpet and made a beeline for the side of the bed where my wife sat with Lisa. He went first to my wife and then moved quickly toward Lisa, going into his figure eight routine with his skinny gray tail standing as straight as a tiny flagpole.

My wife reached down and stroked him along the cheek. "You brought your daddy home." She traced a fingernail from the crown of his head to the base of his tail. Then she turned to Lisa and pointed toward me at the doorway. "He's back," she remarked. "In one piece." Then to me, "How'd it go, Michael?"

Lisa smiled mischievously. "Did you work anyone over?"

I shook my head. "It wasn't like that."

"Did you karate the whole place up?"

"It wasn't like that either."

"Then why are you breathing so hard?"

"Am I?" I listened to myself for a moment: Lisa was right. My breathing was still heavy, my lungs still pulling for air. "When I was in the kitchen," I told her, "I was fooling around on the floor. Before that I jogged up the stairs."

"While running away from Beale?"

I didn't bother replying to that one. I offered her my stone face, instead.

"What did he say when you told him he scared your kitty?"

"Lester?"

"Yes. What'd he say?"

I gave a short laugh but it came out a bit unnaturally. "We didn't get around to Lester."

My wife gave Lisa a nudge. "Some protector we got. What was he doing all that time?"

"Probably dancing with Beale's wife."

"Yeah, then he probably sat in on a couple of hands of poker and lost all our grocery money." My wife and Lisa were sitting towards the edge of the bed, the soles of their bare feet touching the floor. Lisa was still in her underwear and my wife was still wearing her pink nightie. I didn't know why but I had expected them to be wearing something different, something closer to street clothes.

"So tell us," my wife said. "What happened?"

"Not much," I answered. "It was civil. Beale was decent about it."

"Oh, good." She reached past Lisa and took one of the glasses of liquor from the nightstand. "In what way was he 'decent' about it?"

"You mean because he didn't tell everyone to beat you up?" Lisa asked.

"No, because he was willing to stop playing the bongos. And he agreed to keep the stereo low."

"I see," my wife said. "And when, exactly, will he begin keeping it low? Tuesday?"

"He lowered it when I left. What are you talking about?"

My wife smiled, amused by my confusion. "If you weren't breathing so heavy," she said, "maybe you'd hear what I was talking about."

She was right. I hadn't realized that my breathing was still so deep or so loud. I took in a long pull of air and held onto it as, once again, I tried to concentrate on the sounds from downstairs. Right away I could hear what my wife was talking about. The volume of the stereo had been turned back up. Although it wasn't as loud as it had been an hour earlier, it wasn't as quiet, either, as when I first exited their apartment. I stepped out of the bedroom, hoping, perhaps, that the acoustics of our room were playing tricks on us. . . . No such luck. It was louder outside the bedroom than in it. The record by "Queen," Beale's victory song, was back on the turntable. A few members of his crew were singing along with its chorus.

I wondered when they had turned it back up. While I was in the kitchen? Crossing into the bedroom? I couldn't say for sure. All I knew was that I felt suddenly foolish. I took a sip of beer, trying to keep the embarrassment to myself. I could hear some of them starting up on percussion again. Unlike last time, when they had at least attempted to play well, they were simply whacking against their instruments now, beating them as loudly as they could. There was no joy to their playing, no real rhythm. Beale was among them, still on the bongos, slapping them harshly, angrily, like an ill-tempered child trying to prove a point. "Music to press charges by," I heard him shout.

My wife was leaning back on her elbows, watching me. Her look was sympathetic, if a little smug. "It's not your fault, Michael. That's the way these guys are. You can't trust them."

I touched my forehead with the bottle, feeling as flushed as I'd felt in the kitchen. "I'm going to have another talk with him. This time he's gone too far."

"Oh, no," my wife said. "You're not going down there again."

"Of course, I am."

"No, you're not. We've tried your way. Now you try ours." She glanced over her shoulder. There, on the center of the bed, was the telephone book, and, on top of that, the telephone itself. She and Lisa had been making some calls while I was out.

"If you called that guy, Gary," I said, "you can call him back up and tell him to forget it. I'll handle Beale, myself."

"That's what you said an hour ago."

"I know what I'm dealing with now. It'll be different."

My wife closed her eyes, beginning to lose patience. "C'mon, Michael. Gary used to be—"

"A cop. Now he's a bouncer. He has muscles and he knows how to fight."

"Don't take it personally. Nobody's saying Gary's more of a man than you. He's had more experience with this kind of thing, that's all."

"We discussed it, Denise. And you went and called him anyway. After promising that you wouldn't."

"I didn't promise," my wife said and turned to Lisa. "Did I?"

Lisa shrugged; she wasn't sure. After a moment, she raised a finger into the air. "I know something else we could do. Instead of having Gary actually come over, why don't we ask him to give Michael some pointers over the phone? Like a consultant."

My wife shook her head. She didn't like it. "What are they going to do over the phone? Practice choke holds?"

Lisa clapped her hands together. "Like the Heimlich maneuver? Gary can do that. We were at a restaurant once and he performed it on himself in front of the whole place. I forget how he did it but it was funny as hell."

"I'm sure it was," my wife said, dropping her voice into an officious tone as she returned her attention to me. "Would you be willing to speak to Gary over the phone? Take some of his pointers?"

I put my bottle of beer on the dresser. I was growing tired of arguing. I was growing tired, period. I didn't feel like taking pointers from anyone tonight but I didn't feel like calling in a complaint with the police department, either—especially when it came time to provide them with my name and my street address and the letter and number of my apartment. "Alright," l said. "I'll do it for you and Lisa if that's what you want."

"It is", Lisa said. She and my wife were sitting on the bed motionless, hands on their knees. I held my position by the dresser. Not one of us appeared pleased with the idea, nor did one of us appear eager to grab the initiative in calling Gary up.

Eventually, my wife picked the telephone up from the bed and presented it to Lisa. "Do you feel like calling again? This'll be the last time. I promise."

"Sure. If he's not already on his way over."

"What time does he get off?"

"Three o'clock normally. But he might've taken off early. Like I said before, he loves stuff like this." She took the phone from my wife and dialed.

"If he already left, we can—"

Lisa silenced her with a shoosh and spoke into the receiver, asking for Gary. She moved to the head of the bed and gestured for me to squeeze in between her and my wife. When I waved my hand in the negative, she gave me a frown: the reason she was phoning, after all, was for me; so that I could pick up my pointers. "C'mon," she told me. "Nobody likes a wallflower."

I carried my beer and took the spot that she'd indicated. With the three of us sitting there, hip to hip, it proved to be a tight fit. Neither she nor my wife seemed to mind, though. In fact, they appeared quite comfortable.

"Did he leave yet?" my wife asked.

"They're checking."

I put the beer on the floor in front of me. Lisa took a sip from her vodka and tonic and placed it back onto the nightstand. She was tapping her bare foot, I noticed, in rhythm to the music from downstairs. A moment later, she was holding up a finger, her ear to the phone's receiver. "Hi, Gary . . . No. Everything's okay. Michael's back but the party's getting louder . . . No, he's alright. He looks alright. They . . . Denise is fine. We're all fine. The reason I'm calling again . . . What . . . ? No, stay where you are. We just want some point—No, don't bother. We don't want you to come over. We just . . . No, that has nothing to do with it. We only . . ."

My wife nudged me with her elbow and gestured at the phone. "Gary's getting hyper."

I closed my eyes for a moment, picturing the scene: Gary in our bedroom, shirt open to the navel, a Smith & Wesson jammed into the belt of his pants, a tire iron in each hand, waiting for me to lead the charge downstairs. "Hurry up, Michael. Wear what you got on. You don't have to change clothes for these punks."

Lisa was looking at my wife, holding the receiver away from her ear. "Yes," she said into the mouthpiece, "a dozen of them. At least. They're drunk and . . . I know. That's why we're worried. They could be carrying anything . . . No. We don't want you to. We just want some pointers . . . No, please. We won't let you in. We only want . . . hold it. Here's Michael . . ." Lisa passed me the phone. "Careful what you say. He's dying to come over."

I thanked her for the warning and said into the receiver, a little more cheerful than I felt, "Gary, what's going on?"

"What's going on with you, Michael? What's happening over there?"

"Not much. A party downstairs. Lisa said you might have some pointers for us."

"Sorry, man. I got nothing to tell you over the phone. Nothing that's going to help. You need someone there with you. To watch your back. Not give you advice."

"It's not that serious, Gary."

"Anything having to do with Beale is serious. The guy's a psycho. I knew him my last year on the force. You'd make a mistake going down there alone. A prick like that and you need assistance."

"He's no threat," I said, feeling Lisa's hand tugging at the receiver. She put her other hand up to her ear, curling it into a fist, signifying that she wanted to listen in. "Beale's sneaky is all."

"He's sneaky," Gary agreed. "But he's a sick boy, too. You heard about the dog, right? What he did to it?"

"I heard the story."

"It gives you an idea of the guy's character, no? You heard about him and the girl from Scarsdale?"

"From Scarsdale?" I asked . . . Lisa was poking a finger into my side. I pushed it away, trying to concentrate on Gary. "No, I haven't heard that one."

"Then you never will, buddy. The girl's family wants it quiet. I have to respect that."

"That's decent of . . ." Lisa was tickling me, twisting a finger between my ribs. I held her hand and mouthed the words, "Behave yourself."

"The guy's been trouble," Gary went on, "ever since he moved into town. He's got more enemies than he can count. If you wanted to, you could probably throw a bomb into his living room and he'd never figure out who did it. That's how many people hate his guts. When he needs quick money you know what he does? He sprinkles laxatives into small dime bags and sells them out on the street. You'd think the junkies would catch on after a while. They're paying ten and twenty bucks, after all, not to get high but to shit their brains out. But they can't help it, some of them. That's how hard up they get—so desperate they have to trust a swine like Beale. There're five addicts I can name that are pissed off and vicious enough to stick a knife through the back of his neck."

"Why hasn't he been arrested?" I asked, gripping Lisa's fingers tighter.

"He *has* been arrested. More than once. You do know about Chimneys. How he hacked the joint up. Blew out its windows and then did his number with the ax."

"Parts of it. I didn't get all the details."

"Few civilians did. Messed the place up good. Strictly by himself, too. It turned out his wife had left him a couple of hours before that and it really messed up his head. I forget why she left him, exactly—he smacked her in front of her mother, that's what it was. He called her 'diseased.' Said her mind was 'diseased' and her body was 'filth.' Right in front of her mother. . . . It pissed her off. So, she took her mother's station wagon and drove off, leaving his ass behind. Which, of course, ticked him off. He got some car of his own, did some investigating, asked around, cruised the streets and tracked her down, two hours later, at Chimneys."

"Where," I said, "they wouldn't let him in."

"You heard this?"

"They have a dress code. Jackets required."

"Right. And Beale was wearing jeans and a T-shirt . . . a T-shirt, no less, advertising some spark plug company. . . . This is an upscale place but he could care less. He went charging in, found his wife, grabbed onto her and started slapping her face. That's when the bartenders stepped in and rushed him out of the club. They didn't hurt him much—it's a respectable establishment—but he started yelling so loud you'd think they were ripping out his liver. His wife, too, once she got outside, started yelling at the bartenders, telling them to leave him alone. 'Touch one hair on his head,' she let them know, 'and I'll sue . . . I'll burn this place down.' The bartenders couldn't believe it. They're trying to protect her pathetic ass but she's taking her husband's side. They let go of Beale and his wife hustles him into the station wagon, both of them screaming bloody murder, and they go driving off, heading home together."

"Where Beale picked up his shotgun and axe," I said, still holding onto Lisa's hand. She was wriggling her fingers, trying to escape my grip.

"Exactly. He waited till closing time and then drove back to the bar, shotgun and ax on the floor, and parked the wagon directly across the street. First things first, he takes out the gun, aims it high and blows out both front windows. He tosses the gun into the backseat after that, charges into the place and goes to work with his axe. The joint was empty except for a few of the workers. One of the bartenders, I hear, busted him in the mouth with a shot glass—broke his tooth—but that was about it for resistance. I can't blame them. I would've been nervous myself. Beale was totally insane, chopping up tables, smashing bottles, whirling the axe over his head, screaming all kinds of crap. 'Your mind is diseased.' 'Your body is diseased.' 'You're nothing but scum suckers.' Those were his big words that night, diseased and scum suckers. Used them on everyone. He caught one of the kitchen crew under a table and made him crawl across the floor and 'spread the disease' . . . Weird, huh? It goes on, too. By the time we get there he's really over the edge. He drops the axe as soon as he sees us rush through the doors, picks up a chair and comes barreling straight into us. It takes four of us just to get him to the floor. Then we've got to put him in cuffs. . . . As soon as we stand him up, you know what he does? He kicks my partner square in the rocks. Then, and this I couldn't believe, he charges headfirst into his skull. I was on the force for years and that would have to be my strangest sight—head butting a cop. I couldn't believe it. Neither could my partner. I kid him about it every time I run into him. We still go to the same gym."

Lisa had worked her fingers free. She was pulling at my hand now, the tips of her nails scratching against my palm. She was smiling, mouthing the word *please* at me.

I was smiling, too. "Forget it."

"C'mon," she whispered. "Let me listen. I'm nosey."

I covered the mouthpiece. "You're drunk, too. Keep your voice down." I held the receiver between us as she brought her ear closer, her fingers wrapping around my wrist. Her hair smelled like lavender.

"Michael. You still there?"

"I'm here. You were telling me about Beale."

"You don't sound too interested."

"I'm interested."

"Sure I'm not boring you?"

"You're not boring me."

"Where was I," he asked, knowing exactly where he was. "We pulled him off my partner and tackled him to the floor. Some of us went to work on him then, socked him around a bit, nothing much, tightened his cuffs till they really hurt. We were trying to break him down, wear him out. He wouldn't quit, though. When we stood him back up, he was still going at it, kicking his feet, spitting at us, calling us every name in the book. Diseased this and diseased that. The disease is in our minds. We're nothing but filth. We finally dragged him out of the bar, got him to the curb and told him to get into the squad car . . . which he wouldn't do. He spread his legs wide open, refusing to get in. 'Fine', I told him. I pulled out my nightstick and went *whack*! Right on his knee. . . . He let out a howl like you never heard. Stunned. Outraged. 'Filthy fuzz', he called me. 'Stinking copper' . . . coming on like some B-movie, you know? 'I'll murder ya, you pig. I'll stomp your filthy head in. . . .' Turned out I chipped his knee cap. If you guys ever mix it up together, go for his left knee first. Remember that. It'll cripple the punk for life."

Lisa and I looked at one another. She squeezed my wrist and brought her mouth to my ear. "Think you can remember?"

I picked my bottle of beer up from the floor and turned toward my wife. She'd been observing Lisa and I carefully, almost solemnly. Her face had the stern, sour look of a particularly mean nun I once knew. I turned back around and said into the phone, "So, Gary, what happened next?"

"Where was I?"

"You were teaching Beale respect," I said. "You just broke his knee."

"We didn't know it was bro-chipped at the time. We just figured he was yelling to cause a scene. You get that a lot, the police brutality rap. Either way, it got him into the car. Once we pull out, though, he starts carrying on in the back seat, yapping about his constitutional rights and what he's going to do if he ever catches us on the street alone. Routine threats. You hear them all the time. Me and my partner could care less. We're sitting in the front, you know? And we tell him to shut up or we're gonna paint his pecker blue. 'You heard of blue balls' we tell him. 'We'll give you a blue pecker. . . .' The night before, see, we confiscated a few cans of spray paint from some school kids. We tell Beale the paint is indelible and, unless he shuts up, we're going to redo his organs permanently. It doesn't faze him, though. Even with his knee hurting so bad, he's still a wise-ass. He tells us we're a couple of queers and says our minds are diseased. I felt like belting him."

"He can be irritating," I agreed.

"Yeah, tell me about it. As soon as it's time for him to get out of the car, he starts moaning about his knee again, telling me how it's killing him and how he can't walk into the station alone. 'Let's go', I tell him. But he wasn't about to move. He's already laid himself down on the back seat, hands still in cuffs, demanding a stretcher, refusing to get out of the car, jabbering some more about the Constitution. Same garbage as before, right? Except the opposite. Now he won't get *out* of the car. It's what made me bust his knee in the first place. This time, though, I'm more sympathetic about it. I'm starting to understand this might be more than just some ruse he's pulling. He really looks to be in pain."

"A chipped bone," I said. "I'll bet he was in plenty of pain."

"Turned out he was. Who knew, right? I put him over my shoulder and carried him into the station house. Then I sat him in a swivel chair that had wheels on it. That way I could chauffeur him around from the front desk to the office and so forth. He got a big kick out of that part.

Thought it was the biggest gag in the world: wheeling him around in a swivel chair. Once I started pushing, he started in with the quips about 'Home James' and 'Thank you, Godfrey.' All the servant jokes. He loved it. I had to wheel him from the sergeant's desk to the booking office, then take him for pictures. He had a wise crack for every place I rolled him. Said he had a five spot for me if I could get him to prints before midnight."

"Comical guy," I said.

"A real clown. Except he wasn't so funny. I booked him, you know? All the while listening to his remarks. And then the time comes for his phone call. He only had one, so you'd figure he'd use it on his wife or a decent lawyer, right? Someone who'd do him a little good. Instead, he calls some mope named The Professor. He doesn't bother mentioning to him why he's been arrested. He doesn't tell him, for instance, that he hacked up a barroom less than an hour ago. He doesn't tell him about resisting arrest or assaulting my partner with a head butt. All he wants to talk about is his Constitutional rights and his aching knee and what I did to it. How I whacked it without giving him a chance to get into the car. Which is bullshit. Of course he had a chance. But he doesn't care. His mouth is off and running. He starts rambling on about how he's going to slap a lawsuit on the whole police force. How he's gonna go to the newspapers and have my badge taken from me. Meanwhile he's got his legs propped up on a desk, you know, and I'm standing behind him, looking like a real putz, holding his chair steady so he doesn't fall over."

"Like his man, Godfrey," I said.

"Exactly. Like his goddamn manservant."

I took a swig of my beer and returned the bottle to the floor. "Is that why you got kicked off the force?" I asked. "Breaking his knee?"

"It was the start of it, yeah. Broke. Chipped. Whatever. It's what put me on the captain's shitlist. . . . That and another thing . . . when Beale got off the phone, all he wanted to do was sleep. You get that a lot with his type of guy. They think a good night's sleep and it'll all be over the next morning. I wheeled him into his cell, helped him from the chair to the cot and, believe it or not, he nodded right out. It didn't take him a minute—it was remarkable—conked out cold. An hour ago he was a madman and now he was sleeping like a newborn baby. Looking back on it, that was when I should've gotten out of there but my partner, the one who'd been head-butted, he comes tiptoeing in with a can of spray paint. *Blue* spray paint . . . 'Let's teach this worm a lesson,' he says and takes down Beale's pants and shorts. He gave me the can of paint and I knew exactly what to do. I started spraying, aiming right for Beale's crotch. I didn't know why I was doing it. I was a cop. I should've known better. But it was like I was caught up in the moment, you know? Sort of like a mild case of temporary insanity. I kept spraying until Beale jerked awake. He started screaming the second he saw what was going on but it was too late. His thing was already blue. My partner grabbed the paint can and told me to hold Beale down so he could finish up the nuts. He gave them a few squirts, made an "X" across the belly and then, with this big grin on his face, he started wagging his finger at Beale, pointing at his crotch, laughing like a madman, howling, 'One Ball. He's only got one ball.'"

"What did he mean?" I asked, trying to do my part in keeping this a two way conversation.

"Just like he said. Beale only had one ball. Literally one ball. It's rare but it's common. Hitler only had one. Look it up. And Napoleon Bonaparte. Same with a lot of people. It doesn't hurt you, and, unless you got someone like my partner shouting it out loud, who's to know? Except your girlfriend or your wife or something?"

"Beale must have been furious."

"He was wild. Totally psycho. Not only was his missing nut found out about but that his crotch was going to be blue for days. For weeks. It'd wash off sooner or later but scrubbing paint off your manly parts isn't exactly like scrubbing it off of your hands. You got to be gentle. You got to concentrate. Which was something he was in no condition to do. 'Morons,' he called us. 'Frigging fairies. Diseased scum suckers.'" Me and my partner backed out of the cell together and Beale slid over to the sink, pants around his ankles, and turned on the faucet and started splashing water on himself, quarts of it. He tore his shirt off and started using it as a washcloth. Meanwhile he was cursing us through the bars, spitting at us, a total lunatic, scrubbing his thing with the shirt, using it on his pubes. It must've hurt like hell he was scraping so hard. We told him it's too late, his pecker's gonna be blue for life. 'It's like your ball, man. It's permanent. Your own wife ain't going to love you. But the cons up in Attica might.'"

"That must have pissed him off."

"As we were saying this to him, though, he stopped washing. Simply stood there, smirking, real pleased with himself. 'I just thought of something,' he says. 'Thanks for the help, boys.' He tossed the shirt into the sink. His johnson was still half blue but he yanked up his shorts and pants and got back onto the cot. As it turned out, painting that bastard's crotch was the nicest thing me and my partner could ever have done for him."

"Police brutality," I said. "Now he had proof."

"Right. If he had gone to a lawyer about the pain in his knee, I'd have said it got hurt in the bar while he was resisting arrest. His thing was blue, though. And we'd just confiscated a boxful of spray paint from the school kids. What could we say at a hearing? 'The perpetrator made a break for it, so we painted his wee-wee blue.' We had no way out."

"So you let Beale go."

"We had to. My partner and I explained it to the sergeant and then we went to the owner of the bar. Then we talked it over with Beale, made it seem like a big favor we were doing him. Once he agreed, we took him to the hospital for his knee. And that, as they say, was that. He was a free man."

"I'd heard that the district attorney had a hand in releasing him."

"You heard wrong. Beale never spoke to the district attorney. None of it even went on his record. The only one who got in trouble was me —me and my partner. A couple days later, after we thought it was all settled, Beale gets arrested again. This time for torching his wife's hair. Sweet guy, huh? In the detective's office, trying to make things easy for himself, he rats out on my partner and me. Tells everything, how I whacked his knee, how we worked him over in the bar, the whole spray painting business. He pulls down his pants, right in the detective's office, and there's still some paint on him. And, of course, it matches the color we confiscated from the kids. . . . I got called in on it, so did my partner. The rotten part is that Beale didn't have to say a word. His wife mummed up eventually. But by shooting his yap, he got me and my partner in a hell of a lot of trouble. We got a real screwing after that. You don't want to hear about it, I know."

"Another time," I said.

"But you can guess now why I wouldn't mind coming over there. Or why I wouldn't mind meeting back up with that son of a—"

Lisa grabbed the phone from my hand. "So you can wheel him around in a swivel chair again?" She let out a laugh and gave me back the phone.

"*Lisa*?" Gary said. "Lisa? Michael, let me talk to her."

I offered her the receiver but she was shaking her head, grinning broadly, a small tear forming in each eye. Her little joke, it seemed, had gone a long way in amusing her. "Sorry," I said to Gary. "She doesn't want to talk to you."

"What do you mean 'She doesn't want to'? What gives?"

"Nothing gives."

"Why won't she talk to me then?"

"I don't know."

"What does that mean, 'I don't know'?"

"It means I don't know, Gary. Why not call her tomorrow and ask her yourself?"

"Because I'm asking you, Michael. Man to man. Why won't she talk to me?"

"Because she doesn't want to."

"I know that. But why doesn't she want to?"

Lisa had moved her head back next to mine, listening in. She put her hand over the mouthpiece. "Tell him it's because he's a jerk."

"What's the game over there?" Gary asked. "Lisa's on the extension? What's the scoop?"

"No scoop. She's not on the extension."

She took the phone again. "Hi, Gary. What's up? No, I was just teasing. I know you don't want to wheel Beale around. . . . There isn't anything going on. We're okay. We're fine. No. Don't start that again. Really, you don't have . . . you better not. You'll just be wasting your time . . . I mean it, Gary, don't! We won't let you in . . . what are you—? Don't be like that. I don't have an . . . I'm not the one with the attitude. You're the one with the . . . Hello . . . ?" Lisa held the receiver from her ear, looked at it a moment and then dropped it onto the bed. Her expression was one of utter shock. "He hung up on me," she said to my wife. "The fink. I wanted to hang up on *him*."

"Then call him back," my wife told her, rising from the bed. She took a step towards us. "Tell him, 'Thanks for the pointers,' and then slam down the phone. That'll fix him." She tweaked the tip of Lisa's nose. Her mood, once again, appeared to be on the upswing.

"Except I won't thank him for anything. He can keep his measly pointers. I'll just slam the phone down and leave him wondering who it was." She stood up next to my wife and did a little stretching movement: knees bent, butt out, arms stretched overhead. She stood up straight and folded her arms in front of her, a pinch of flesh protruding from the bottom of her panties.

"So, he told you nothing useful," my wife said to me.

"Just a story from his police days. Some of it was interesting."

"I didn't think so," Lisa said. "Nothing Gary says interests me. It's like I told you before, there's only two things he cares about—being a cop and his muscles. Luckily we cut him off before he started blabbing about his muscles."

"I thought it was *him* who cut *you* off," my wife said.

"You know what I mean. It doesn't matter anyway. Hanging up on people is a rude thing to do."

"You're young. You'll get over it."

"I hope not. I want to remember him this way for the rest of his life. It'll serve him right."

I lifted my bottle from the floor and stood up next to my wife and Lisa. Downstairs, Beale's party was back in full swing, as loud as it had ever been. An old Four Seasons record, "Let's Hang On," was playing on the stereo. Beale and his pals were drumming along to it. Over their music I could hear someone hollering for Smooth Albert to "Quit hogging the bathroom." The card players in the bedroom below us were growing louder; there was an argument going on. Valerie, apparently, was disgusted, "grossed out." She was refusing to deal the next round of cards until Glass Eye Dick stuck his glass eye back into its socket. Without it, she said, he was the most repulsive thing she had ever seen ... "Gimme a break," he said in reply. "I play better like this."

My wife lifted the telephone directory off of the bed and held onto it with both hands. She moved towards the bedroom door. "Let's go into the living room. It's cooler in there."

Lisa took her drink from the nightstand and followed my wife's steps. "What's with the phone book? We're going to call someone else?"

"We have to do something."

"Why not call Beale's number then?" Lisa asked. "Get him on the phone and let him know this is his last chance."

"How many chances are we going to give this guy?"

"Two. And this is the last one."

"No," my wife told her. "It's a step backwards."

"But this way we've given him every chance we could. If he ends up with cops at his door he's got no one to blame but himself. Plus, and most important, it'll keep Michael from having to go down there again."

"Will it?" my wife asked. She and Lisa were standing in the doorway, watching me. "What do you think, Michael? Would you settle for calling him up?"

"Not Michael," Lisa said. "Me and you'll call. No more Mr. Nice Guy, either. We'll tell Beale what a sleaze he is. Make him feel like dirt."

My wife smiled at the thought and then shook her head. "No. We should just call the police and leave it up to them. By calling Beale—"

"It'll be fun," Lisa told her. "I'm drunk enough to do it, too."

"I know you are. But cursing him out isn't going to do the trick." She turned to me. "What do you think, Michael?"

"I think I should go down th—"

"About the phone call. Should we call him up?"

"If you and Lisa were to call," I said, "he'll think he had me beat. It'd look like I'm handing it over to two women to solve. He'd love it."

"No, he wouldn't," Lisa said. "Not once me and Denise get through with him. We're a couple of bitches when we want to be. You should hear us when you're not around. We've got mouths like dump truck drivers."

I followed them into the living room. "If we're going to call," I said, "let me do the talking."

"What are you going to say," my wife asked, "that you didn't say last time?"

"I'm going to tell him he's a liar and he's got thirty seconds to shut it all down. No more compromises."

"Why can't we just call the cops?"

"The police have bigger things to worry about, Denise. And even if they did come by and address it—which would surprise me—they'd wind up letting him go anyway. At worst, he'd get a summons and maybe pay a small fine on it. Which would leave me, sooner or later, still having to face him by myself. And then it'd be on his terms, not mine."

"You think calling him will avoid all of that?"

"If he listens, yes."

I followed my wife and Lisa into the living room, my wife carrying the directory under her arm. "What do you think?" she asked Lisa as they both sat down on the couch.

Lisa shrugged; she didn't know.

I settled into the chair opposite the couch. In front of me was the coffee table. I kicked off my sneakers and began to place my feet onto it. With them midway in the air, however, I caught a disapproving look from my wife and lowered them back down to the carpet. The table, like most of our furniture, was relatively new, purchased about three years ago when we were first married. My wife tried to keep it looking that way. "Almost forgot the rules," I told her, wanting to lighten the conversation. "I must be losing my mind."

"It's late," she said. "We're all getting a little stupid." She placed the directory on the table next to the fan and curled one leg beneath the other. "I'm exhausted," she said to no one in particular and dropped her hands into her lap and started to fidget with her nightie, tugging at its hem, trying to pull it past the tops of her thighs.

"Don't poop out on us now," Lisa said.

"I'm tired all of a sudden."

"You better not be," Lisa told her, sauntering over to my chair, putting a bit of movement into her hips. "You leave me and Michael un-chaperoned," she said, "and I can't guarantee that we'll behave ourselves." She sat down sideways on the armrest of the chair and laid a hand on my shoulder for support. "When the frump's not around," she told me, "maybe I'll let you feel my tattoo."

My wife gave me a look. "You better not, Michael," she said. "I'll find out about it."

"Oh, really?" Lisa asked. "How's that?"

"Because I know you," my wife said. "One way or another you'll let me know. You let me know about everything. . . ." She pointed a finger at me. "You're not saying much, Michael."

I took a long chug of beer, tossing back my head as I swallowed the last few drops. I placed the bottle onto the table and ran a hand beneath my collar. My wife had been mistaken about this room; the air was no cooler in here than in the bedroom. If anything, it was heavier, more stagnant. "Not to change the subject," I said, "but isn't it hot in here?" Lisa, sitting so close, only seemed to make it warmer. I looked at the fan on the table and watched it rotate towards us. I inched forward in the chair as it approached and shut my eyes as I felt a puff of its breeze just graze my chin. It began its rotation back towards the couch then, taking its meager wind with it. "Let's turn it up," I said and reached to the fan and turned the knob from Low to Medium to High.

"Thank God," said Lisa. "It's torture in here."

"I know," I agreed. "It's like a sauna."

My wife flicked the knob back to Low. "It's not that bad," she told us.

"It's worse," Lisa said. "Have a heart. We're suffocating."

"I feel fine," my wife said.

"Then aim it at me and Michael."

"It's better to leave it oscillating," my wife explained. "The air stays fresher that way. The fan keeps it whirling around."

"I don't feel anything *whirling* around," Lisa said. She pulled at the front of her bra and snapped it back against her chest. "The only thing I feel whirling is heat." She made a move for the fan but my wife gave her wrist a smack.

"Come on," Lisa said, "I'm bubbling."

"You're always bubbling."

"Really, I mean it."

"Tough."

"Tough on you. . . ." Lisa let go of my shoulder and reached past me for the fan. "It's not fair," she said to my wife. "Hot people have no rights in this world. It's always the cold ones that get their way."

My wife pushed Lisa's hand from the fan and then let out a little shriek as Lisa pushed her hand in return. "C'mon," she laughed. "Cut it out."

"*Me* cut it out?" Lisa asked, "How about you?"

"I'll cut it out as soon as you do."

"Yeah, sure, Denise. You must think I'm really—"

"*Dumb,*" my wife said. "You're right, I do. You're ugly, too."

"Boy," Lisa groaned happily, "you've got to be in charge of absolutely everything." She was laughing, jerking back and forth in front of me, struggling with my wife. I couldn't see, exactly, what they were doing. All I could see was the smooth tanned flesh of Lisa's bare back— that and the washing instructions on her bra: Hand wash/Hang dry.

"Let's be adults about this," my wife said. "It's *my* fan. So, we keep it set at *my* preference. Low."

Lisa settled back on the armrest, returning her hand to my shoulder. "Okay," she said, "but if I get any hotter, I'm going to strip down in front of your husband. Panties and all . . . You wouldn't mind that, would you, Michael?"

"If you're trying to embarrass him," my wife said, "you're wasting your time."

"I'm not trying to embarrass anyone, Denise. What I'm trying to do is piss you off."

"Well, it's not working, so let's get down to business. You wanted to make a phone call, right?" My wife reached toward the directory on the table and flipped it open. She started thumbing through its thin, noisy pages, searching for "Beale, N", flipping backwards through the pages, stopping finally at page 72, BEAKMAN-BECK. She ran her finger slowly down the left hand column and then slowly back up. She repeated the motion twice, tapping her finger against the book before closing it up. "He's not in here," she told Lisa. "He must be unlisted."

"I don't blame him," Lisa said. "He's probably been getting nasty calls his entire life."

I picked Lisa's drink off of the table and took a sip. I smacked my lips and took another. It tasted surprisingly weak, as if it'd been made with several parts of mix for each part of vodka. Perhaps that was how she and my wife had been able to go on drinking all night without falling on their faces.

"So, what do we do now?" my wife asked.

"Let's weasel the number out of Information," Lisa said. "Pretend we're Beale's long lost grandmother or something."

"Information would never give it to us. I've tried it with other numbers. They've heard every story in the world."

I put Lisa's drink back on the table. "When I was downstairs," I said, "the first person I spoke with was Beale's wife, Rosanne. She told me she gave you her number once, a long time ago. Do you think you might still have it?"

My wife leaned back into the couch, shut her eyes for a moment and then nodded her head. "It's in my address book. She gave it to me when she first moved in. I met her in the laundry room."

"Lucky you," Lisa said.

"She seemed nice. I feel bad now for never calling. I think she wanted to be friends."

"Good thing you're a snob," Lisa said. "Otherwise, we'd all be down there banging the bongos."

My wife rose from the couch and went to the bedroom, adjusting her nightie as she went. She returned a minute later, carrying a pack of Marlboros and her address book. "Any idea," she asked me, "what you're going to say to him this time?"

"I haven't given it much thought," I told her. "With this kind of thing you're better off winging it. You'd come off as phony if you had some indignant speech prepared." I stood up and went into the dining room for the telephone, not as sure of this as I sounded. Who knew if I'd even be able to get Beale on the phone? If his wife or Junior or Lenny answered, they might not put him on, knowing that it was me, anticipating a fight. The music down there was so loud they might not even hear the phone ring. For that matter, I might end up getting nothing but a busy signal; the receiver might be off the hook or, just as likely, the caller for Smooth Albert might still be holding.

I flicked on the light switch and went to the half-wall that separated the dining room from the kitchen. I took the phone off its stand and grabbed a book of matches next to the candles on the dining table. At the head of the table was a setting of our new silverware from Bloomingdale's, laid out neatly on a white cloth napkin: my wife showing off her new purchases for Lisa. I pulled the napkin from beneath the silverware and stuck it into my rear pocket. "Anyone want something from the kitchen?" I called. "Chips? Something to drink?"

"Liver and onions," Lisa said. "And a Pink Squirrel."

I shut off the light and carried the phone into the living room, unwinding its cord as I walked.

"What's with the napkin?" my wife asked, pointing to my rear pocket?"

"It's to disguise my voice. In case someone besides Beale answers the phone."

Lisa leaned forward, still sitting on the armrest of the chair. She pulled the napkin from my pocket and held it up to her face bandito fashion. "Pretty tricky," she said.

"He's been going to secret agent school," my wife told her. "Surveillance Tactics and Napkin Use."

Lisa lowered the napkin. Her lips were parted in a half smile. "We should be nice to Michael. He's got a tough phone call to make." She folded the napkin in half and raised it to a point just below the bridge of her nose, turning it into a sort of harem girl's mask. "How," she asked me, "may I please you, Master?"

I settled down beside her, not bothering to answer, my thoughts drifting back to Beale and his crew. The steam was running out of their percussion section but the party, as a whole, was as loud as it had ever been. I lit a cigarette and stuck the match into the empty beer bottle at my feet.

"So," Lisa said, handing me the napkin, "are we going to make that call?"

My wife opened her address book and picked up the receiver. She cradled it between her ear and shoulder. "Are you ready, Michael?"

I nodded in the affirmative and so did Lisa.

My wife dialed a few numbers then. She checked the address book and dialed a few more.

"This is exciting," Lisa said. She laced her fingers around my forearm. "It's lucky I thought of it."

"What would we do without you?" My wife dialed the final number and offered me the phone.

"Here goes . . ." I took the receiver from her and draped the napkin over its mouthpiece. I listened to the first soft ring.

"Let me listen," Lisa said. She shifted her weight on the armrest.

I heard the phone ring another time. "Alright," I said to her. "You can listen but no funny business." I switched the receiver from left hand to right and held it an inch from my ear.

Lisa angled her head next to mine. "I can't hear," she said. "Is it still ring—oops."

A voice came on the line; it belonged to a male, slightly hoarse, with a tough street accent. He sounded tired and pissed off, like I'd just woken him from a long restless sleep. "Beale's," was all he said.

"Nicky home?"

"Who's this?"

"Who's *this*?" I asked in return.

"I'm asking you," he said. I heard his mouth working on a piece of gum, slow and sassy, sounding a lot like the first guy I'd spoken to when I was down there, the guy with the sleeveless sweatshirt and bad attitude.

"Stop wasting my time," I said.

"You got a problem?" he asked me. "Something I can help you with?"

"Christ," I said. "Here we go again."

"Say what, smart guy?"

I rolled my eyes for the benefit of Lisa. "Let me talk to Nicky."

"Try your mother's house."

"What?"

"She's giving Nicky something for dinner. Something special."

He let out a noise close to a cackle, his voice fading as he moved his mouth away from the phone. It gave me the idea that, like myself, he had someone listening in next to him.

"That's a good one," I told him. "Mind if I use it sometime?"

"You won't tell me who you are, so screw off."

"I'm an acquaintance of Nicky's."

"Like bullshit you—"

"Who is this . . . ?" It was a different voice asking me now. It sounded like Rosanne's.

I wrapped the napkin tighter around the mouthpiece. "Nicky home?" I asked.

"Yeah, he's home," she said. "You want to talk to him, all you got to do is tell me what's going on." I heard voices muttering behind her, voices ordering other voices to quiet down. I heard the volume of the stereo turned lower then; the last of the percussion playing came to an end. "You have three sec—"

"*Give me that thing!*" Another voice was on the line. "*Who is this?*"

It was Beale asking this time. I covered the mouthpiece and looked at Lisa. "It's Beale," I whispered to her.

She nodded, eyes closed, indicating that she had already figured it out.

"Beale," I said into the phone, "you messed with me."

"What are you talking about?"

"I'm talking about you. You can't be trusted."

"You're talking like you know me."

"I know you."

"You don't know squat."

"I could write a book on you, Beale."

"Who is this?" His voice was a mixture of bravado and uncertainty. "Mambo?" he asked. "Stinky?"

"You have a lot of enemies," I said.

"Meatballs, if this is you, I'm—"

"You're not even warm," I told him.

"Ain't Donny?" he said, "are you?"

"Who is it?" a voice in the background hollered. I heard Beale's voice trail off from the phone. "I think it's Meatballs," he said. "Maybe Donny the Douche. He's not saying."

I heard a soft clicking noise, someone picking up on Beale's extension, probably one of the card players in the bedroom. For all that I could tell, Beale was unaware of it. He finished addressing the voice behind him and returned his attention to me. "If you're one of those junkies, you better quit calling here. I got nothing more to say. I explained it ten times. I knew nothing about it."

"Save it, Beale. You're getting cold."

"How'd you get my number?"

"It wasn't hard."

"You dial it again and I'm gonna break your fingers. How'd you like that?"

"You're scaring me," I said.

"What's your problem, anyway?"

"You make people's lives uncomfortable."

"Is that so?"

"I'm through playing it your way, Beale. You proved you can't be trusted."

"I don't know what you're talking about."

"We had a deal," I said.

"Whoever you are, you're—wait a minute." He laughed loudly, heartily. "I know who this is. It's Five E, ain't it?"

"What's a Five E?" I asked.

"It's a moron who's going to get himself hurt if he doesn't get off my phone."

"Your mind is diseased, Beale."

"Where'd you hear that?"

"You're a wife beater."

"I'm a *moron* beater, too," he said. "You're wasting your time if you're trying to hurt my feelings."

"You're a scum sucker, Beale."

"I'm going to kick your teeth in, asshole. You don't get off my phone, I'm gonna rip your face off."

"Spread the disease, Beale."

"I'll tear your ears—"

"Dog killer."

"Right off of your head."

The guy who'd been listening in on Beale's extension broke in on us. "What're we listening to this jack-off for, Nicky? We ought to smash his f—"

"*Paulie!*" Beale shouted. "Get off the phone. Get off it now."

"Nicky, I'm just say—"

"You hang up, Paulie. This is between me and ass-wipe here. Nobody else."

I looked at Lisa. Gradually, she'd been sliding from the armrest towards me; she was practically in my lap now, sitting sideways across my knees. She laid her hand over the mouthpiece. "Let me talk to him," she whispered. "There's something I want to try."

I shook my head and pried her fingers from the mouthpiece. "Lie to me," I said into the phone, "one more time, Beale, and I'll break your other knee."

"What do you know about my knee? Who are you? A cop?"

I looked back at Lisa. Her mouth was one large grin.

"You've got to be a cop," Beale was saying. "How else did you get my number?"

"I'm not a cop, Beale. And I'm not Donny the Douche. You were right about—"

Lisa grabbed the receiver from me. "Nicky, Nicky," she said, "how's your dicky?"

"What the fuck?"

"How's your dick, Nick?"

Beale cleared his throat. "You really want to know?" he asked her, lowering his voice into a smooth, suggestive purr. "Why don't you come over, honey, and see for yourself?"

Lisa handed me back the phone. She straightened herself on my lap, laughing like a little kid.

Beale was still going through his patter, coming on like some juiced-up porn addict. "You wanna play with it, honey? We'll work something out."

I switched the receiver from my right hand to my left. "A blue dick like yours?" I said. "With one ball? She prefers whole men, Beale."

"What do you know about—? You *are* a cop. I knew it was a cop."

"Listen, One Nut," Lisa shouted, "you one-balled creep, either—"

A loud whooping horselaugh sounded at the other end of the line: the eavesdropper, Paulie, had been listening in again. "Nicky's got one ball" he announced to whoever was in earshot. "He's only got one ball"

"*Paulie*," Beale yelled, "I'll whip your ass like—"

"One ball! He's short one ball!"

Beale let out a scream. "I'm going to come in there, Paulie and I'm gonna punch your face out."

I took the empty bottle from the floor and rapped it twice against the phone's mouthpiece. "Bongo time's over, Beale. I'm giving you—"

He was no longer on the line. Nor was Paulie. A dial tone was all that I could hear."

"Beale," I said into the phone, "are you there . . . ?" But it was obvious that he wasn't. More than likely, he was in the bedroom now shutting up Paulie. He was probably taking care of him the same way he had taken care of the drunk in the Hawaiian shirt. In a few minutes, once he had cooled down, he'd be back in the living room, huddling with his friends, piecing together what had happened, trying to figure out who the caller might have been.

I put my bottle back on the floor and handed the receiver to Lisa. "Sounds like he took it personally," I said.

She was laughing, rocking lightly on my knee. She supported herself with an arm across my shoulders. "He had it coming," she said. She brought the receiver to her ear, listened for a moment and then set it into its cradle on the coffee table. "If anything, we let him off too easy."

I slid a hand around her waist, steadying her on my knee. Through the corner of my eye I stole a glance toward the couch. My wife was watching us; her look was grim, irritable. I turned my attention back to Lisa. "I wouldn't say that we let him off easily."

"You're right. He's probably in the closet now, hiding behind the coats, too ashamed to come out." Several beads of perspiration had formed on her brow. She wiped them away with the backs of her finger-tips and turned to my wife on the couch. "Is something wrong, Denise? You seem angry."

My wife didn't answer. She was still looking at us, staring at us. She attempted a smile but it only made her angry face appear angrier.

Lisa reached over and waved a hand before my wife's eyes. "Yoo-hoo, Denise. I'm talking to you."

"I can hear you," my wife said.

"And . . . ?"

"And I *am* angry. You two acted like a couple of nitwits."

Lisa pointed an innocent finger toward her chest, incredulous. "Me and Michael? Nitwits?"

"You were juvenile," my wife told her. "Idiots."

"Us? Me and Michael?" Lisa asked again, requiring further clarification.

"It was immature. And stupid. Especially 'How's your dicky?' You sounded like a twelve-year-old."

"It made you laugh. I saw you, Denise. You were laughing just as much as me."

"Maybe for a second," my wife told her. "And only because it was so stupid."

"It wasn't stupid. It's what he needed to hear. We wanted to get him upset, embarrass him."

"Lisa's right," I said. "It worked, too."

My wife lowered her head to the side and concentrated for a moment. The stereo remained shut off. There was no more instrument playing. The only real noise that could be heard was that of the party disbanding, people bidding their goodbyes as they left the apartment, the front door closing behind them. Unfortunately, however, not everyone was leaving; maybe half. The ones staying behind were the diehards, Beale's closer chums, the gruff voiced males that I was used to hearing on most Friday and Saturday nights.

"You see?" Lisa asked my wife. "They're quieter now. It did work."

"They've been quiet before. It doesn't last long."

"This time it will," Lisa said, "You should've heard what me and Michael said to him."

"I heard. I was sitting right here."

"Then you should have heard what Beale said to us. He was fuming. I knew he wouldn't feel like partying after what me and Michael put him through."

"Maybe you got him quiet for now, Lisa. Maybe for the whole night. But It doesn't mean anything about the future and it doesn't mean—"

"It's a start," Lisa said. There was a bit of a whine in her voice. "What do you want from me, anyway? You want me to come over here every weekend and tell him to be quiet for you?"

"Are you serious? That's the last thing I—"

"If they get too loud again just do the same thing I did."

"Right," my wife said. "I'll just call up and ask him, 'How's your dicky . . . ?' How many times do you think he'll fall for that one?"

Lisa lifted her hands, disgusted. "Then do what you want, Denise. Next time handle it yourself."

"I wish that I could," she said. "Except we can't call the police anymore because it was *us* who just harassed *him*. We can't go to his door anymore because he'll murder us. Who knows what our car will look like tomorrow. Now I'm worried about even riding the elevator again."

"Gimme a break, "Lisa said. "You're really overdoing it."

"Oh, am I?"

"He's not even sure it's us, Denise. He only thinks it might be us. He also thinks it's a cop named Meatballs."

My wife looked at me. "Is that right, Michael?"

"He isn't sure who it is."

She folded her arms. "No, but he'll figure it out. Give him time."

"It could have been anyone that called him," I said. "There're other people besides us holding a grudge against him."

"That's right," Lisa told my wife. "And even if he did figure it out, he'd never do anything about it. After all the trouble he's caused us, he wouldn't have the audacity to accuse us of anything."

"Don't tell me about Beale's audacity."

Lisa moved a little further into my lap. "You're such a worrywart. Even if he does know it's us, and even if he does do something like ruining your car, your insurance company will pay the damages. And then you can give them Beale's name and they'll have him arrested. Who knows? Maybe you can sue Beale yourself and come out a little ahead on the deal."

My wife shifted forward on the couch. "That's easy for you to say, Lisa. You don't have to go without a car for a week. Or pay the hike in insurance. Or go to court to testify against him. Or hire a lawyer to defend yourself against Beale's countersuit."

"His *countersuit*?" Lisa asked, incredulous. "He's not going to countersue."

"Don't tell me what he will and won't do. Tomorrow, you walk away from this. I've got to live here. You have no place telling—"

"Look, Denise, even if he countersues it doesn't mean he has a case against you. All you've got to do is call all his friends to the witness stand and have your lawyer break them down, one by one. Get them to confess about everything he did."

My wife groaned. "What are you doing, Lisa? Playing devil's advocate? Or are you really that stupid?"

"I'm trying to help. I'm trying to show you—"

"No," my wife said. "Don't show me anything. Don't tell me anything. It's not doing any good."

Lisa removed her arm from my shoulders. "Then I don't know what else you want me to do. I'm only trying to help."

"No, you're not. You're making excuses for your stupid behavior."

"I'm not making—what do you mean 'stupid'? I'm beginning to resent all these insults about being dumb."

"Tough," my wife said. "You *were* dumb, you were selfish, too. You had no right."

"I had every right," Lisa said. "Just because you don't want to get involved doesn't mean I can't."

"You're talking stupid again, Lisa. You whimper when I call you stupid but you continue saying stupid things."

Lisa brushed the hair from her face. "You know, Denise, you've been calling me that ever since I've known you. I'm sick of it. I've got just as good a job as you. I earn as much money as you. I went to college the same as you."

"You didn't exactly make the dean's list."

"So, what?"

"So, nothing," my wife told her. "Anyone can *go* to college. It's another thing to do *well* in college."

"I told Beale what I told him because I thought it would help. And because I thought it was funny."

"Well, it wasn't funny. And it didn't help. Not in the least."

"Alright," Lisa said. "Then I'm sorry. I apologize. What more can I do?" There was a certain scratchiness to her voice. Tears were beginning to form in her eyes. I can't stand to see a woman cry.

"Next time," my wife said, "consider the consequences before screwing everything up. Think before—"

I raised a hand, pointed a finger at my wife. "Drop it," I said. "Let it go." My tone was low; measured. "Do you understand me, Denise?"

"What are you doing now? Taking her side?"

"I said to drop it. Just lay off her."

Lisa touched my arm. She blinked several times as the tears began to run down her cheeks. "It's okay, Michael. You don't have to defend me."

"That's right," my wife said. "Lisa can take care of herself."

"No." I looked into my wife's eyes; I felt them lock into my own. "You're in a lousy mood, Denise. You're tired and you're upset with Beale. Don't take it out on Lisa."

She stood from the couch, hands on hips. "Don't tell me what sort of mood I'm in. And don't tell me what to do either. Not in front of her."

"Tell *you* what to do?" Lisa demanded. She wiped the tears from her cheeks and rubbed a hand against her thigh. "You've been dishing out orders all night long."

"Oh, have I?"

"You sure have," Lisa answered, her voice starting to crack. "You've been doing it for a lot longer than that, too."

"What does that mean?"

"You've been bossing me around," Lisa said, "for as long as I can remember."

"Is that so?"

"You're a bossy person, Denise. You can be a real bitch."

My wife nodded. "Anything else about me that's been bugging you?"

"Plenty. But I'm not going to sink to your level by mentioning it."

"Good," my wife said. "Now do me a favor. For the last twenty minutes, you've been sitting on top of my husband, looking like a perfect slut. Why don't you act like a lady for once and get the hell off him?"

Lisa made no move to get up. She did her blinking thing again as a new group of tears began to form in her eyes. "That has nothing to do with it, Denise."

"Would you get off of his lap, please?"

"I'm not bothering anyone."

"I mean it, Lisa."

"If you're worried, Denise, that there's something going on between me and Michael, let me assure you that you're quite mistaken."

"Get off of him."

Lisa held firm. "I will not," she said. "Not until—"

"Will you puh-leeze get out of his lap?"

"No," she said. "You've been pushing me around for ten years. You insult me whenever you feel like it. In front of everyone. You call me stupid. A slut. I'm sick of it."

"Then act like a lady," my wife told her.

"I'll do what I want," Lisa said, "when I want. . . ." Her words were stubborn but the voice she said them with was fragile, on the verge of breaking. She ran the backs of her fingers across the side of her face and rubbed her eyes. They were in bad shape: red, sore looking, still moist with her tears. What mascara hadn't run down her cheeks was beginning to cake at the end of her lashes. "You're the worst hostess," she told my wife, "that I've ever known."

"Lisa," I said. I shifted my legs and placed my palm against the base of her back. I applied a little pressure, hoping to coax her from my lap. She wasn't budging, however; not an inch. "Lisa," I said again, "it's late. You've both had too much to drink."

"No, Michael," she said. "This has been building for a long time. If you're caught in the middle, I'm sorry."

"That's hardly the problem," I said.

She took her arm from around my shoulders. "I won't get up for Denise, but if you ask me to, I'll get up for you."

My wife let out a laugh. "Don't hold your breath waiting. I'm sure Michael just loves having you as his little lap ornament."

Lisa swiped at her eyes and then she began to sob. "Stop it. Just go away and leave me alone."

"No," my wife told her. "*You* stop it. *You* go away." She grabbed onto Lisa's wrist. She gave it a twist, a quick jerk, and yanked her from my lap, standing her up straight. "I might be a rotten hostess but this is still my home. When you're in it, you'll behave according to my rules, not yours."

"Denise," I said. "Easy."

Lisa wrenched her wrist free from my wife. She took a step to the side and moved backwards around the coffee table. "I'm leaving," she said, coughing out the words. "I don't need this abuse." She was crying freely now, soft tears flowing from her eyes, running down her face. Her nose, her cheeks, were flushed with blood. She inhaled deeply, making a delicate sniffling noise as she wiped away some of the tears with the tips of her fingers.

"Listen," my wife told her, "no one is asking you to leave. All I'm asking is that you show a little more maturity, a little more respect for my home."

"I know what you think of me now."

"C'mon," my wife said. "We're friends." She walked to the center of the room. Her pace was slow, arms at her sides, eyes cast down. She looked, suddenly, very sad and very alone. I rose from the chair and stood beside her.

Lisa looked at the two of us together and then she looked at me. "I don't know what to do," she said.

I took a step towards her and touched her shoulder. "Stay," I told her.

My wife nodded, seconding it.

Lisa rubbed her wrist and then shook it a couple of times. She held it out for our inspection. It looked similar to her eyes: red and sore. "You hurt me," she told my wife. "I think you sprained it." She pulled it back and, with the full length of her hand, wiped her face once again. "I've got to wash up," she said. "Where's my stuff?'"

My wife pointed to the floor at the far end of the couch, where, in a small neat pile, all of Lisa's belongings were stacked: her powder blue skirt, her white pullover blouse, her shoes, her purse, and, on top of it all, her "Foxy Lady" beach bag.

Lisa grabbed the beach bag and her purse. She sniffled one last time and headed for the bathroom. For a moment, I felt like following her in there, sitting her on the side of the tub and dabbing away her tears with a cool wet washcloth. Instead, however, I sat back down in my chair and lit a fresh cigarette. "You came down on her kind of hard," I told my wife.

"Since when has she been Miss Sensitivity?"

"She was only trying to help."

"So she said."

"You think she had other motives?"

"I don't think she had any motives. She never does. Like she told us, she does what she wants to do when she wants to do it. . . . the hell with the consequences."

"She made a mistake, Denise. Period. You're turning this into something more than it is."

"I'm not turning it into anything. It was a dumb thing to do. She acted stupidly. You both acted stupidly. It's over now. I'm willing to drop it."

"It might be too late. She was pretty upset."

"What do you care?"

"I care because she's your friend."

"Spare me, huh?" She took Lisa's drink from the table and finished it off in one chug. She sat back down on the couch.

"Not much of a drink," I said, pointing at the glass, hoping to change the topic. "It goes down like water."

"She fixes them that way on purpose. So she can drink them longer."

"Makes sense."

"Not to me," my wife said. "Why doesn't she just make them normal and drink a little slower?"

I shrugged, not knowing, not caring.

"She has no discipline," my wife went on. "It's another one of her faults."

I reached over and took her hands between my own. "Try to relax," I said. "You've been friends for twelve years. You don't want to throw it away because of one bad night."

"What are you taking her side for?"

"I'm not taking anybody's side. Mostly I just feel bad for her. She made a mistake. Let it go."

My wife separated her hands from mine and drew one of the Marlboros from the box. Her face was tired, sunken. She lit the cigarette and blew out the match. "I'm just worried. I'm scared about Beale. Are you sure he didn't know who you were?"

"He knew a couple of minutes into the talk. Then I threw him off track by quoting some of the history Gary gave me. I doubt if he knows who it is now. His wife might be able to put it together for him . . . if she remembers giving you their unlisted number last year and then remembers that she told me about it tonight. Otherwise, Beale can't be positive. He can't prove anything."

I picked the empty glass and beer bottle off the coffee table and brought them into the kitchen. I grabbed a fresh beer from the refrigerator and twisted the cap open. Once again, I wasn't as confident about Beale as I'd pretended to be. It wouldn't be long before he figured it all out. Downstairs things were still quiet but that didn't mean much. He and his friends could be huddled in a corner right now going over their plan of attack. Or, just as likely, they could be outside in our building's parking lot, putting the finishing touches on my Toyota. There was no telling what they were up to.

I brought the beer to my lips and took a long swallow. My mouth was dry and my stomach was beginning to feel empty. Except for the beer, I hadn't much in me tonight: a "Hungry Man" dinner when I'd gotten home, an ice cream sandwich and some green olives and that was it. I flicked on the kitchen light and looked around for what was good. On top of the refrigerator, behind the liquor, there was a small box, a "Fun-pak," of miniature chocolate doughnuts. Behind it, lying on its side, was a large bag of potato chips. I chose the chips, poured half of the bag into a silver bowl and took them out into the living room with my bottle of beer. I looked at my wife as I entered the room. She was on the couch, leaning over, playing with Lester. He'd come out of hiding apparently; he was hovering around her, doing his figure eight routine between her ankles. I took my spot on the chair and set my beer and the bowl on the coffee table. "Chips," I announced.

My wife paid me little notice. She stroked Lester behind the ear. After a while she said, "When Lisa comes out of the bathroom, I'm going to apologize to her."

I took a swallow of beer, saying nothing.

"She can be a jerk," my wife said. "And a flirt. But she means well."

I offered her the chips but she showed no interest. "You look tired," I said.

"I'm exhausted. And I feel like a mess."

"It's been a long night," I said, "and it's not over yet." Downstairs, the people that remained were beginning to raise their voices. They weren't so loud that I could hear exactly what they were saying but they were loud enough that I could get a fix on their mood: it was a mean one. The party, for most purposes, was over, and these loyal few, it seemed, were staying behind for a reason. I couldn't hear any of the friendlier voices I'd previously encountered, Junior's or Lenny's or even Rosanne's. The only voices that I could make out were the hostile ones. I took a long breath and held onto it and sat perfectly still, trying to pick out whatever conversation that I could. The words "junkie" and "asshole" kept coming up. So did the names "Meatballs" and "Five E." It was Beale doing most of the talking. His voice was throaty, pissed, and it came out in short violent bursts: "I'll find out . . . Scumbag thinks he's smart . . . I'll beat it out of him."

"Michael?" my wife asked me. "Are you feeling okay?"

I let out my breath of air and took a sip of beer and offered the bottle to my wife. She shook her head no. "Look," I said. I pointed to the floor where Lester now laid against her feet, his chin resting on her big toe. "Pooped kitten."

She nodded. "We're both tuckered out."

"Do you feel like another vodka and tonic? I'll fix it."

"I don't think so. I've had enough to drink."

"If you're sure. . . ." I heard the bathroom door open. A moment later, Lisa's feet were padding down the hallway. She stopped just outside the living room and zipped up her beach bag. Her face, from what I could see, looked different. She had washed up, put on a little blush and some lipstick. Her hair was pulled away from her face on one side, sort of flamenco style, held by a small brown comb. "You look good," I told her. As an afterthought, I added, "for three o'clock in the morning."

Lisa smiled, eyes cast down. "Is it that late?"

"Close to it."

My wife reached for my beer and took a swig: a rarity for her; she never drinks beer. "Lisa," she said, "about our argument . . ." She paused a moment as she placed the bottle back on the table and then coughed into her hand. I had the feeling that she was stalling, waiting, perhaps, for Lisa to jump in and say "Unnecessary," or "If anyone should apologize, it's me." Lisa, however, said nothing of the kind and so my wife continued. "About before, I realize that you meant well. I shouldn't have said the things I did."

"We're all tired," I put in. "Words were said that weren't meant."

Lisa placed her beach bag next to the coffee table. She reached for the box of Marlboros and then pulled back her hand. "Okay to take one?"

"Sure," I said.

"Of course," my wife said.

I flipped open the box. "They're for everyone."

Lisa drew one out, put it between her lips and lit it with the matches from the table. Her movements were slow and fluid, almost elegant. "I've been grubbing all night," she said. "I probably owe you two a carton by now."

"Don't be silly," my wife said. "You're welcome to anything we have."

Lisa lowered her eyes again, holding the cigarette between her fingers. She made no move to sit down.

"Anyone for another drink?" I asked. "A nightcap?'"

Lisa shrugged, indifferent. She tried a smile but the strain was obvious. "What do you feel like, Denise?"

"A drink will put me right to sleep. I'm ready to crash out now."

I clapped my hands and rubbed them briskly together. "I'll make them myself," I announced. "Teach you girls how to make a real drink." I polished off the remainder of my beer and held up the bottle to show that it was empty. For us to go to bed now would be the worst thing that we could do. "One last drink," I said. "It'll be the best thing for everyone."

"Let me pee and wash up first," my wife said, rising from the couch. "No, actually, you know what I'd like to do? I'd rather take a nice hot shower. Wash the stickiness off and wake myself up."

"Anything you want," I said. "Me and Lisa'll make the drinks."

My wife moved around the table. She made it halfway out of the room before looking back at Lisa. "Again," she told her, "I want to say . . . well, I know that you didn't mean any harm." She smiled quickly and disappeared around the corner.

I leaned back into the chair, hearing the bathroom door shut behind her. I looked up at Lisa. "You'd probably prefer to hear it from Denise," I said, "but she *is* sorry. She regrets having said those things."

"She can say what she wants. I don't care."

"Of course you do."

"No. It doesn't matter. I'm going to have another drink. Maybe two. And then I'm going to hit the sack for a couple of hours. I'll be out of here before Denise wakes up."

"Don't do that. You've been friends too long."

"I thought it over in the bathroom. She's been putting me down since I've known her. I'm not going to take it anymore. If I didn't have so far to drive, I'd probably go home right now."

Actually, it wasn't that far a drive—five miles tops, half of it highway. I held onto the thought, however, and said "I'll drive you home if that's the problem. But I'd prefer that you'd stay."

"I will stay. Like I told you. I'm going to have another drink. Maybe—"

"Two," I finished. "And then you're going to hit the sack for a couple of hours."

She smiled. "You have a good memory."

"You have a memorable way of saying things."

She lifted her head. "Are you trying to compliment me, Michael?"

"Absolutely," I said.

"Well, it's not doing any good. I'm still leaving first thing in the morning."

I crossed my legs. "It's three a.m.," I told her. "Right now is first thing in the morning."

"You know what I—You're starting to sound like Denise." She took a step towards my chair, her mouth a tight grin. "You're calling me stupid, too. Just like your wife."

"I'd never call you stupid."

"Oh, yeah?"

"I'd never say anything to hurt you."

She looked at her bare feet and then she looked at me. "You're telling the truth?"

I nodded that I was.

"It's not just Denise," she said. "A lot of people make fun of me. I don't know why. They just—it's because I let them, isn't it?"

"Not anymore you don't."

"That's right," she said and took another step towards my chair. "Not anymore." She said the words quietly, her temper subdued. I was sorry about the events that put her in this mood but I had to admit that I liked her this way, too; more mature, more feminine. She turned towards the table, dipping a bit at the knee, and stabbed her cigarette out in the ashtray. "A minute ago," she said, "you mentioned something about a drink. About making a *real* drink."

I pushed myself up and grabbed the empty bottle from the table. I heard noise coming from downstairs: another fight was flaring up. I put a finger to my lips, asking Lisa to be still. I could hear shouting, swearing down there. The fight was between Beale and his wife. They were arguing about Beale's friends, his parties. Rosanne was sick of them; she'd had enough. "And I've had enough of you," he told her. It sounded like it was just the two of them. There were no derisive words coming from Beale's pals, no hoots of laughter. There was no sense of Beale playing to them, either. His voice was different now; it was more personal, more intimate; his words were aimed solely at Rosanne, not at an audience.

The observation relieved me some. Unless his friends were outside vandalizing my car right now, I was through with the bunch of them, at least for tonight.

"Right," I said to Lisa. "Let's make those drinks."

She looped her arm around mine and turned us toward the kitchen. "I'm dying for one," she said.

I heard my wife in the bathroom, the faucets being turned on, first the heavy drone of tub water, then the quieter spray of the shower. The noise stirred Lester from his sleep. He did a stretch and followed Lisa and I through the dining room and into the kitchen. As soon as his paws touched the linoleum, however, he turned around and scooted out.

"Eccentric kitten," I said. I flicked on the overhead light and dropped my bottle into the trash can.

"What'd you say?" Lisa pulled her arm from mine and reached for three fresh glasses from the cabinet above the sink. She placed them on the counter, setting each one down gently. Her face was emotionless, rather somber. There was a faraway look to her eye, as if her mind was elsewhere, deep in thought. Idly, she fingered one of the glasses.

"You feel okay?" I asked.

She looked at me and nodded. "Just thinking." She clicked a fingernail against one of the glasses. "About these. They have a nice quality, a good weight. You know who bought them?"

I pointed at the glasses. "These?" I looked them over: three ordinary tumblers. I had no idea who bought them. My wife, I supposed. I couldn't be sure.

Lisa smiled. My face must have revealed my uncertainty. "It was me that bought them. The whole set. Last April for Denise's birthday . . ." She let out a muted laugh. "We threw her a party, me and some friends."

"I heard about it."

"You should have come, then. It was fun."

"No one invited me."

"I know. It was a no-men-allowed party."

"Just the girls, aye?"

"That's what it was. Just the girls." She lifted one of the glasses from the counter, looked it over and placed it back down. "There were about six of us," she said. "Me, Denise, a few ladies we knew from school and someone whose name I'm always forgetting, one of Denise's old friends."

"Donna?" I asked.

Lisa shook her head. "No. This one had blonde hair, no makeup, sort of dumpy looking. She dressed weird, too. Lots of layers."

"Gertrude," I said.

Lisa nodded. "Gretchen, you mean . . . Klondike Gretchen." She let out another laugh. "I have trouble remembering because she only stayed for the first half of the party, the dinner half. After that she was afraid to go out with us."

"Poor Gretchen," I said. "She's sort of timid."

Lisa shrugged. "It was just as well. She would've had a rotten time, anyway. We all ended up getting pretty wasted after she left. Especially Denise. She turned into a whole different person that night."

"My Denise?" I asked.

"You wouldn't have believed your eyes."

I took the bottle of vodka from the top of the refrigerator and set it on the counter next to the glasses. I held it at the base and unscrewed its cap.

"You should've seen the things she ended up doing," Lisa continued. "She was nothing like the person you know. Nothing prim or proper about her that night."

I tinkered with the glasses, arranging them on the counter.

"I'm not exaggerating," she said. "She kept coming on to the bartender, the DJ, some cops we met through Gary. She even came on to this guy in a cowboy hat. Let him buy her drinks, kept dancing with him, letting him touch her. It really surprised me. She never told you about it, huh?"

I nodded my head indicating that she had. In truth, however, my wife had told me very little about the night of her twenty-seventh birthday. She had returned to our apartment the following morning just as I was preparing to leave for work. She looked rather sheepish then and rather hung-over. She told me that she'd had a good time with her friends, that she was extremely tired and that she needed to get some sleep. After phoning in sick to her office, she went straight to bed and never discussed the night again. I had always known that she'd spent a good part of that night with Lisa and several other girlfriends. I had known, too, that they'd gone to dinner and then hit some of the local bars. Other than that, the night had been a mystery to me. . . . It could stay that way, too, however. If Lisa had a little dirt on my wife, I didn't want to hear it. Not tonight.

"Denise calls *me* a slut," Lisa said. "You should have seen *her*. She was no angel herself—no Virgin Mary if you know what I mean."

I poured a shot of vodka into each of the three glasses, not enjoying the direction this conversation was taking. "Let's not discuss it," I said. "Not right now."

She shrugged and leaned against the counter. "Alright. If you don't want to." She extended her legs a bit and stuck both hands behind her butt. "I was making conversation. That's all."

"No harm done."

"Good," she said, "because none was meant."

I doubted this but I said nothing. What would be the point? I returned the bottle of vodka to the top of the refrigerator and turned back to her.

"You aren't going to mention anything to Denise," she said, "are you?" Her voice was almost a whisper.

"There's nothing to mention."

"I know," she said, "but sometimes husbands and wives have a way of talking about things like that."

"Not in this case."

"Good," she said. "Because I wouldn't want her to misunderstand." She crossed one foot over the other and lifted her head just slightly. Her movements were slow, relaxed. There was a sleepy sort of look to her eye.

I turned back to the refrigerator and opened the freezer door. "Do you like it with a lot of ice, your drink?"

"Sure. Who doesn't?"

"There're a few people," I said.

"Well, I like it with loads of ice. The colder the better." She brought a hand to her shoulder and slipped a finger beneath the strap of her bra. "I've been dying of heat all night."

I grabbed a handful of cubes from the freezer and dropped a few into each glass.

"Denise had a good idea," she said, "with the shower. I wish I'd taken one myself."

"It's too late now. Once she's in there it's tough getting her out."

"I hope she doesn't fall asleep. You hear about that sometimes. People falling asleep in the shower."

"She's okay. She likes them long, that's all."

Lisa nodded. "I know," she said. "We were roommates. Remember?"

I turned back to the refrigerator and took a bottle of beer from the top shelf. With the side of my foot I pushed the door shut.

"By the way," Lisa said, "you were good on the phone before. With Beale. I liked the way you handled him."

I opened the beer and said nothing.

"It was overdue," she told me. "You really stood up to him."

"It's too bad it had to come down to that."

"No, it's not. In a way, I'm happy it all happened. It was fun. I was nervous, you know? But I felt safe, too. Protected."

"Not by me, I hope."

"Yeah, by you," she said and touched my face. "It gave me a good feeling. The whole thing did. I thought it was exciting.'"

I laughed. "Exciting?"

"Uh, huh. You really told him off. What's wrong with getting excited about it?"

"Not a thing." I took a swig of beer and held the bottle against my forehead. "What else," I asked her, "gets you excited?"

"What do you mean?"

"Just what I said."

She bit a nail, smiling. "A lot of things," she said, "get me excited. What's it to you?"

"Wondering."

"Certain men get me excited," she said, "if that's what you're driving at."

I wasn't sure what I was driving at. I brought the bottle to my forehead again and rolled it from one side to the other. Its chill was invigorating, a nice little shock.

Lisa was watching me. "Does that help," she asked, "to cool you off?"

"It feels good," I told her.

She held her hand out for the beer. "Let me try . . ." There was a different sort of smile on her lips, her eyes brightening.

"You like to try stuff," I said.

"I'm curious. It's my nature."

I held her hand in mine and brought the neck of the bottle to her wrist. She made a sound of surprise, a soft "oooh" as the cool glass touched her skin.

"Cold?"

"Yes," she said. "It feels good."

A thin blue vein was visible from the center of her wrist to the end of her forearm. I traced the bottle along it towards the crest of her bicep.

She let out a shiver. "It's giving me a chill," she said.

"Oh, yeah?"

"A good one. I like it."

I held the bottle away from her arm and touched a finger where her skin had broken into a patch of small rounded goose bumps. "Your skin is allergic to beer bottles," I said.

She looked at her arm and nodded. "For as long as I can remember, Doctor." She raised her eyes to me; there was mischief in them, a certain devilment. "Are you going to examine me?"

Her hand was resting lightly on my own. "Yes," I said. "In a moment."

"Then I'll disrobe."

I ran the bottle from her bicep to the top of her shoulder and back again. "No," I told her. "I'll do that myself."

She watched as the bottle grazed her skin and she let out another "oooh." Her face was heated, slick with perspiration. "Have you ever done this to Denise?"

I didn't answer. I drew her body to mine, slid my hand from her wrist to the curve of her hip. "Denise doesn't like things that are cold," I told her. "You know that." I brushed my lips against her cheek, kissed the warm salty skin of her throat. I rested the bottle against the base of her spine and ran it across her back.

"We shouldn't be doing this," she said. "We really shouldn't." Her voice lacked conviction, however. No heart at all.

"Is there something else you'd rather be doing?"

"I don't know," she said. "What did you have in mind?" A smile came to her lips as she said the words and I kissed her softly. Her mouth was wet and fresh and had the flavor of mint. She'd brushed her teeth while in the bathroom.

"You taste good," I told her.

"Do I?"

I held her partly away from me and moved the bottle to her chest, tracing it down between her breasts, along her belly to the small pink rosebud at the top of her panties. The lip of the bottle hooked against her waistband. I lowered it slightly, a quarter inch, then a half inch, then all the way.

"That's a handy gadget," she said, looking down at the bottle and what it had revealed. "Sort of multi-purpose."

I placed it on the counter and moved my hands behind her, sliding them down her back, across her buttocks, cupping the warm meatiness of her cheeks.

"We shouldn't be doing this," she said again. "We really . . ." But this time there was laughter in her voice. I stepped in closer and brought my mouth to hers. I felt her hands working at my zipper. I lifted her onto the counter and slid off her panties as she raised her hips to assist me. "I'll bet," she said, "Denise's never done it in the kitchen."

Looking back on that night, it was obvious where we were headed. If I didn't see it at the time, I have no one to fault but myself. Lisa, if she chooses, can blame some of her behavior on the alcohol. My wife can do the same if she wants an excuse for her part in that night. My own mind, however, had never been clearer, especially during those few minutes with Lisa.

I regretted what we'd done afterwards—seconds afterwards.

"Hold me," she'd said, once we were through, her legs wrapped around me. "I need to be held." She was nude, feeling no urgency to dress. Her bra and panties were balled together on the far burner of the stove. The way she clung to me now, so tranquilly, so lazily, you'd think my wife was a hundred miles out of town rather than twenty feet away in the bathroom. She'd be in the shower a few minutes longer, maybe less. I'd hear the loud flow of water turned off, the metallic creak and then the clunk of the pipes shutting down. She'd dry herself slowly and powder her neck and chest and arms. If she hadn't done so before, she'd then brush her teeth, paying as much attention to the gums as to the teeth themselves. Then, winding down, she would rinse her hands, slip into her bathrobe and step out into the living room, an anxious smile on her face, curious to discover if I'd smoothed things over for her with her best friend.

"What's wrong?" Lisa asked me. "Why don't you hold me?"

I couldn't. I could barely touch her. I wished, at that moment, that one of us could simply vanish from the earth, preferably myself, dispatched to some sound, eternal sleep.

The thought, however, lasted only a moment. "Nothing's wrong," I told her. "I'm thinking." I kissed her nose, hoping to display some sign of affection. Then I kissed her cheek and then the crown of her head. There was no warmth to the gesture, no real tenderness.

"I feel nice," she said. "So peaceful. You made me come good."

"Thanks."

"You were just like I thought you'd be. It's kind of naughty what you did with—"

I put a finger to her lips, silencing her. A recap of our screw was the last thing I wanted right now. I disengaged myself and yanked my shorts and jeans past my hips, one quick motion, not bothering to tuck in my shirt.

"Is something wrong?" she asked. "Something I did?" She leaned back on her hands. Her legs were parted. There was a dull, sluggish look to her face. She reminded me of someone just hanging out, sitting on a concrete wall, relaxing, another hour to kill before their bus arrived.

"Nothing's wrong." I heard the water in the bathroom being turned off, the metallic creak and then the heavy clunk of the pipes. I looked at the clock on the kitchen wall: 3:17. Lisa and I had, perhaps, five minutes to dress and come to some kind of understanding.

I grabbed her bra and panties from the stove. Both felt damp, still moist with her sweat. I held them out for her to take but she simply glanced at them and made an expression of pain. "They're a little grubby," she informed me. "I've worn them enough today."

"You have to put something on," I said, dropping them onto her thigh.

She looked at me as if I were a dope. "I brought another pair. Two other pairs. They're in my beach bag. It's in the living room. A big canvas bag. It says—"

"Foxy Lady."

"It's by the couch. Both pairs should be on the bottom, under my bathing suit. You want to get them? I'll wait here."

"Yes," I said. "Don't move."

She folded her arms across her breasts. "Don't worry," she said, gazing down at her bra and panties. "I'll stay right here . . . me and my undies."

There was a joke there somewhere, I assumed; just Lisa being playful. I held up my forefinger—"One second"—and headed out of the kitchen. I tucked in my shirt as I went, patted down my hair and buckled my belt. The apartment was darker, quieter than I remembered it. I flipped on the light in the dining room and switched on the floor lamp as I entered the living room, trying to erase all appearances of intimacy. Lester was lying in his old spot beneath the couch, two feet from Lisa's beach bag. I scratched him behind the ear, not looking into his eyes, feeling somehow that I had betrayed him.

"Go back to sleep," I said as I lifted Lisa's bag from the floor. It was heavier than I'd expected, filled almost to the top. I rested it on the coffee table next to the bowl of potato chips and pulled it open. I could hear sink water running in the bathroom: my wife brushing her teeth, only a minute from rejoining us. I reached into Lisa's bag, hunting for the underwear. Towards the top of the bag were a few magazines: *Cosmopolitan*, *Glamour*, and *Mademoiselle*. I put the three of them on the coffee table and spread them open, suggesting to my wife, perhaps, that Lisa and I had been reading while she'd been in the shower. I turned back to the bag then. A pair of brown leather sandals was the next thing I came across, followed by a makeup kit and some suntan lotion. Beneath these were Lisa's beach towel, an empty thermos and a pair of oversized sunglasses. I found the underwear, both pairs, where she had said they'd be: on the bottom, beneath her bathing suit. I studied the two pairs carefully; the beige and the baby blue, wondering which pair would look less conspicuous, more suitable for our situation. The beige ones appeared more modest, fuller cut and not as transparent as the baby blue, not as—wait a second; was I losing my mind? How could I go through the motions of turning on lights, spreading open magazines and then expect my wife to overlook the fact that Lisa had slipped into a change of underwear?

I tossed both pairs back into the bag and closed it up tight. I could hear my wife in the bathroom. The sink water was turned off now, the room relatively still. She was humming a tune to herself, a light, happy melody that I wasn't able to identify.

I left Lisa's bag on top of the table, hoping that it might give the room a little more of that cluttered, lived-in look that I was hoping to project. I scanned the area for something to add to it. The bowl of potato chips made an appealing target. I grabbed a handful of them off the top and scattered them about the table. Then I rubbed my hands together, letting the salt and crumbs fall around the bowl. I might have been overdoing it but it was better than leaving everything exactly as it was.

"Michael," Lisa called from the kitchen, "I'm cold."

That was doubtful. Nude or not, it was still eighty-plus degrees in the apartment. Within the enclosed area of the kitchen, the temperature was even warmer. I stuck my hands into my pockets and went in to talk it over.

"What took so long?" she asked. She was still on the counter, arms folded across her chest. "I thought you were going to get my bra and panties. Where are they?"

"In your beach bag," I told her. "Wearing different underwear would make Denise suspicious. She'd ask why you changed."

"So?" Lisa said. "I'd tell her the truth. I'd tell her I felt grubby. And sweaty. So, I changed. What's the big deal?"

"No big deal. But it could draw attention to us."

"Don't be so paranoid," she said. "You're new to all of this, aren't you?"

I shrugged, hardly knowing how to respond. After all, what was she to all of this? A seasoned pro? I grabbed her ball of underwear from the stove and presented it to her once again.

She took it this time and gave me another of her pained expressions. "This is so dumb," she let me know. "I'm going to feel cruddy for nothing." She looked me square in the eye, making little effort to disguise her annoyance.

"Why take chances?" I asked her.

"Why wear sweaty underwear when you don't have to?"

She had a point I was sure but, at the moment, it was beyond me. I picked up the beer next to the refrigerator and brought it to my lips. It was lukewarm and tasted slightly of Lisa. "Let's just put it back on the way—"

She was holding out her hand, wanting a sip of the beer for herself.

"It's warm," I told her.

"I don't care. My mouth is dry."

"Warm beer will make it even worse."

"I want some, Michael."

I handed her the bottle then, wondering if she was ever going to get dressed. She tossed back her head and took a long, slow gulp. She made a smacking noise and took another gulp. I watched her as she drank. I watched the way her eyes moved as she swallowed and listened to the little noises her throat made. She let out a sigh and had a third pull from the bottle. Several strands of her hair were matted, sticking to her forehead. On her upper lip, I noticed, there was a small line of peach fuzz; nothing serious; it neither added to nor detracted from her appearance; it simply surprised me that it was there.

She handed me back the bottle and I poured the remainder of its contents into the sink. "Let's get dressed," I said. "Once Denise has had a look at you in these, you can change into whatever you want."

"Alright, once she sees me, I'll tell her I want to take a shower, myself. She won't suspect a thing. I'll bring my bag into the bathroom and change after the shower."

"That's fine," I said. I was grateful that Lisa wanted to help me deceive my wife. But it felt unpleasant hearing her talk about it.

"I'll be casual about the whole thing," she continued. "Make a joke out of it. I'll tell her that I feel like I've been in the coal mines all day. Maybe I'll pretend I'm jealous that she had a shower while I didn't. She gets a kick out of it when I'm jealous of her. It makes her feel superior. Like her life's better than mine."

"Michael?" my wife called from the living room. "Lisa? Is everything okay?"

"Everything's good," I called back. "Be out in a second."

Judging from my wife's voice, from the words she chose, I had the impression that she'd been out of the bathroom for a while now. Chances were good that she was recalling her quarrel with Lisa and so was in no hurry to face her. She was probably on the couch now spending time with Lester, perhaps feeling a bit immobile with him napping or making dough on her lap. It gave me a jolt: any other time she might have walked directly by the couch and straight into the kitchen, finding Lisa holding onto her damp underwear, naked on the counter.

"Let's go," I said and touched the ball of material in her hand. "It's getting late."

She dropped the panties into her lap slowly, almost lethargically, holding onto the bra.

"Let's move, Lisa. Hurry up."

"I am hurrying," she said.

"If it was your spouse out there, you'd—"

"*Spouse*?" she asked, lifting an eyebrow.

"Yes, *spouse*," I told her. "If you had someone waiting out there, I'd be dressed for you in a second."

"Girls take longer than men," she informed me. "It's not our fault."

Why were we bickering? Perhaps it was our new intimacy. "Listen," I said, "I'm going out there. To keep Denise company. And to keep her from coming in here."

Lisa slipped on her bra and clipped it in front, one clean, deft move. "Stay," she said. "I'm getting dressed now."

"No, it's safer this way."

She lowered herself off the counter. "Please, Michael, I'll feel funny going out there alone." She pulled at the shoulder strap of her bra and made an adjustment. "Please. For me . . ."

I watched as she slid a foot through her panties. One of her toes, I noticed, overlapped the other. There was something about her toenails, too: some were long and sharp; others short and jagged; all were unpolished. "Alright," I said. "But let's be quick."

"That's what I'm being." She was bent at the waist, standing on her right leg. She slid her left foot through the panties and yanked them to her hips. "There," she said. "Ready."

"Now try to act nonchalant."

"Michael?" my wife called. "What's going on in there?"

"We're talking," I said. "Be out in a second."

"Yes," Lisa called. "We'll be right out." A smile came to her mouth; she seemed to be enjoying the suspense. "Give us one . . . more . . . minute, Denise . . . okay?" She ran some fingers through her hair, fluffing it up at the sides and towards the back. She pursed her lips and then licked them, her mouth free of lipstick.

I wondered, for a moment, where it had gone, her lipstick. I wiped my palm across my mouth and cheeks in case it had rubbed off on me. I started to ask Lisa to check me over and then thought better of it. "Ready?" I asked her. I made a motion to give her forehead a quick kiss but she raised her head, anticipating one on the lips. The kiss, therefore, came out rather awkward; a bit clownish.

"Yes," she said. "I'm ready. Time to face the music."

I looked at her, not knowing what, exactly, she meant by that.

She gave me a look in return and said, "Come on. All set." She hitched her panties past her hips and wrapped her pinkie finger around my own.

"You feel up to this?" I asked her.

"I'll be fine."

"Let's just behave as naturally as possible." I separated my pinkie from hers as delicately as I could. "We have to be careful," I warned her. "No touching, alright?"

She shrugged to show that she didn't care about it one way or the other. We walked out of the kitchen together, our eyes aimed directly ahead. As we passed through the dining room, I picked up my pace and led the rest of the way into the living room.

"Here we are, Denise," Lisa announced from behind me. "Safe and sound."

"It's about time." My wife was sitting on the couch, looking pretty much as I had pictured that she might: she wore no makeup, her hair was freshly washed and she was wearing her light green bathrobe. Lester was resting comfortably in her lap. "What were you two doing in there?"

Lisa moved beside me. "Michael was screwing my brains out," she said. She paused for a moment, then let out a laugh. "What do you think we were doing? We were talking. Nothing else."

My wife nodded, accepting it.

"And making drinks," Lisa added. "Michael was teaching me how to make a real drink. A *man's* drink."

"Uh huh," my wife said. She stroked Lester along his back. "Where are they?"

Lisa looked at me, her eyes opened wide. She appeared confused, startled by the question. We'd forgotten to finish making the drinks. "What do you mean?" she asked my wife.

"I mean, where are the drinks?"

"The what?"

"The drinks. Where are they?"

Lisa released another laugh; it came out a bit too quickly, a bit too loudly. "We dumped them down the sink," she replied. "This guy you're married to, Denise, is no bartender. He makes drinks terrible. Just horrible." She fidgeted with her hands and laughed again, a little more quietly this time. "The first batch he made tasted like moonshine. The second tasted like turpentine."

My wife wrinkled her nose. "You know what turpentine tastes like?"

I stepped in front of Lisa, shielding her from my wife. "The drinks were kind of strong."

"I never tasted turpentine," Lisa answered from behind me. "But I tried moonshine once. Real hillbilly stuff. Down in Kentucky . . . yuck," she said. "No wonder those people are always yodeling."

My wife traced a finger across Lester's cheek. "Hillbillies yodel? I thought it was the Swiss . . . over in the Alps."

"The Swiss yodel, too," Lisa said. "But so do hillbillies. I read a book on it once."

"On hillbillies?" my wife asked her. "Or yodeling?"

"Neither," Lisa said. She laughed once more and again it came out too loudly. "I'm sorry," she continued. "I'm a little nervous. I was making up the whole thing . . . the moonshine . . . being in Kentucky . . . Michael teaching me the drinks . . . I'm sorry."

My wife remained seated on the couch, stroking Lester, a bewildered grin on her face. "I don't understand," she said.

I smiled with her, imagining what my own grin must have looked like. "Lisa's putting us on," I told her. "She's just having fun."

"That's right," Lisa added. "Just goofing around."

"Nothing like a kidder at three in the morning, huh?" I sat down, taking my old spot on the chair. Lisa followed quickly, about to assume her former position next to me on the armrest. I stuck my elbow there and checked her back with a stare. "Try the couch," I whispered through the side of my mouth.

She remained standing, sort of inching sideways to the center of the room. I couldn't figure out her frame of mind. It was difficult to tell if she was fooling around, if she was deliberately acting suspicious, or, as she had said, if she was simply nervous. In any event, I wished that she would grab her beach bag as planned and head into the bathroom.

Slim chance. She lowered herself down to the floor instead. She sat with her arms behind her, legs set out in front, slightly parted, similar to the posture she'd had on the kitchen counter.

"Why don't you take that shower?" I asked her. "It'll help you feel better."

She lifted her head. "In a few minutes." she said. "Unless you want me to take it now."

I shrugged. "It doesn't matter to me. Whatever you want."

"In a few minutes then. I don't feel like being alone right now." She looked down at her chest and adjusted one of her bra cups, tugging it to the left.

My wife watched with curiosity. "I don't get you two," she said. "What's the secret? You're acting so . . . sneaky."

I crossed my feet and took in a breath, needing a moment before I could respond. "There's no secret," was all that I could come up with. "We don't look sneaky."

"Yes, you do. You both do." My wife turned to Lisa on the floor and then she turned back to me. "Something's up, Michael. What is it?"

"Nothing's up," I said. "While you were in the shower, we read a bit." I pointed to the magazines opened casually on the coffee table. "We had a few chips." I pointed to the potato chips scattered next to the magazines.

"And patted the kitty," Lisa added, and she pointed a finger at Lester.

My wife shook her head with the bewildered smile still on her face. "Something's going on. I can feel it."

"Nothing's going on," Lisa told her. She brought her hands in front of her and played a little more with the cups of her bra. "Sorry to disillusion you, Denise, but there's noth—"

"Then what were you doing in the kitchen?"

I reached over and touched my wife on the knee. "Easy, Denise. You don't have to cross-examine her."

"Stay out of this, Michael. I'm talking to Lisa."

"Then *talk* to her," I said. "Don't give her the third degree."

"Denise can ask me whatever she wants," Lisa told me. "I don't care." Then she addressed my wife. "Michael and I weren't doing anything in the kitchen."

"What's that supposed to mean?" my wife asked her.

"It means," Lisa said, "that we weren't doing *anything*."

"You had to be doing something."

"But that's the thing. We weren't. We were just—"

"Then what took so long?"

"Nothing did."

"Tell me the truth."

"Nothing took so long."

"I heard talking," my wife said. "You were talking about something."

"No, we weren't."

"You were. I heard you." My wife leaned forward. Lester stirred in her lap. "You weren't making drinks. You weren't talking. Then what *were* you doing?"

"Nothing," Lisa said. "That's what I've been trying to tell you. We weren't doing *any*thing."

"So why can't I believe you?"

"You can do whatever you want but I'm telling the truth."

My wife sat back into the couch, Lester gone now from her lap. She appeared tired; drained. Tears were forming in the corners of her eyes; I couldn't tell if they were from anger or sorrow or sheer frustration.

Lisa got up from the floor, rising unsteadily to her feet. "I need a shower, too," she said. Her voice sounded stiff, unnatural. "I'm a little jealous of you, Denise, smelling so clean and fresh. Compared to you it's like I've been shoveling coal all day."

My wife smiled but her face lacked amusement. "Sure," she said. "Go ahead. Enjoy."

Lisa grabbed her beach bag from the coffee table. She picked her dress off the floor, her purse and then her shoes and she moved swiftly towards the bathroom. A minute later, I was certain, she would exit it, fully clothed, ready to go. Before she went in, however, she looked back at my wife. "I don't know what you expect me to say, Denise."

My wife shifted on the couch. "How about the truth?"

Lisa looked to me and then at my wife, that wounded expression was back in her eye as she turned toward the bathroom door. "I'm sorry," she said. "I can't."

As time passes, the details of that night become hazier to me, harder to recollect. My wife, I'm certain, recalls things differently than I do. Lisa, too, must have her own version of events. For that matter, so must Beale. Here, at any rate, is the way that I remember the rest of it.

After coming out of the bathroom, Lisa announced that she would be leaving our apartment. Her head was pounding, she explained, and her stomach was feeling queasy: when her body turned on her like this, only her own place and her own bed would do.

My wife agreed, saying that she understood and she quickly called a taxi for her.

Keeping up appearances, wanting to play it as straight as possible, I offered to escort Lisa down to the street and stay with her until the cab arrived. It seemed like the appropriate thing to do: it was dark outside; she was feeling ill.

My wife, choosing to play it straight, as well, agreed. "By all means," she told me. "Go with Lisa. I'd appreciate it." Her voice was quiet, no emotion. To Lisa she said, "Hope you feel better."

The following minutes passed slowly, waiting silently with Lisa for the elevator, riding it down the five floors, avoiding one another's eyes, exiting the lobby and walking together to the curb. The strain between us was a heavy one. By the time the taxi appeared, I was prepared to turn around, say nothing and go back to my apartment, never to see or to speak with her again. Instead, I opened the cab's door and glanced at the dark, cloudy sky above. "It looks like rain," I observed.

She raised her head and took in a long pull of air. "Hmmm," she said as she slipped into the back seat, placing her beach bag onto her lap. "It smells like it, too."

"Let's hope it cools things off. It's been too hot for too long."

"And humid, too," she added without enthusiasm, as disinterested in the topic as I was "That's what's really been making it uncomfortable —the humidity."

I bobbed my head in agreement and closed the door for her. When she rolled down the window, we were ready to change the subject. I leaned forward and asked if she was feeling well enough to make it home alone.

"I'll be alright," she said. "Tell Denise I'm sorry about getting sick, okay? And let her know I had a good time."

I nodded that I would.

"Maybe I'll stop at the diner near the police station. Gary goes there after work. I think I'll drop in on him."

"He'll be there this late?" I checked my wrist to verify the time but, unfortunately, I wasn't wearing a watch.

"He'll be there. It's his favorite hangout. He talks with the cops that come in, trades stories with them. If he's nice to me, I'll let him treat me to breakfast."

"He'd like that," I said.

She lifted her eyes and smiled. "A lot of guys would."

I tapped the taxi's roof and waved my fingers goodbye. The car pulled from the curb, a thin line of gray exhaust streaming from its tailpipe as Lisa waved her fingers back at me. "Take care," she called.

It was a quarter past four when I returned to the apartment. My wife was sitting on the couch. A scan around the living room told me that she'd been busy tidying up while I was out. Gone from the coffee table were the potato chips and ash tray. The fan had been shut off and put away in a corner. All glasses and bottles had been removed from the room, probably brought back into the kitchen.

I took a step towards the couch. My wife was reading a magazine, too enthralled in it, apparently, to look up. Not knowing how else to break the ice, I coughed into my hand and told her that it smelled like rain.

She nodded her head once, precisely, acknowledging the statement. A look of silent hatred was on her face.

I took another step toward her. "Interesting article?" I asked, feeling a wave of exhaustion cross my body. The last thing that I wanted right now was to speak to her. I felt, however, that there wasn't a choice. If we didn't speak in these next minutes, things between us might never be the same. I stood in front of her, giving her no alternative than to look up. "Do you want to talk?"

She closed the magazine and laid it beside her. "Talk? Yes, I want to talk. What were you and Lisa doing in the kitchen? Can you answer me that?"

I rubbed the back of my neck and turned it from side to side.

"Forget it," she said. "I already know what you were doing. Lisa lets me in on all her secrets. One way or the other, she was going to make sure I found out. I tried to warn you about that."

I nodded briefly, saying nothing. My mind, at the moment, felt leaden, drained.

"I don't know how you could have done it to me. Do you really despise me that much? Does our marriage mean that little to you?"

"I didn't do anything to you, Denise."

"No. Just to our marriage."

"Nothing was done to our marriage, either. It's the Eighties. Things are different."

"Spare me. Don't start coming on like Hugh Hefner, okay? Even he wouldn't put the moves on his wife's best friend. Not in her own apartment. Not in her own kitchen. Not while she's taking a goddamn shower."

"I wasn't putting the moves on Lisa. It just happened. It was natural."

"Please. No details. Not necessary."

"What I'm saying is that I didn't have any ulterior motives. I wasn't doing it to hurt you. I didn't even consider you."

"That's pretty obvious."

"It's not what I mean. My point is that you're taking this as a personal affront when none was intended. I only did what I did—"

"To get laid. While our friend, Lisa, wanted both—to get laid and to hurt me. Fortunately for her, she had you to assist her in both.".

"She wasn't out to hurt you. There are other ways to do that. She wouldn't cheapen herself just to hurt you."

"Don't defend her to me. She wanted to prove that she could take from me whatever I have. And you helped her do it."

"She's not that devious," I said.

"Maybe not. Or maybe you're just protecting your own ego. It doesn't matter either way. You're my problem now, not her."

I brought my hand to my mouth, stifling a yawn, and sat down in the chair. I don't think I was ever so tired in my life. All I wanted to do at that moment was to fall straight into bed, draw the covers over my head and sleep until this whole thing blew over. "Please, Denise, can't we discuss it in the morning? I'm exhausted."

"Sure. Go to bed. Go to sleep. But don't expect to find me here when you wake up."

"What does that mean?"

"Figure it out yourself."

"Don't do this to me. Not tonight."

"Do this to *you*? How about me? God, you're self-centered. You're an immature jerk. You can't look outside yourself for one minute, can you?"

I raised my head, trying to focus my eyes. "Not now," I said. "Not that crap about my adolescence again."

"I'll give you any crap I want, Michael. Especially now. You're acting like I'm some nit-picking housewife. Some bitch on the rag. This is serious stuff. Our marriage is on the line here."

"Denise," I said, "we'll work it out. Nobody's marriage is on the line."

"Don't be so sure, Michael."

"Why keep harping on it?"

She stood up, a hard mean look to her face. "You bastard," she shouted. She lifted her foot and stamped it on the floor. And then she stamped it once again. The lamp by the far end of the couch shook with the vibrations. "*Harping*"? Is that what you call it? You're belittling everything I say, every point I make. You'll either listen to me now, Michael, or I'll walk right through that door. That's a—"

"SHAAADDAAP UP THERE! WE'RE TRYING TO SLEEP!"

It was Beale. His voice was a loud crude slur. He sounded groggy, disorientated, as if, indeed, he actually had been trying to sleep. He rapped something, a thick board or a baseball bat, against his ceiling. "If you're playing with me, Five E, you're playing with the wrong son of a bitch." He slapped the wood once more against his ceiling, twice as hard as the first slap.

"Beale," I called back down, "I've had enough of you."

"You haven't even had a taste of me. I got a bat down here and if you don't shut up I'm gonna ram it straight up your ass." He slapped his ceiling again. I felt it with my feet. He was directly below me. "You mess with me," he shouted, "and you pay the price."

I went to the hall closet and looked inside for my own baseball bat. After a quick search I remembered that I didn't have one. It'd been years since I last played ball.

"People toy with me" he was going on, "and they end up hurt. They end up with their brains damaged."

I felt around the closet and flipped on the light. Behind the vacuum cleaner was a long-handled broom, the industrial kind. I unscrewed the pole from the end with its bristles and rapped it a few times against the floor. It had a decent weight to it; a solid piece of wood. I lifted it above my shoulder and brought it down against the floor once more, feeling the hard reverberations travel through my arm.

"Michael," my wife said, "I'm warning you!" She stood in the center of the living room, a fist on her hip and a finger aimed at my chest. "Don't you start up with him. He is no longer the problem."

He was the only problem as far as I was concerned. If it wasn't for him and his out of control party, my wife and I would be sound asleep right now; in a couple of hours she and Lisa would be waking up, preparing for their trip to Long Island. I struck the floor with the end of my pole. "Beale," I called down, "I'm ready for you."

"You're ready for squat, Five E. I'll teach you to play with me."

"You're talking too much, Beale. You either do it or you shut up."

Lester darted from beneath the couch, heading straight for the bedroom. My wife stared at me, her eyes glaring a flat hatred. "Stop it," she shouted. "Both of you, stop it!"

"Stay out of this, Denise. It's not your affair."

"I know," she spat. "Man business."

"That's right." I rapped the pole against the floor. "Man business."

She shook her head, letting out a long harsh laugh. "You're a child, Michael. Trying to prove something. Trying to do the manly thing. Is that what you were doing with Lisa in the kitchen?"

"Denise," I said, "we'll talk about it later."

"No, goddamnit. You screwed up and we're going to talk about it now."

"Later," I told her.

"So you can have your fight with that maniac? Two self-centered children. You're pathetic. Both of you."

"That's enough," I said. "I'll deal with you later."

"You'll deal with *me*?" Her face was incredulous. She turned and stomped into the bedroom. The door banged like a gunshot behind her. "Asshole," she shouted. "I hope he kills you."

I felt another wave of exhaustion strike me just then. It hit me at the top of my head and swept straight down to my feet. It took whatever fight was left in me but I decided to go through with it anyway. I went to the telephone, opened the address book and dialed Beale's number.

He answered on the first ring. His voice was quieter than I'd anticipated. It sounded hoarse; listless. It sounded, in fact, as if he was as weary as I was.

"Beale," I said, as if by rote, "you've gone too far."

"How'd you get my number?"

"Your mother gave it to me."

"It was you," he said. "I knew it all the time." He paused for a moment, coughing away from the receiver. It was a loud, wet-sounding cough that seemed to come from somewhere deep inside his chest.

"Listen, you punk," I said, "you've been messing with people's lives for too long."

"Who are you calling a punk? I'm going to kick in your head, Five E."

"You're doing nothing, Beale."

"I'm going to put this bat right up your ass."

"You already told me that."

"I'm coming up there, dick bag."

"I'm waiting, Nicky Boy." I put down the phone and listened to my wife banging around the bedroom, rustling through our things. I heard a thud and then a zipper whipped open. She was getting a suitcase together. I didn't know if she was packing it for herself or for me. Either way, I'd have to make things up to her later. Right now, if I wanted to or not, I had to deal with Beale.

"*Five E,*" I heard from below. "*I'm coming for you.*"

I tightened my grip on the pole and walked towards the door, my legs moving sluggishly, feeling heavier than they should have. Where, I wondered, was my adrenaline? Why wasn't I getting worked up?

I heard Beale's door slam shut, his wife, Rosanne, shouting at him from behind it. I opened my front door and listened to his feet clomping up the staircase. I heard him striking the bat against its concrete steps. Within a minute, he was on the fifth floor, dragging his bat along the hallway as he walked, striking it against the tiles. His movements sounded slow, plodding, as tired as my own. "This is it, Five E. Your time is up."

I stepped out into the hallway and squeezed both hands around my pole. I tried to remember the phone call with Gary, tried to remember what he'd said about Beale's knees, which one had been chipped the night of his arrest: his right one or his left?

"Five E," Beale called again. "You're a dead man. When I'm done with you, they're going to be scraping your brains off the wall."

Once more, he slapped his bat against the tiles and then he moved into view. His appearance surprised me. As weak and fatigued as he had sounded on the phone, he appeared, now, even worse. He was winded, his face drawn and listless. If I didn't know any better, I might have taken him for a sleepwalker. He just stood there, shoulders slumped, belly out, arms at his sides, holding onto his baseball bat. He wore pajama bottoms only; no top. A pair of black loafers were on his feet; no socks. He had been boozing, fighting, shouting, on and off, for close to a dozen hours. It looked now as though it had finally taken its toll. He appeared to be as exhausted as I was; maybe more so. "Five E," he said, his voice sounding something less than powerful, "your ass is grass."

I squeezed the end of my pole and rapped it once against the hallway floor. "Is that the best you can come up with?"

"Make your move and find out." He motioned me towards him with his fingertips. His legs were spread about eighteen inches apart; they looked shaky, capable of buckling if struck with one good whack of my pole. "Come on," he said. "Make your move."

I raised the pole shoulder-high. "You make yours."

"No way," he said. "You first." He beckoned me again with his fingertips, not moving an inch toward or away from me. "You start. I finish."

"Wrong," I told him. "You've got it backwards, Beale."

"Uh, uh. You're the one with it backwards, Five E."

I held my position outside of the doorway. He didn't want to fight any more than I did. Like me, he was simply going through the motions, spinning his own wheels, tossing out lines learned in schoolyards and the streets. Maybe my wife had been right about us two. I stepped back into my apartment and started to close the door. "Let's fight tomorrow, Beale. Outside. At noon. In the playground . . . behind the swings."

August, 1985

a certain seductive charm

AS SOON AS WE GET HOME," she announces, "I'm calling my lawyer. I want a divorce."

Her words come to you slowly. Your attention is on the traffic, on the road conditions of the expressway, on the Oldsmobile speeding past you to the left and the tractor trailer approaching to the right. A hit of water splashes the windshield of your car and you flip the wipers to High. When the glass is clear, you give her statement some thought. She had said that she wants a divorce and that, as soon as you arrive home, she will be calling her lawyer. You consider this as you switch into the right-hand lane. You glance at the dashboard's clock: 9:09. It will be another moment before you wonder, *what lawyer? She doesn't have a lawyer.*

You will wait, however, before mentioning this. You are collected; nonchalant. "If you want a divorce," you tell her, "go ahead. I won't stop you."

"I know you won't. No one's going to stop me."

"You've thought this through, I imagine."

She snaps open her purse. "You imagine correctly. I've been thinking it through for months." To punctuate her point, she pulls a cigarette from her purse and lights it up. "If you've known it or not, you've been on probation."

It is a cold November evening, a Saturday, and you are driving home from a party neither of you had particularly wanted to attend. The expressway is heavy with traffic and it is slick with a rain that has been falling, on and off, for the past hour. Both of you have been drinking: you since seven, she since five. You check the rearview and see the glare of a dozen headlights behind you. "What's his name?"

She looks at you, eyes perplexed.

"Your lawyer? What's his name?"

She blows a stream of smoke your way and lets out a mirthless laugh. "His name is none of your business. But I've got a lawyer. A good one. Don't worry about that."

"And he'll accept your call?"

She tilts her head, the look of puzzlement back in her eye.

"It's after nine," you explain. "We won't be home till ten. He's going to accept your call after ten o'clock on a Saturday night?"

"I'll call him tomorrow then. He can wait."

She is in *one of her moods*, you realize, but you pursue the argument nevertheless. "Why bother with a lawyer? If I'm half as bad as you say, any judge in the state will give you a divorce based on your words alone."

She adjusts herself in the seat, making herself comfortable. "Nice try," she says. "But that's not the way I want it. I've gone out and gotten myself the meanest lawyer I could find. And he's going to take you for every dime you've got."

You don't respond immediately. You play with her words (*meanest lawyer, every dime you've got*) churning them about in your mind (*meanest wife, meanest divorcee*), wanting to throw her words back at her in an insult. . . . It is not to be, however. Not tonight. Your mind is lacking wit this evening while her mind, it appears, is on a roll.

"And once my lawyer's done with you," she continues, "I'm going to get myself a new husband. Someone with manners and a ton of class. A Frenchman. Someone named François. Or Pierre."

"Sure," you say. "If he needs you for a green card."

"No way. I'm not going to be made any man's fool ever again. I'm tired of being used by you creeps." She takes another drag on her cigarette and stabs it out in the ashtray.

"Used by you creeps," you repeat.

"That's right. From now on, I'll be the one calling the shots. I can do better than you." She traces a finger along the curve of her chin and tells you, "There is a certain, seductive charm that I have. You won't be hard to replace."

"No one's irreplaceable," you agree.

She sits back into the seat, crosses one ankle over the other. There is a dreamy look to her eye. "My man is going to have manners," she says. "He's going to have character. Sophistication. Pizzazz. And he's going to be hung like a horse."

"Frenchmen have big dicks?"

"A lot bigger than yours. That's for sure."

You release a strained but patient sigh. This conversation is getting dumb. "Then write it down," you suggest. "More ammunition for your lawyer . . . *Your Honor, he just couldn't keep her satisfied.*"

"That's right. You're much too small. If I ever led you to believe otherwise, I apologize. I was lying."

You exchange a swift, significant look with her. Then you set your eyes back on the road. Hearing this kind of talk does not disturb you, necessarily. You understand that it is nothing personal, that it is only, as they say, her liquor speaking. If this marriage has nothing else going for it, you remind yourself, it at least has healthy sex. Still, no man likes it said of himself that he is *small*. You consider a retort (*Listen, Manhole*), but then you refrain. Why aggravate matters? For the time being, why not try to simply ignore her?

"Do you know what I want to talk about now?" she asks. "Let's see if you can guess."

You haven't the slightest idea, nor the least bit of curiosity. You notice the windshield beginning to fog and you turn on the defroster.

"I want to talk about God," she informs you. "I think he gave us the crappiest marriage in the world. And then he made us hate each other." She draws a fresh cigarette from her purse, lights it with her disposable Cricket lighter and blows a puff of smoke towards your face. "Damn it," she says, lifting the cigarette into the air, studying it, "I think this is my last one." She pulls a pack of Virginia Slims from her purse, examines it, confirms that, indeed, it is empty, and then she crushes it in the palm of her hand. With an over-the-shoulder flip, she tosses it into the back seat of the car.

Slowly, for her benefit, you glance toward the area she has just littered. To illustrate your disdain, you shake your head sadly.

She barely notices. Taking a drag on her cigarette, she laments to you, "That's my life. Right there. Crumpled. Nothing inside. My life is a piece of garbage." Then, really spelling it out for you, she adds, "My life is a pile of shit."

From the corner of your eye, you can see her peeking over for your reaction to such a soliloquy. You offer no acknowledgement, however, and remind yourself of the strategy: ignore her.

"I mean it," she says. "My whole life sucks."

At this moment, you do not know if you can disagree. Certainly, you would not want to trade places with her.

"I know what you're thinking. You're thinking that I'm just drunk. That tomorrow I'll wake up and make you a big lumberjack breakfast. Climb into the sack with you and plead for your forgiveness." She flicks an ash to the floor. "Well, I got news for you—it's not going to happen. Not in a million years."

When she is angry, you've noticed, she has a tendency to speak in these common phrases: "I've got news for you, Bub." "Not in a million years, Pal." During past disagreements she has gone as far as "This is the way it's gonna be," and "You bet your sweet life." You slow the car. The road has expanded from three lanes to four. You flick on your signal and change into the newest lane.

"Cripes," she says as she shifts in her seat. "Why do you have to drive so slow? You drive like a nun. Like a *dead* nun."

For spite, you ease your foot off the gas pedal and watch as the speedometer descends to 45.

"Cut it out, huh? I'm going to need more cigarettes soon."

Hearing this, you'd like to drop the speed another five miles per hour, maybe another ten. But, then, why drag out this excursion any longer than it needs to be? You check the rearview, see the lights of several cars approaching and, gradually, you increase the pressure on the pedal until the speedometer's needle touches 60.

"Come on. Move this thing. I've got no more cigarettes." Either she didn't notice the fifteen mile per hour increase in speed or she is, once again, just testing the level of your tolerance. But you will not react further. You neither increase the speed past sixty, nor do you decrease it. Nor do you pay attention to her now as she yanks on your jacket sleeve.

"Hey, Nun! Can't you go any faster? Try one of the lanes on the left."

You take in a deep breath, rub at your eyes, and let out a soft, wheezing cough. The car is getting smoky. "Would you mind blowing your—" But you catch yourself. No speaking to her. You touch the control button on your door's console and crack your window open an inch.

This, for whatever reason, angers her. "Poor little baby," she says without sympathy. "You don't like my smoke?" She touches the control button on her own door's console and holds it until her window is opened fully.

The cold November air whips through the car, insulting you like a smack in the face. You can seal the passenger window, of course, with the master control on your console and lock it shut. But you decide to leave it alone. Let her have her fun.

"Oh, I get it," she says. "You're ignoring me. Is that the idea . . . ?" Poor little baby is a little martyr, too." With that she closes her passenger window halfway. Then opens it. Closes it. Opens it. "Pretty annoying, right?" She shuts her window one more time. Opens it again and then leaves it that way. She takes a last drag on her cigarette and tosses it out the window.

You think for a moment, try to recollect what started this fight. You cannot honestly remember; it seems so very long ago. You recall that both of you left the party in good spirits, that both of you admitted to having had a better time than either of you had anticipated. At the beginning of your drive home, you compared notes on the different people you had spoken to. There was a rundown on who she thought was getting fat, what couples were candidates for separation, who might be fooling around on whom. Perhaps the problem began when you started comparing one another to the various guests at the party, then critiquing each other's individual performances. It evolved harmlessly enough. You told her that she was one of the best-looking women at the party, quite possibly the best looking. Of the men she thought you, also, were one of *the* best looking, and to boot, one of the wittiest. It went on in this fashion until you suggested that, "although it hardly matters," maybe she shouldn't have had so much to drink towards the end of the evening: all of that wine, you explained, seemed to have caught up to her, had taken an adverse effect on her "party etiquette" (i.e. she had asked some rather awkward questions of the host, had snubbed several of the women who'd attempted to befriend her, and, perhaps most inappropriate of all, had spent the final hour of the party lingering at the portable bar).

She scoffed at the charges. "Ridiculous." And then she countered with a couple of suggestions for you: you shouldn't have spent so much time in the corner with that "streaked blonde in the fishnet stockings," or, for that matter, you should not have been so obvious about trying to "chat up the hors d'oeuvres waitress."

You busted out laughing, flabbergasted. "Are you kidding? What waitress? It was a buffet. Serve yourself."

"Who do you think set up the buffet? It was the waitress. The one you were trying to hump."

And so it went, one accusation leading to another, one outraged denial on your part leading to one on hers. Indeed, it would not be long before the conversation turned to the subject of a lawyer, of a divorce and of well-hung Frenchmen blessed with sophistication and pizzazz.

"Listen," she says, "what's the deal? Are we talking or are you still ignoring me?"

You drum your fingers against the steering wheel, more for the purpose of keeping them warm than to be musical. It does no good, however. You bring your hands to your mouth, blow into them, rub them together, then wish instantly that you had not done so; you've just demonstrated to her that her antics with the window are affecting you.

"What? You're getting cold?" She turns around and kneels on the seat. "Sorry," she says, "but you're forcing me to do this." She stretches over the top of the seat and reaches into the rear of the car. She grunts, going for the window behind you. Her backside is arched perpendicular to the top of the seat. It moves toward you to a point not three inches from your ear. Your impulse is to give it one good shove with your elbow, sending her over the seat and into the rear of the car.

But you resist. Instead, you keep an eye on the road as she opens the window directly behind you, then the one opposite it. It is a chilled and bitter wind that strikes you. You turn up the collar of your jacket and, for the next moments, sulk in silence.

"So, are you going to talk to me now, or what?" She sits back down. She folds her arms together, holding them close to her chest. It appears as though she is suffering this cold as strongly as you. Perhaps more so. She lets out a shiver and asks again if you are going to stop this "childish game" of ignoring her. When she receives no reply, she says, "All right then," and turns on the radio. She cranks the volume to Nine, turns the bass all the way up, then increases the treble. She starts shooting through the stations: Heavy Metal, Country, Talk Radio, Soul, Top Forty, and back to Heavy Metal.

This strategy of ignoring her has not proven as successful as you imagined. Outside the temperature is barely above the freezing mark. As the air from the three open windows whips through the car, you wonder if it might not be even colder inside than outside—wind chill factor and all. The radio is blaring an advertisement for a muffler-repair shop: its lifetime guarantee is being sung in verse, Doo-wop fashion. Your exit is about five miles up the expressway. You decide to hang in a while longer.

"Don't blame this on me," she is shouting above the noise booming from the speakers. She points to the radio, then gestures around the interior of the car, towards the three open windows. "It's your fault. Not mine. Because you're being such a baby. If you'd just talk to me, I'd cut it out."

Maybe she would, you think, but what a talk it would be. You can picture it now. Within minutes you'd be commenting on one another's flaws, cutting on one another's mothers, dredging up old insults, tearing scabs from wounds that should have healed years ago. No, you refuse to speak to her again tonight, at least for the duration of this ride home. She can leave the windows open, turn the radio's volume to Ten if she chooses, but you will not give into her; not this time.

"And it's your fault, too," she shouts in your ear, "if I go deaf tonight. Or if I die of pneumonia." She reaches into the glove compartment, fishes through it—tossing around your registration and insurance papers, your loose sticks of Doublemint chewing gum, your flashlight, wrench and screwdriver—until she finds the packet of Kleenex tissues. She sets the packet in her lap and draws a tissue from it. "If I so much as catch a cold," she tells you, "my lawyer will be hearing about it." She blows her nose into the Kleenex, folds it in half, snorts, and blows again. She crumples the tissue into a ball and starts to give it the over-the-shoulder-flip into the back seat. Halfway into the movement, however, she stops herself. "*Here*," she shouts. "*You take it*!" And with that she aims and flings the crumpled wad at your chest.

This is too much. The hell with your strategy. "Classy," you mutter. "Very classy."

"Well, well," she says. "I see you're talking to the old battle-axe again." She pulls another tissue from the packet, blows into it and—"Here you go"—pitches it into your face.

She hadn't even bothered crumpling that one, just threw it, wet and exposed, right at you. Bull's-eye!

"You're a gem," you let her know. "So dainty."

"You want 'dainty'? Try that hors d'oeuvres girl of yours. I never claimed to be *dainty*, Bub."

You drag a hand across your brow. "What a bore you are. Why don't —" You see another tissue coming your way. You weave your head to avoid it but a gust of wind catches it in mid-flight, blows it against your cheek. "You're going to cause an accident," you warn her.

"So? You could've caused me pneumonia and you didn't care about that."

This can't go on. It is getting dangerous. You will have to pull the car to the shoulder and park until she gets hold of herself.

The thought depresses you. It is only a few more miles to your exit. You check the rearview and find that you are in a patch of sixty-miles-per-hour traffic that might stretch as far as half a mile. The process of pulling your car to the shoulder could be as risky as carrying on with the drive. "*Listen*," you shout over the music blaring from the speakers, "you're going to have to—" You shut off the radio. "You're going to have to cut this out."

"It's my car, too," she tells you, seemingly missing your point. "I can do what I want." And, to prove it, she turns the radio back on, cranks up the volume and blows a deep wet one into a fresh tissue.

"Don't you dare!" You raise your arm and show her the back of your hand. This is simply for effect, of course; a threatening gesture, no more. You have never struck her and have no intention of doing so now. Still, you feel violence through your arm as you hold it before her, adrenaline racing through your heart. "Cut it out. Now!" Once again you shut off the radio. You lift your arm back up, returning your hand to a point just inches from her face. "I mean it. You're dangerous."

She slaps your hand from her face. "Who the hell do you think you are? Don't you ever threaten me again." She pulls out a new tissue. "You want to see dangerous?" She folds it into fours. "I'll show you dangerous." From her purse, she grabs her yellow Cricket lighter, flicks it, adjusts its flame and holds it to the Kleenex, setting it on fire. "Now this," she says, "is dangerous." She holds the burning tissue before her and then throws it onto the dashboard. "See what I mean?"

You slap at it several times with your open palm, tamping it out. What is wrong with her? Is she insane? She has thrown tantrums before, plenty of them; never, though, were they as severe as this one. You take a quick look at her, wanting to say something, but she is lighting up another tissue.

"Here's one more for you." She tosses it onto the dashboard.

"What are you doing?" The wind blowing through the windows catches the burning tissue across the dashboard and deposits it on the floor by your feet. "You're suicidal," you tell her. "You're going to get us killed." As you stamp the tissue out, you see another one coming; this one towards your lap. You snatch at it, and then try to block it, but it falls between your legs onto the seat of the car. You lift your hips from the seat, feel around with your hand, still keeping an eye on the road. Once you find the tissue, you put it out with your right hand, holding the wheel with your left. You see the cars behind starting to flash their brights, the drivers passing on the left are giving you the finger, honking their horns at your erratic driving. Up ahead, you spot the sign for your exit: 1/2 MILE. RIGHT LANE. "That was brilliant," you tell her. "You almost got us killed."

"With a wizard like you behind the wheel? Not a chance. You're too skilled a driver."

You almost start to laugh the situation is so out of control. But then you see that she is about to set fire to another tissue. "That's it. Enough!" You hear your voice begin to crack, hear the blood pumping through your brain.

"All right," she says, "all right." She drops the tissue and the lighter into her purse. "But get me cigarettes."

Unbelievable. You shake your head as you hit the signal and turn off the expressway. "You're not serious," you tell her.

"Yes, I'm serious. Why not? There's a gas station up the road. They'll have a machine."

The traffic light ahead is turning red. You slow the car to a stop.

"Forget it," you say. You place your hand on your door's console, touch the master control and listen as all three windows close simultaneously. Within seconds, you feel the car start to warm.

"Come on. I'm dying for one."

"There's chewing gum in the glove compartment. Try that."

"It sticks to my dental work."

"Too bad," you tell her.

"Yeah, well, too bad for you. Because I've also got to go to the bathroom."

"Sure you do."

"I do. I've had to go since we left the party."

"Hold it till we get home."

"Nope. Stop at the gas station. I've got to go pretty bad."

"That's unfortunate," you say, turning to look at her. "Number One or Number Two?" She's acting like a child, you'll treat her as such.

She makes a face. "Yuck! You think I'd do a Number Two in a gas station?"

You shrug. "After tonight, I haven't the slightest idea of what you would and wouldn't do."

She lets out a pleasant laugh. Apparently, she has taken this as a compliment. "I'm pretty unpredictable, huh?"

There is warmth to her voice; friendliness; it takes you by surprise.

"Come on," she says. "It's Number One, okay? And if I don't go now I'll get cystitis." She taps your shoulder and points to the traffic light; it has changed to green. "My magazines say bacteria starts floating around down there in some women. If they don't go to the bathroom right away it gives them cystitis. Something like that."

As you put your foot to the gas pedal, it occurs to you that she is making this up as she goes along. The cigarettes are her first priority, you realize, not the bathroom, but you agree to pull into the station anyway.

"You're right," you tell her. "We can't risk having bacteria floating around *down there*."

She touches your hand, then your knee. "You're a honeybunch," she says as you pull the car into the station. "*My* knight in shining armor." She opens her purse and picks around for change. "Got any quarters?"

You pat the front pockets of your pants. You hear no jingle; feel no coins, no quarters. "The attendant will give you some," you tell her.

"Not after nine o'clock. Gas stations lock up all their money. So they don't get robbed."

You park several yards from the pumps, shut the lights and then the engine. "Ask anyway. The guy will have some."

"All right. But pull up to the island. Buy some gas." You look at the gauge: almost three quarters full. "I don't need any."

"Come on. Buy some. Or he won't let me use the bathroom."

"Flatter him," you suggest. "Use that gift you were telling me about, that *certain seductive charm*."

She gives you a face. "Funny," she says and steps out of the car, purse in hand. "I'll be a few . . ." She wiggles her fingers at you and walks around the car and out of your mirror's view.

This has to have been, you think, one of the more bizarre evenings in recent years. You close your eyes and take in a long breath of air. It's odd: deep inside you feel yourself chuckling a little, don't you? Now that the drama is over, you can appreciate some of the evening's humor: mucous-soaked tissues, wide-open windows in thirty-five-degree temperatures, talk of lawyers and divorce and well-hung Frenchmen. You review the key details of this evening, embellishing them somewhat as you reel them through your mind: "There we were, shooting down the expressway at eighty-miles-per hour, these flaming Kleenexes flying all over the car, falling onto my crotch, hitting me square in the face."

Perhaps you will recount this evening to friends sometime. You imagine yourself at your next party, a small crowd surrounding you as you spin your tale of marital conflict and expressway daring-do. "The way the radio was blasting, sixty watts minimum, it's a miracle we're both not deaf. . . . You should've seen it. Everyone was giving us the brights, blowing their horns, giving us the finger. It was fifty-fifty, really, our chances of getting killed that night. . . . This gal I'm married to, what a kook."

You ponder it for a while, the narrative and the dialogue that you will recreate for your friends, the descriptions, the emotions you were feeling at the time. You pause a moment, think it through once more; then you decide to put your little story aside. It is not really that amusing, is it? Nor is it that interesting. Nor, for that matter, are your characters all that appealing. Why waste everyone's time?

November, 1988

three
please, god, make her say no

CAROL GATHERS the kittens into a cardboard box that is lined with yesterday's newspaper. Paul, her nine-year old, looks on from the hallway. He's been quiet all morning, unusually so. "Come on," she says to him. "Don't give me those eyes. You knew we'd be doing this." She gives his head a rub, gets a box of Friskies from the kitchen cabinet, a couple of bowls and a container of milk from the refrigerator. She puts these into a grocery bag. It's almost noon; time to go. "You ready?" she asks.

Paul carries the grocery bag and the "5 FREE KITTENS" sign that he had drawn up the night before. Carol carries the box of kittens and her purse. They put everything into the back seat of her car. "If nobody likes them," Paul says, "do you think we can keep them for ourselves?"

"These adorable things?" she asks, keeping it light. "Everybody's going to like them."

It's a decent day outside: large white clouds, a crisp autumn wind in the air. Carol pulls the car onto the highway and, for the most part, they drive in silence: Carol behind the wheel, watching the road, Paul, head tucked low, examining the scuffed-up Keds on his feet.

As they approach the town line, Paul begins to move in his seat. "Mom? Let's say that no one does like them. Then can we keep them? Or if nobody's at the store?"

"It's Sunday. We're going to Sears. Everybody'll be there."

After another mile or two, they pull into the parking lot. "You see?"

she says. "Look at all of the cars. It's packed with people." They find a space close to the store. They place the boxful of kittens into a shopping cart, the sign, her purse and the grocery bag, and they wheel the cart to the store's front entrance.

The first hour passes slowly. Rather than attracting people with the "5 FREE KITTENS" sign, it seems to be scaring them off. People see the sign and, instinctively, turn away their heads, assuming, probably, that she and Paul are selling something like chocolate bars or greeting cards for a Little League fundraiser.

"Mom," Paul says, "can we go now?" There's an optimism to his voice, as if this might actually be a possibility.

"Let's give it a while more. Try to look cheerful, okay? No pusses. We don't want to scare everyone away." The problem, of course, is deeper than the matter of Paul's puss. Maybe they should move from the entrance doors to the exit doors. And, instead of holding up just the sign, maybe they should hold up one of the kittens, too. And, as much as she dislikes the idea, maybe she should try to be more aggressive; try some salesmanship.

"Paul," she says, lifting one of the kittens from the box, "let's bring the cart down here." She spots a man and a woman, mid-twenties, leaving the store. She raises the kitten into the air, makes eye contact with the man. "Free kittens," she says, putting on the grin. "All healthy. Easy to take care of."

The man just smiles and brushes her off with a wave of his hand.

"Sure you don't want to take a look?" Carol widens the grin, lifting the kitten higher. This is not her type of thing, she knows, but she carries on anyway. "They don't bite. They keep themselves clean. . . ." What else? "And they don't take up much room."

The man and woman keep walking but another couple, an older pair in their fifties, is right behind them and they seem eager to have their look at what's inside the box.

"Free kittens," Carol tells them. "Eight weeks old." She returns the kitten into the box with the others.

"They're so cute," the woman says, taking a peek. "Eight weeks you say?" She gives each of them, one at a time, a scratch behind the ear, and then a stroke on the crown of each of their heads. "Some people give them away at six weeks, or seven, because they're just a tad cuter then. But that's too young. Eight weeks is perfect." She turns to the man she is with. "Come on, Art. What're you afraid of?"

Art is standing off to the side. He gives a chuckle, then steps towards the boxful of kittens and takes a peek himself. "They're playful," he says. "Especially this guy." He points to one of the two black-and-white kittens. "It reminds me of myself when I was eight weeks."

"*Art*," the woman laughs. She takes the kitten from the box and cradles it against her breast. "Do you have a name for it?" she asks Paul.

Paul raises his chin from his chest. "Kind of," he tells the woman.

Carol looks at him, makes a frown. Both her mother and ex-husband had advised against giving the kittens names since they wouldn't be keeping them. She had told Paul this and listened to him promise that, indeed, he wouldn't give them names.

"Well?" the woman asks Paul.

He hooks a thumb into his pocket and then he says, "Ralph. I call it Ralph." He glances at Carol to see if he'll be punished for this.

Carol smiles. "Ralph, huh? That's a nice name for a girl cat."

The woman lifts the cat up to her nose and gives it a kiss. "Actually, I'm glad to hear it," she tells Carol. "I prefer female cats." She lowers her voice confidentially. "Their urine doesn't smell as bad as a boy's."

"You know about cats?" Carol asks.

"Oh, sure. Me and Art—I'm Fran, by the way—we've never been without a cat. Not until last month, anyway. When we had to put ours to sleep."

Carol tsssks softly. "I'm sorry."

"Leukemia," Fran tells her. "Don't ask me why but it's one of the leading killers of cats."

"Right after steel-belted radials," Art puts in.

Fran gives him a shot to the shoulder for that—"Be nice"—and they all chuckle together. "You'll have to excuse my husband. He thinks he's a comedian."

They chit chat awhile longer, Fran and Carol, discussing the care of cats, whether it's better to make them *indoor* or *outdoor*, what's the best age to switch them over to canned food . . . and, by the time Fran and Art have left with their black-and-white kitten, and Carol has changed the sign from "5 FREE KITTENS" to "4 FREE KITTENS," there is a horseshoe of onlookers around herself and Paul. Within the next hour, the sign will be changed three more times, until there is only one kitten remaining.

She looks at her watch: a quarter past two. It shouldn't be much longer before the last one is picked up. With a little luck she and Paul might be out of here in a few minutes. Maybe, once they're through, she'll take him to the Burger King across the street. She'll keep it to herself for now and surprise him with it later.

"*This is wrong*." A short, matronly lady is staring into Carol's eyes. The lady is wearing blue sweatpants, a baggy yellow sweat shirt and, on her feet, a pair of white sneakers. She gestures with a half-smoked cigarette to the "FREE KITTENS" sign and then to the box holding the last of these kittens. "For one thing, you should have had their mother spayed. That way none of this would have happened. There are too many cats in this world already, over half of them homeless. No one needed you to bring another five into it." Carol fidgets with her hands, saying nothing. "Furthermore," the lady says, blowing a puff of smoke into the air, "since their mother did get pregnant, you should have brought the kittens to the animal shelter. Not to the nearest Sears. I don't mean to tell you what to do, of course, but this isn't the way to rid yourself of a litter."

Carol listens to the lady, feigning interest, nodding her head when appropriate. More than once, of course, she had considered bringing the kittens to the animal shelter. At the moment, however, she can't recall what had caused her to decide against it. It must have been the thought of the poor things trapped inside of cages; scared stiff, lonely. She explains this to the lady, trying to help her visualize the scene as she, herself, had visualized it—"cramped steel cages," "dogs barking all over the place"—but it does her no good.

"With cats this young," the lady says, flicking an ash from her cigarette, "it would have been, at most, only a week before they found good homes. And the people that adopted them would have done some planning on the matter. They would have known for sure whether they wanted a pet or not. You give cats away at a place like this and people bring them home on impulse. They haven't thought it through. They'll end up getting rid of the things the first time they climb up the curtains. They'll drive them to the woods or someplace and dump them out into the cold, leaving the helpless things to fend for themselves." She sticks the cigarette back into her mouth and waits for a reply.

Carol exchanges a look with Paul. This kind of talk is the last thing she wants him to hear. She'd like to tell this lady to take a hike, to mind her own business, but she does not. She isn't, she knows, as assertive as she'd like to be. With the exceptions of her son and her ex-husband, she has a difficult time confronting anyone, let alone rude and insulting strangers. "Well, I just thought by doing it this way, it'd be—"

"I know what you were thinking. It's not necessary to explain. You thought it would be nice for your boy to see who'd be getting the kittens."

Carol nods her head. "That's right. This way he'd see that they were going to good homes. He wouldn't worry about—"

"And you thought you'd enjoy seeing the people's faces as they looked at your cats. And instead of handing them over to some volunteer at the shelter, you thought you'd be able to share in the fun of the whole adoption process."

Again, Carol nods. If her expression shows it or not, she is getting pretty annoyed. What is it with this pest?

The lady drops her cigarette to the pavement, stamps it out and coughs into her hand. "Think of it this way . . . let's say that you were putting your son up for adoption. Would you give him to an adoption agency, an agency with credentials and regulations? Or would you bring him to Sears and hang a sign over his head? FREE BOY? What I'm say—"

"Alright," Carol tells the lady. "Fine. Thank you for your input." She lays her arm around Paul's shoulders. "Now leave us alone, please. Really. Go do your shopping."

The lady's eyes widen as she tightens her mouth. Slowly she shakes her head. "Well, you should have had their mother spayed. That's all I wanted to say. It was selfish of you not to do so."

"And all I want to say is that any cat in the world would rather live in the home of an impulsive Sears shopper than never to have lived at all."

The lady dismisses this with a wave of her hand. "You're being arrogant," she says. "And I think you've missed my point entirely."

"Well, good," Carol tells her. "It was a lousy point." The lady turns and heads for the store. As she nears the entrance doors, Carol calls after her, "It was a *terrible* point." It sounds dumb, she knows it does, but she doesn't care. She feels a pleasant rush inside. She stood up to the bitch—sort of. She pulls her arm back from Paul's shoulders. If there's one regret it's that he was the one to witness the exchange. She would have preferred it was her ex-husband to have seen it or, perhaps, her mother, who used to tease her as a child by referring to her as "Mouse."

Carol looks at the kitten and traces a finger along the side of its face. She checks her watch: 2:40. "When we're done," she tells Paul, "I was thinking we might go to Burger King and you can get anything you . . ."

Paul isn't listening; his focus is on a man approaching from behind.

"Old fart had it coming," the man says. "I'd have told her to screw off a long time ago." The man is accompanied by a woman, a boy about seven years old with a gauze pad taped over his eye, and another boy about three. How long have they been standing there? How much have they heard? She has no idea. She tries a grin but it's difficult.

"You got one left," the man says and points to the box holding the kitten. "How old?"

"Eight weeks," Carol tells him.

"Got any teeth?"

"Huh? Oh, sure."

"Ain't housebroken, I bet."

"It's on cat litter, if that's what you mean."

"Uh, huh," the man says. "Is it big?"

"Well, no. Not yet. It's a kitten still."

"Uh, huh," he says again. "Healthy?"

"Yes. No problems."

He stuffs his shirttail into the waistband of his pants. He is a thin man, medium height, with longish brown hair and a complexion in need of sun. It's hard to get a fix on his age: thirty-five, maybe, or early forties . . . or late twenties. Carol really can't tell; she is usually good with ages.

"What's its color?"

"It's black," she tells him. "And white. But mostly black." She opens and closes her hand. She feels a headache coming.

"Mostly black," he says to the woman that he's with. There is disappointment in his voice.

Carol watches as he rubs at his chin. She looks at his left hand and sees no wedding band, just a faded tattoo of a snake or a lizard or some other sort of reptile.

"What do you think?" he asks the woman. "You want it?"

The woman lowers her eyes and shrugs. "It's hard to say." She rests her hands on her hips and looks to her two boys for their opinions. They, however, don't seem to know what to think, either. She glances in the direction of Carol. "Can we look at it first? Before we go making up our minds?"

Carol attempts a smile, not really inviting them to inspect the kitten but not denying them the opportunity, either.

As it turns out, it doesn't matter. The man is already at the box, moving Paul out of his way. "It's kind of scrawny looking," he tells the woman, lifting the kitten by the scruff of its neck.

"Wait. You shouldn't—" Carol has heard that holding a cat this way is painless for it (it's the way their own mothers hold them, after all) but it looks painful and it's always given her the creeps to watch. She sees Paul inching towards her, intimidated by this man, as is she.

"Who wants to hold it?" The man looks at the woman he's with and then at the two boys, exhibiting the kitten at arm's length.

After a series of glances and counter-glances, the older boy, the one with the gauze pad over his eye, takes the kitten and holds it in cupped hands against his stomach. "I think it's scared of me," he says.

The man doesn't respond. To Carol he says, "You had five of them, huh?" He points to the sign advertising FREE KITTENS. "Giving them away for nothing . . . you should've charged money." He thinks for a moment. "Ten bucks a pop would have made you fifty."

"I guess so," Carol says. "I didn't really think about it that way."

He shrugs. "The way I look at it, money's money, you know? Fifty's fifty."

Carol tries a grin again. She spots Paul coming closer and takes his hand.

"Well," the man says to the woman, "what's the verdict? You want it or what?"

Carol bites her lip. *Please, God, make her say "No."*

The woman glances at the kitten still cupped in the hands of the boy. "I'm not sure," she says. "What do you think?" She's studying the kitten as she says this; it's difficult, therefore, for Carol to determine who the question had been addressed to: the man or herself.

"Moment of truth," the man says. He gives Carol a slow wink with his left eye. Then, for the benefit of the woman he's with, he makes a face and turns his head from one side to the other. "Your call, Cupcake. But hurry it up, huh? We're wasting this girl's time."

Reflexively, Carol gives a quick laugh and raises her hands in front of her, the *don't-mind-me* gesture. "Take as long as you need" she says. "There's no—" She catches herself: *don't encourage them.*

The woman lifts her gaze from the kitten to a point about three inches below the man's head. "I guess, maybe, we should keep it," she tells him. "Ends up we don't like it, it's not the end of the world, right?"

He's not listening. He's poking around the shopping cart, looking into the grocery bag. *Jesus*, Carol thinks, stay away from there. Along with the grocery bag and the empty cardboard box, her purse is also in that shopping cart. She makes a move to grab it from the cart but stops herself halfway: it would appear too obvious, like she doesn't trust the man.

"Do we get the rest of the food?" he asks, "and the milk? Seeing that we're getting the last one?"

Carol takes Paul's hand back into her own; it's sticky with perspiration. She tightens her grip on it. "Well, yes," she says. "I suppose so. But . . ." she clears her throat. "You see, I've been thinking about it. And I'm not really sure this is a good idea."

The man arches an eyebrow, tilting his head quizzically.

"You two seem uncertain," she explains. "What if I give you my number? And when you've decided for sure, you can give me a call."

"Yeah. Five-five-five, right? One of those bullshit numbers."

"What . . . ? No," she says. "I wouldn't do that. It's seven, six, two —" She stops herself. *Don't be a dope.* "What I'm saying is that this is a big decision."

"Right. And we just made it. We want the cat. You have a problem with that?

"No. Not at all. Not necessarily. But maybe you'd want to talk it through when you all are alone. Sleep on it."

"Uh, huh," he says. "Have a family meeting. Set up a little committee."

"I'm not saying that. But you might want to talk to friends, neighbors, other pet owners. Find out what it's like owning a cat."

"We know what we're doing," the woman says in a tone meant to comfort. "We've had cats before. Plenty of them."

Carol looks at the kitten in the hands of the boy. Maybe she can snatch it from him—one quick grab and run like hell with Paul . . . or should she wait until she has her purse out of the cart and back in her hand? "What I'm saying is that there's a lot for you to consider. Like this cat, for instance, is a male. And some people don't like male cats"—damn, she hates this—"because their urine smells bad."

The man pulls at the waistband of his pants and then drops a hand to his crotch. "Well," he says, "mine don't smell so hot, either."

The woman laughs; so does the boy holding the kitten.

"It doesn't matter anyway," the man says. "It'll be doing its dirty business outside."

"You're going to make it an *out*door cat?" Carol asks. She turns her head, takes a look around, hoping to see another crowd of onlookers gathered about her. This is not the case, however. There is no crowd. The shoppers entering and exiting the store are paying them little attention. She releases Paul's hand and approaches the boy who's holding the kitten. The boy draws it close to his chest, frightened, and takes a step behind his mother. "I'm sorry," Carol tells the man, "but you can't have it, then. Maybe I didn't mention this beforehand, but I wanted it to be an *in*-door cat. I've only been giving them to families that promise to keep them *indoors*."

"How about its mother, then? You let its mother out."

"What?"

"How'd its mother get herself knocked up if it wasn't an outdoor cat?"

Carol shakes her head. "I don't know. I guess it snuck out one night."

The woman lets out a short hoot—it sounds like half a hiccup—obviously impressed with her man. "Pretty sharp," she says.

He acknowledges the compliment with a nod, impressed with himself, as well. "It's called a built-in crap detector, Cupcake. I keep it turned on twenty-four seven."

"Please," Carol says, "I've changed my mind, okay? Nothing personal but I want to keep the kitten for myself."

"It's a little late for that," the man says. "You can't go giving away cats, wait for a seven-year-old boy to get his heart all set on the thing and then go changing your mind about it, wanting to take the thing back."

Carol moves to the shopping cart and grabs her purse. She can feel the thump of her heart; her stomach is mush. "Listen," she says, "why don't you and I talk for a minute? Alone." She walks into the parking lot, motions with her head for him to follow. When they are out of hearing distance of the others she unclasps her purse. "What if," she says, "I was to give you twenty dollars. . . ? To leave my son and me alone? And to leave us with the cat?"

The man rubs his chin, amused. He runs his hands across his waist, making sure his shirt is tucked in all the way. "Twenty bucks, huh? These days, that isn't much." He thinks a moment, takes a look over his shoulder at the woman and the boy holding the kitten. "Maybe if you threw in that phone number of yours, a real one, maybe then I'll—"

"Come on. Just the money. Twenty dollars."

"I don't know. It looks like the boy's gotten pretty fond of the thing."

"Please," Carol says.

He clucks his tongue against the roof of his mouth, thinking it over, enjoying himself. "Make it fifty. That's the lowest I can go. I couldn't square it with the boy otherwise."

"I don't have fifty."

"What do you have?"

"I don't know. But it's not fifty. I just paid my rent."

"Is that supposed to be something special? Like nobody else's got rent to pay?" He stretches his neck from side to side as if working out stiffness and then he points to her purse. "Open it up. Let's see what you got."

She unclasps it and looks inside. She can't believe this is happening. It's like being held up at knifepoint: less frightening but just as degrading. Perhaps it's even more degrading. After all, she doesn't really have to be doing this, does she? Opening her purse for this man? Forking over every dollar that she has?

"Let's hurry it up," he says. "I got shopping to do."

Carol takes a step backwards and opens her wallet. A twenty, two tens, a few singles. Forty-three dollars. Forty-five if it comes down to her quarters and dimes. She takes a minute, trying to figure her cash expenses for the coming week. Five dollars for gas. Another five for dry cleaning. Two dollars more, forty cents a day, for her morning buttered roll at work. She already gave Paul his allowance and did her grocery shopping yesterday, so she'll need just another seven or eight dollars if she and Paul are to go to Burger King . . . So that's five and five and two and eight . . . Twenty dollars. She searches through the other compartments of her wallet, checking to see if she has any emergency money stashed away.

"Well?" the man asks her. "What's the good news?"

She checks the final compartment: empty. "Sorry," she says. "I don't have much to spare."

"Then tough. You don't get the cat."

"I can give you twenty-three. Twenty-five if you want the change."

"Yeah, I want the change. But twenty-five ain't gonna cut it." He shoves his hands into his back pockets, turns his head to the side, pissed, not looking at her. "You rich types, you're all the same. You think you can buy off everyone. Then, once you get saps like me to name our price, then you try to talk us down."

"I am not rich," she tells him. "And I didn't try to talk you down. I offered you twenty dollars and it was you who tried to talk the price *up*. To fifty. It was me who named the first price."

"Whatever," he says, again not listening. "It slays me, too, the way you people never keep enough cash on you. It's always credit cards and checkbooks and money markets and portfolios. You never have the cold green stuff when you need it."

"I am not rich," she repeats. "And I don't have money markets or whatever you mean by portfolios. I earn nineteen thousand a year. That's it. And I get another five hundred a month in child support."

The man snorts. "Well, that's five hundred more than I get. And I got *two* kids to take care of." He pulls his hands from his back pockets and shoves them into his front pockets. "You're divorced then . . . child support. You're a *divorcée.*" He accents the word, making it sound almost sexual.

She stares into his eyes, saying nothing, and reaches into her wallet. The hell with the dry cleaners. The hell with Burger King. The hell with her stupid buttered rolls. She pulls the bills from her wallet and crushes them into a ball. "Here. It's been a real treat meeting—"

"*Don't give that man a cent! Put your money away.*" It is the short, matronly lady Carol had argued with earlier. She's holding the kitten against her shoulder. Trailing a few steps behind her is Paul, trying to maintain pace with the lady as he struggles with the grocery bag, the sign and the empty cardboard box.

The man pushes out his chest and straightens his posture, glaring at the lady. "Stay out of this," he tells her. "It ain't your affair."

"You're extorting money from this poor girl. With an animal as your hostage. That's my affair alright."

"I didn't extort anything. I'm not forcing her to give me money. She offered it."

The lady ignores this. She takes the kitten from her shoulder and passes it to Carol. Two security guards, in dark blue uniforms, are jogging towards them from the store's exit doors, their silver badges bouncing on their chests.

"Rudy!" Cupcake calls out. "*Cops!*"

"Go on, Dear," the lady tells Carol. "Go home. You keep the cat."

Fiercely, Carol nods her head. "Thank you," she tells the lady, step-ping backwards. She drops the ball of crushed bills into her purse, clutches the kitten tight and, with Paul, starts walking to the car, double time.

"What about my dough?" the man calls after them. "You owe me twenty bucks."

This makes them walk even quicker. After several stiff-legged paces, they break into a trot, heading straight for the car. Once inside, they lock the doors, roll up the windows and slip on their seat belts. Carol sets the kitten between them and starts the car. Paul, his face flushed and freckled with perspiration, pants for breath through an open smile as they exit the parking lot without looking back. There will be a few traffic lights to deal with before they make it to the highway. Once they've reached it and are headed south, there is nothing but an open road in front of them. Paul, eventually, turns on the radio. He lifts the kitten onto his lap and shimmies toward Carol. There is mischief in his face, a happy glint to his eyes. "Hey, Cupcake," he says, adding a goofy accent to his voice, "are we going to Burger King or ain't we?"

She smiles toward him, but it is a smile without energy. "You think you're pretty funny, don't you?" She pokes a finger at his ribs, giving him a tickle, and listens to his little squeal as he shields his torso with his arms. After a while, as they're about to turn off the highway, she slows the speed of the car. "You want to drop in on your dad for a bit? Tell him about our adventure?"

Paul's eyes brighten at the question and he nods his head, yes, grinning broadly.

"Good," she says. "We'll ask him to join us. It'll be fun."

September, 1988

four
to know an other

LIZ STRUCK the dashboard with an open palm. "What more do you want, Mark? A sign out front? This is their place. It's got to be." She pointed towards the house. "They said a brown and white house on the left-hand side. A gingerbread-style house. That's got to be it."

I thought for a moment and then shook my head. "No," I told her. "Not necessarily." I shifted the car into park and shut off the wipers. Snow gathered quickly on the windshield. "Look . . . all the lights are out."

"So? Maybe they lost power. Or maybe they're just trying to save a watt."

I shook my head again. "I don't think so, Liz." I rolled down the window. "Look at their driveway. There're no cars."

"So? Maybe they loaned it to someone. Maybe they're having it repaired."

I placed my hand on hers. Why, I wondered, must she and I have these disagreements whenever we travel someplace new? We had been arguing, on and off, since we left home. I reached into the glove compartment and pulled out the flash light. "What's their last name? I keep forgetting."

"It's English sounding. Sort of Anglo Saxon-ee. Something with a P . . . Parker or Peterson. Something like that."

"This is the wrong house, then." I aimed the flashlight at the mailbox for her, spotlighting the name on it, *Monteleone*.

"Let me see." She shimmied across the seat and leaned towards my window, raising her fingers to her forehead like an Eagle Scout, almost as if shielding her eyes as if it were high noon outside and not a dark, snowy night. She peered out the window, reading aloud the name I had illuminated for her. "Mont-e-le-one," she said. "Right. That's not it."

I turned off the flashlight, flipped on the wipers and shifted the car into drive. Slowly, we traveled along the road, scanning the houses on the right-hand side, keying on the houses to the left. A quarter of a mile down the road I saw it: a brown and white gingerbread-style house, well lit, with a large Christmas tree visible through the living-room window. And there, standing outside the front door, waving his arm at us, was the man who invited us here this evening, Tommy Pubman. The name, upon seeing his face, returned to me instantly.

I parked the car out front and poked around in the back seat for the bottle of wine we had brought with us. "Pubman," I said. "That's their name." Then, in spite of myself, I added, "Pubman isn't Anglo Saxon-ee."

Liz shrugged her shoulders and gave me one of her drier looks. "He's *your* friend, Mark. Not mine. It's not up to me to remember his last name."

"I never said that he was my friend. I barely know the guy."

"Well, I know him even less," she answered, and then, in a lower tone, added, "and what I know of him I don't like."

"Now's a nice time to tell me."

"I told you when we first met him that I didn't like him. I said the man has no presence. He's a bore."

"No, you didn't."

"Yes, I did."

I shook my head. I couldn't believe this. "Liz, you were the one who wanted to come here tonight. You were the one who accepted their invitation."

"I didn't know what else to say to them. I was being gracious."

"You at least liked his wife, I thought."

"His wife? Me?" She laughed. "I can't even remember her name."

"You two hit it off great together."

"Me and her? No, Mark, hardly the case."

This was not true. They had a fine time together. "Yes," I said. "After the Christmas party. On our drive home. You said she was a lot of fun."

"She was *alright*, Mark. She wasn't a total drag. But nobody said she was a lot of fun. Nobody said we hit it off great."

"That's not what you said on the way home from the party. You told me that if it wasn't for her the night would've been a waste of time."

"No, Mark. Wrong. I think it was you who liked his wife. Not me. The big jazzy hairdo of hers. The pouty lips and all that mascara and blush . . . and that little Betty-Boop voice of hers. It was you who liked her, Mark, not me. Because, as I told you, I can't even remember the woman's name."

"Her name," I said, "is Antoinette." And then, just as quickly as saying it, I wished that I had not.

Liz was smiling. "Oh, yes. Antoinette," she repeated. "That's right. So you see, Mark? You remembered her name when I couldn't."

"So, what? It means my memory is better than yours. Nothing else." I pulled at my chin, a reflexive move, losing patience.

"Maybe. But it also means that they are *your* friends, Mark. Not mine. That's all I'm saying."

I set the bottle of wine between my legs and turned in the direction of Tommy Pubman who was still standing outside his doorway, hands in pockets, knees close together. He was shorter than I remembered him: a couple of inches under six feet, slumped shoulders, heavy around the waist. He was also older than I remembered him: he was several years my senior, somewhere, probably, in his early forties, which made him, I realized, more than a dozen years older than his wife, Antoinette. I watched him as he raised his gaze to observe the snowy sky above. He must have been getting cold out there; it was late December and yet he was wearing only a festive green sweater, adorned with several reindeer and Santa on a sled. He called out to us and motioned with his arms for us to come inside.

I lowered my head and turned away. Maybe coming here was a mistake. Although I was not about to admit it to Liz, I wasn't particularly enchanted with Tommy, myself, on the night that we'd met him. And now, to make matters worse, I discovered that she didn't particularly care for Antoinette.

I tinkered with the keys in the ignition and gave it some thought. It was last week at my company's Christmas party that we had made their acquaintance. The party was a massive affair, a couple of hundred employees plus their spouses. Liz had met Antoinette while waiting in line to use the Ladies Room; the line had been so long that they ended up speaking together for as much as a quarter of an hour. I, in the meantime, by sheer coincidence, was in the middle of some chitchat that Antoinette's husband, Tommy, had initiated with me at one of the portable bars set up in the reception hall. Our topic of conversation: *what was taking the wives so long in the Ladies Room?*

As I say, it was sheer coincidence. But, for that one moment in time, when the wives had returned together from the Ladies Room to find their respective husbands in the midst of conversation, that coincidence was interpreted as common ground, as the spark of a new friendship.

The cocktail portion of the evening was winding down around then. Dinner was close to being served. We decided to grab a table together and eventually, found one close to the dance floor. Conversation with Tommy Pubman was easy enough but it was not necessarily enjoyable. In too short a time I was to learn more than I cared to about his life and his career path. Over soup, I learned that he had been with the company for a little more than a year. He was a "bigwig," his word, not mine, in Engineering. His office was tucked away somewhere on the top floor of C Building. "Probably why you never ran into me before, aye, Mark?" He lived in Rockland County, an hour's commute to and from work each day. He had attended college out west and graduated with a three-point-eight grade average. "Fourth highest in my class, Mark." And then he had returned to New York to complete his master's.

Over salad, I was to learn that, after completing his education, he had worked for a couple of years up in Syracuse. Then he'd spent several more years up in Buffalo where, through a private contractor, he had done some work for the government. "I'm afraid the project was hush-hush, Mark. Rather confidential. It's a shame, because I'd really love to tell you about . . . well, what the hell, maybe if you twist my arm hard enough, maybe I could let you in on some of the details." He had moved to northern New Jersey after leaving "the project" due to professional differences. Then he had moved to Rockland County where he met Antoinette. They'd been married for over five years now: every night, though, seven nights a week, they still did it "like rabbits." "But who can blame me, aye? She's a fox, isn't she, Mark? Not that she's a goddess or anything. She could use a little more in the bosom department, I admit, and a little less in the rump but you'd do her, wouldn't you, Mark? If you weren't a married man, yourself . . . ?" All of this, as I say, over soup and salad.

The man was tiresome, plain and simple: the caustic remarks about his wife, the unending references to himself. By the time we had started on our entrees, he was rattling on about his material possessions and their respective costs: his two BMWs, his in-ground swimming pool and his Chris-Craft motorboat and his new set of golf clubs and his membership fees to the Westwind Country Club. At times even Tommy himself seemed to realize how limited and unsuitable his conversation was becoming. Unfortunately, he appeared incapable of censoring himself. "I paid two-eighty for my house back when we first got married, Mark. Guess what it's worth today. Go on, take a guess." "Hey, Mark? Have you noticed that rock on Antoinette's necklace there? Three grand it cost me. I kid you not. But, hey, so what? Moneywise, I'm having a good year. What can I tell you?"

He was a strange bird, Tommy Pubman. But, in his way, he wasn't altogether unfamiliar to me. Through the years I had come across his type many times before. He was the kind of guy who, back in high school, always seemed to be getting his butt kicked. He was the kind of guy who, later in life, always seemed to be getting on other people's nerves, making them uncomfortable without knowing quite why, without really caring why. He was the kind of guy who, I was sad to realize, always seemed to be befriending me at these sorts of corporate affairs, whether I welcomed it or not.

In truth, however, the night was not a total loss. If it was utter boredom on my part, it did have, at least, one good side to it: my wife, Liz, looked to be having a fine time for herself. She and Antoinette were, as the saying goes, getting along famously. They laughed often. Their conversation was varied, their faces animated. Towards the latter part of the night, after Tommy and I had continually ducked Liz's and Antoinette's requests to dance, they both said "Screw it" and ended up walking onto the dance floor together, choosing a spot directly in front of the band. For the most part, the music they danced to was from the '50s and early '60s. They did the Twist together, grinding down low, throwing their arms and their hips into the movements. They did the Pony, the Swim and the Shing-a-Ling. They did steps to dances that I had forgotten about long ago. They danced without inhibition, making a scene of themselves, now and then, but they were enjoying themselves, too; which, to me on that night, was the important thing.

"They sure cut a mean rug," Tommy had said, as we observed them from our table.

I nodded. My mood was improving. I laid my palm on his shoulder and said, "They sure do, Tommy."

After a few more songs, they returned from the dance floor and it wasn't long afterwards that the party began closing down. The four of us left the dining area together. I made a safety trip to the Men's Room before the long ride home, meeting Liz and the Pubmans at the coat check counter.

"Hi, Mark," Tommy said to me as I held Liz's jacket open for her.

"Hi, Mark," Antoinette repeated, her freshly glossed lips parting into a bright and happy smile.

Liz slid her arms into the jacket's sleeves. Then, in front of them both, in a voice loud enough for all three of us to hear, offering me no escape, she said, "Tommy and Antoinette invited us over to their place for next Friday, Mark. I told them, '*Sure.*' Is that okay with you?"

"Nothing fancy," Tommy put in. "Just a get-together. Highballs. Some noshes."

"And maybe a game of Pictionary," Antoinette added in that little Betty-Boop voice of hers.

And I, having had my share of drinks, feeling that artificial intimacy only alcohol can induce, I had told them, "Absolutely. We'd love to come." Why not? I had thought. Liz wanted to go, and, for that one moment in time, so did I. "Yes," I had said. "Of course we'll come. What time do you want us there, you crazy Pubmans?"

~

That was a week ago.

I played now with the bottle of wine between my legs. The car was growing cold. I turned towards the house. Tommy Pubman was still standing outside in the falling snow. He was blowing into cupped hands, shifting his weight from one foot to the other. He noticed me looking at him and gestured with his arm for us to hurry and come inside.

"Listen," I said to Liz, "this is getting kind of rude. Look at him. The poor guy's freezing out there."

"Well, I'm freezing in here."

"So, what do you want to do? It's your choice."

"What does that mean?"

"It means what I said. Do you want to go inside? Do you want to stay here in the car? Or do you want to turn around and go back home?"

She let go of a hard laugh. "Right. Sure thing, Mark. We'll just turn the car around and go back home. Who's to know, right?"

I lifted the wine bottle with my right hand and opened the car door with my left. "Then we'll go inside."

"Whatever you want," she said. "You're the boss. It's up to you."

I pulled the keys from the ignition and stuck them into the side pocket of my pants. "But let's try to have a good time. Be polite and we'll beg out early."

"Not a problem. I'll be polite the whole night long. I won't say a goddamn thing."

"Good," I said.

"Good," she repeated, having the last word.

In retrospect, we should have left Tommy standing out there in the snow. We should have turned the car around and headed back to Westchester, sending him, perhaps, a letter of apology the following day:

Dear Tommy,

What can we say? It wasn't until this morning that we realized it was actually you standing out there in the freezing cold, in the falling snow, waving your arm at us, signaling for us to come inside.

With regrets,
Mark and Liz

But, of course, our manners, our sense of propriety, would allow us to do nothing of the sort. We had, of course, gone inside.

"Having a bit of a tiff in the car, aye, Lovebirds? Some trouble in paradise?" Tommy hung our coats in the hallway closet, taking the bottle of wine as he led us into the living room. "Husbands and wives should never fight," he continued. "Me and Antoinette never do. We have a simple rule in our marriage—*count to ten and do what Tommy tells you.* It makes things so much simpler. Especially," he added, "for Antoinette."

I looked at him, his round pink cheeks lifted above a cheerful smile. I could have been wrong but my perception was that he had expected me to laugh with him. "Where is she?" I asked.

"My better half? In the bedroom. Putting on her war paint . . . and a new outfit she bought last week. . . . Well, maybe I should let her surprise you with it. You know how women are."

Liz observed him quizzically. "No," she said. "I *don't* know, Tommy. How *are* we women?"

He chuckled. "You're just different, is what I'm saying. The way you like surprising people with clothes and makeup and hair-dos and the like. No offense."

She didn't offer a reply, just scanned the living room, taking in the long black-leather couch and matching loveseat, the recliner and glass coffee table and matching end tables and the large-screen television. She moved towards the unlit fireplace and examined the several knickknacks on its mantle.

"Well?" Tommy asked her. "What's the verdict? You like?"

"What? The furniture?" she asked him back. "Sure. It's nice."

"I'm glad you approve. It's sort of cozy, isn't it?"

"Yes. It's nice. I just said so."

"Most of it I picked out myself. At Bloomies. It cost me a tidy sum, that's for sure." He waited for her response; when none was forthcoming, he turned to me.

"Very tasteful," I told him.

"Thanks. And how about you guys?"

"Hmmm?" I asked.

"What sort of furniture do you guys have? At your home?"

The question struck me as odd. "Sort of the same," I told him. "A couple of chairs, dark brown. A brown couch. Lamps. A few tables . . ."

He wasn't listening. He moved towards his lounge chair as if to sit in it, but, halfway into the movement, he seemed to change his mind. He remained standing and pointed to a long bank of photographs lining the wall behind the couch. "Check out these pictures, Mark. I can tell. You have an eye for this sort of thing."

The photographs were of Antoinette, more than a dozen of them. Eight by tens. Ten by fourteens. A few of them were in color; the remainder were in black and white. All of them were studio photographs, taken, most likely, by a professional photographer. There was a shot of Antoinette sitting on a ladder, licking an ice cream cone. Another shot had her in a bathing suit, about to toss a multi-colored beach ball, looking cheerful and energetic. There was a black and white shot of her, shoulders bare, staring straight into the camera, challenging the viewer with her eyes. Some of the photographs were interesting, but, for the most part, they struck me as nothing more than standard portfolio material. There was happy Antoinette. There was woebegone Antoinette. There was startled Antoinette. There was sultry Antoinette, her eyelids lowered, her hair being blown by a high-powered fan, her pouty lips puckered into a moist red kiss.

"Not bad, aye?" Tommy asked. "I had them taken last summer. Down in the city. The whole shoot cost me a couple of grand, but it was worth every penny, Mark. Don't you think?"

"She's an attractive woman, Tommy."

"Which one's your favorite?"

"Favorite photo? I really couldn't say."

"I know what you mean. They're all kind of sexy. But let's say you had to choose, Mark. Let's say you *had to*."

I didn't know, exactly, how to answer this. I shrugged and pointed to one of the shots at the far end of the wall, one of Antoinette clutching a small towel against her bare chest, looking intruded upon, her privacy violated. There was nothing outstanding about the photograph, nothing particularly dramatic or beautiful about it: it just amazed me that someone would actually hang it on their living room wall.

"Good choice," Tommy said. "Not that I consider that one my own favorite but it definitely makes my top three, that's for sure." He hunched his shoulders and rolled his neck from one side to the other. With a quick and discrete turn of his head, he glanced at Liz still standing by the fireplace. He looked her over briefly and glanced back at me. Then he turned his head towards her once again, lowering his focus. I could have been mistaken, it might only have been my imagination, but it appeared as though he was checking out my wife's ass. "You know, Mark, this might sound funny, but me and Antoinette weren't sure if you guys were going to make it here tonight."

I looked at my watch: a quarter past eight. "It was for eight o'clock," I said. "You weren't expecting us sooner, I hope."

"Not at all. It's just that I looked up your extension at work the other morning. I gave it a call. They told me you hadn't been in the office all week."

"Right. I took the week off."

He shoved his hands into his pockets. "Super. Good for you, Mark. A little vacation, huh?"

"It was fine. I didn't do much."

"No? You didn't get away for a few days? You didn't scoot the little lady down to an island somewhere?" He tucked in his stomach an inch or two and expanded his chest. "Have you guys ever been to Aruba? Me and Antoinette went there last winter."

"No," I said. "Aruba. We've never been there."

"You should go. Who knows? Maybe the four of us can all hop down there together sometime. It was gorgeous. Eighty-degree temperatures every day. Clear blue waters. These long-legged beauties scampering up and down the beaches in their teeny-weeny string bikinis. I was in heaven, Mark. I recommend it to everyone."

Liz turned her attention from the mantle to exchange a look with me. She said nothing, just raised a brow.

"It sounds wonderful," I said to Tommy without enthusiasm.

He raised his eyes towards the ceiling and exhaled deeply as if trying to remember something. "Oh, yes. So excuse me, Mark. How was it, then?"

"How *was . . . ?*"

"Your vacation. How was it?"

"It was pleasant," I told him once more, "if a bit domestic."

He nodded knowingly. "Say no more, Mark. A stay-at-home vacation with nothing to do. It drives you nuts, right?"

"It wasn't bad. Liz had to work. December is a busy month for her company. So, I just puttered around the house by myself, tended to a few chores. Nothing major."

"I didn't *know that.*" His voice was low, sympathetic. He turned to Liz. "Too bad," he said to her. "You work, Liz?"

Slowly, she turned back from the mantle. She gave him a long, quiet stare and answered, "Yes, Tommy, I do."

"I didn't know that," he said again. "Not that there's anything wrong with it, *per se*. A woman's got to do, of course, what a woman's got to do." He attempted a grin. "Every little bit helps, I suppose."

She raised a finger to her chin. "Is there a point," she asked, "that you're trying to make here?"

"Not at all. No point. Even Antoinette used to work. During our first year of marriage, that is. These days, I guess, lots of gals work."

"It certainly seems that way," she agreed.

He winked an eye. "I guess the trick, then, is to marry rich, aye? Or prod your husband into getting off his duff and start earning some real dough."

She offered him a tight smile. "We can't all be bigwigs, Tommy."

"Of course not," he said, showing a smile of his own. "You make your choices in life. You take what risks you can afford to. It's not for everyone. Especially, I guess, for guys like yourselves. What with three kids and all."

"Two," I corrected, not knowing what, exactly, he was driving at. "A boy and a girl."

"That's right. Two kids." He held up two fingers. "How old are they again, Mark?"

"Ten and seven."

"Me and Antoinette tried to have one once. We spent a whole year at it. No luck, though. Antoinette says I'm shooting blanks. I tell her she's got a hole in her catcher's mitt." He said this with a straight face, his voice a monotone. "Who knows? Maybe it's for the better. The cost of raising kids these days. The hassles involved. The way they bog down your freedom and your life. They ruin a gal's figure, too. Their muscles go right to—oops. Excuse me, Liz." He peeked over at her and made a gesture with his hands. "I didn't mean to imply, of course, that there's anything wrong with *your* figure."

She didn't respond. She moved towards the Christmas tree set in front of the windows. She stood before it, silently, hands behind her back. Eventually, I would hear her sigh.

I looked at Tommy. He adjusted the sleeves of his sweater and fussed with a loose thread near the cuff. Was he nervous about something? Was there something distracting him? I didn't know. And, at the moment, I didn't care. My wife was uncomfortable. In part, it was due to our spat together on the drive up; under normal social circumstances, however, that spat should have been forgotten about by now; her mood should have rebounded as soon as we had walked through the door. I looked back at Tommy, feeling a peculiar and immediate anger toward him. In one way, it wasn't really his fault; in another way it was. I had realized, before coming here this evening, that he was insensitive, that he could be something of a jerk. But that, I figured, was to be my problem for the night, not Liz's. She was supposed to have a pleasant time with Antoinette. It was to be only me who'd suffer Tommy's obtuse and never-ending remarks.

"Mark," he whispered, keeping an eye on Liz. He gave me a nudge and pointed toward her still standing by the tree. "Is she upset or something?"

I lifted my hands and gave a shrug. "Tommy, why don't you check on Antoinette? I'll talk to Liz."

"Good idea," he said, still in a hushed voice. He nodded his head but he did not move. He did not depart for the other end of the house. He just stood there before me; his eyes fixed on Liz as she examined the ornaments on the tree. He walked over to her, crossing the room.

I followed.

"Usually," he said to her, "me and Antoinette put up our artificial tree. This year, though, I said, 'What the hell? Let's get the real McCoy.'"

I waited for her to reply. When she did not, I said, for want of anything better, "It's a large tree, Tommy."

He considered the tree himself. "Thanks. The guy at the lot wanted sixty for it. I yanked his chain a little, haggled him down to fifty." He plucked a long green needle from one of the branches and held it between thumb and forefinger, displaying it for my inspection. "In my opinion, Mark, the tree's worth every dime of it. It's from Canada." He said this as if it was something special. When he sensed that I was not impressed satisfactorily, he added, "It's from the Yukon Trail."

I glanced at Liz. She stepped back a pace, eyeing all of the wrapped gifts beneath the tree. There were dozens of them, all shapes and sizes, but all of them wrapped in either the same red or the same blue Christmas paper. The red boxes were stacked into several large piles under the left-hand side of the tree; the blue boxes were stacked under the right-hand side.

Tommy chuckled, appreciating our interest in the gifts. "All for me and Antoinette. In the Pubman household, we pull out all the stops for Christmas. We're like a couple of kids." He swept his arm broadly across the many stacks of boxes. "There're sixty-eight separate presents you're looking at there, guys. Thirty-one for Antoinette. Thirty-seven for Tommy." He chuckled again, this time a bit impishly. "I counted them up last night. Ole Tommy is a little boy at heart."

I slid a hand into my pocket, trying to think of a response. I came up dry, however, nothing to say. For better or for worse, I had no rapport with this man; I was not relaxed in his presence. I pondered it a moment longer. Then, without any real interest, I said, "Did you ask Antoinette for anything special this year, Tommy?"

"Actually, yes." He lowered his voice confidentially. "I asked her to, um, shave a certain patch of her anatomy for me."

It was going to be a long, uncomfortable evening for us. The man was a nuisance, a frustrated jerk still working out his adolescence. Time dragged on slowly as Liz and I remained standing with him by the Christmas tree. All together, we studied the gifts beneath it. We listened to him speculate aloud as to what might be inside each of the thirty-seven blue boxes that Antoinette had wrapped for his Christmas morning. One at a time, he held each of the boxes in his small soft hands, testing their weight, shaking them close to his ear, pressing at their corners with his fingers. "I wonder what this one is, Mark. Think it's a wristwatch? And how about this one? Feel the weight of it. A set of golf balls, maybe? Or how about this here? Think it's a fishing rod?"

"Tommy," I said, "we shouldn't be doing this. Antoinette wouldn't like it."

"Who's going to tell her? Not me, that's for sure. Hey, check this one out. I think it's some kind of clothing. Gloves and a scarf, maybe?"

The man had, I realized, no sense of others. He was incapable of looking outside himself to see how others were experiencing him. I glanced at the photographs of Antoinette hanging on the wall, feeling a short pang of sympathy for her. What a chore it must be to live with this man.

"Check this out," he said to Liz, moving on to the stacks of red boxes that he had for Antoinette. "You'd love this one, Liz. The long box. It's cutlery. For the kitchen. All tempered steel. And, in that large box towards the back, that's a set of Revere Ware. And that one with the silver ribbon—guess what that is."

"Gee," she said, "I don't know, Tommy."

"That's a makeup kit. Eye cream and liner and lip gloss. All from Lancôme. They're the name in makeup, as you probably know."

"No," she said, rolling her eyes. "I wasn't aware."

"Well, they are. The crème de la crème." He dipped down to pick up another red box, this one adorned with a golden ribbon. "This present here is my favorite. It's for Antoinette but it's for me, too. It's a little something I picked up for her at Foh's."

"At *Foh's*?" Liz asked.

"F-O-H . . . Fredrick's of Hollywood."

She let out a short laugh. "My, my, aren't we the naughty one?"

"I can't help it," he said. "Sex is my vice." He turned to me and passed me the box. "It's a French maid's outfit, Mark. It's a skimpy little piece of nothing, all lace and silk and elastic. The thing doesn't weigh more than eight ounces, but, come Christmas morning, it's sure going to give Tommy, old Tommy boy, a lot of pleasure."

I exchanged a glance with Liz and then lowered my eyes to the box in my hand. I did not appreciate the turns, the detours of hints and innuendo that these conversations continued to take. Where were the drinks? The *noshes*? That game of Pictionary they'd spoken about?

"The bra is one of those push-up jobs," he said, "which, believe me, Antoinette could sure use." He lifted his eyebrows, wiggled them a bit. "And the panties have one of those strategic openings in the, uh, pubis area. The crotch area, if you get my drift."

"Tommy," I said, "you have no business tell—"

"Who knows, Mark. If we play our cards right, maybe we could talk Antoinette into modeling it for us tonight. That'd be a treat, aye? You wouldn't be averse to seeing that, would you?"

Was he for real? I was no prude, of course. I had, in my day, heard my share of crude remarks. From time to time, even I had swapped with friends certain gags and tidbits concerning our respective love lives. But it was with friends, I reminded myself, not with new acquaintances; and it was always done with humor, with a sense of lightness. I observed his expression now, searching for that sign of humor, that touch of whimsicality. I saw none, however; only a dull, all-too-serious face.

Coming here, I told myself again, was a mistake. We should leave this house immediately. I knew that we should but my sense of decorum, my civility, was holding me back.

"Mark?" He was tapping me on the wrist. "What about you guys? Do you go in for the lingerie bit? The accessories thing? Or is that a little too kinky for your tastes?"

I handed the box back to him. Something else now, something more important, was bothering me. "Tommy," I said, "where is Antoinette?" We had been here for longer than a half an hour and still there was no sign of his wife. Was he actually married to the woman? Did they live together? Was the woman at the party just a friend brought along for the sake of appearances? Was she a hired escort? I glanced at the photographs, the dozen photographs of Antoinette hanging on the wall. "Tommy," I said again, "where's Antoinette? What's going on?"

"What do you mean?"

"Where is she? Where's your wife?"

"Antoinette?" he asked me back. "Like I told you, Mark, she's in the bedroom."

"*Putting on her war paint. . .* really? For thirty minutes?"

"You know women. You know how long they take with these things." He bent at the knees and placed the box of lingerie back under the tree, setting it just right.

"Maybe you should look in on her, Tommy. See if she's okay."

"She's fine, Mark. She's just taking her time." He straightened himself back up, smoothing down the crease of his pants.

I didn't understand. "What do you mean, Tommy?"

"Just taking her time. Dawdling. There's nothing wrong with that, is there?"

Maybe not. The idea of it, however, struck me as being more than a little rude. Liz was watching me. Her eyes were confused. Was I over-reacting? Was I talking too emphatically, too loudly?

"Look," Tommy said, "I'll go hurry her up and get her down here. Then I'll fix us some highballs. And make up a tray of noshes. How does that sound?"

"It sounds," Liz said, "like something you should have done thirty minutes ago."

Briskly, he rubbed his hands together. "So, what'll it be, then? For drinks. Beer? Wine? Booze?"

"Anything that's quick," she told him.

"Michelob," he said, "and a pitcher of Bloody Marys. How's that?"

Liz nodded and so did I. I heard activity coming from the hallway above. I heard footsteps, a door closing and then the sounds of a bathroom fan turning on. To a degree, the sounds comforted me. "Michelob is fine. Thanks, Tommy."

"Likewise with the Bloody Marys," Liz said.

"Excellent. And, as you can hear, Antoinette is on her way. Maybe, once we all get cozy, maybe we'll try a game of Pictionary together. Losing team gets a spanking." And with that, Tommy ambled off.

I walked to the window as he disappeared into the kitchen. Outside, snow continued to fall. I peered towards our car and saw that as much as two inches of snow had settled onto its roof. I closed my eyes for a moment, trying to recall the last weather report that I had heard. The forecast had a number of uncertainties to it. The weatherman, his voice popping with excitement, explained all of the various scenarios: "If the strong front pulls along the coast. . . . If the moisture from the Carolinas arrives before midnight. . . . If the winds from the northwest . . ." I should have paid more attention. Under most circumstances, traveling in snow doesn't concern me. Tonight, however, I was thirty miles from home. There were hills, unfamiliar roads to deal with. I should have listened for updates.

"It looks so peaceful out there." Liz moved behind me. Her voice was soft, low-key. "I love snow."

I held out my hand and waited for hers to come into my own. "And I," I said, "love you." It sounded trite but the sentiment came naturally.

"Really?"

"Really and truly," I told her. "For always and forever."

"Do you love me madly?"

"Insanely. Deliriously."

"Unquestionably?"

"Out-of-this-worldly."

She brushed her lips against my ear. "So," she said, "are you having fun with your new buddy?"

"What do you think?"

"I think that he's a pea brain."

Gently I squeezed her hand. Tommy's problem, of course, was more complex than simply being a pea brain. Still, I saw no choice but to agree with her. "The man," I said, "is an ass."

"Like me?"

I turned and looked at her.

"During the car ride. I was an ass."

"Car ride?" I repeated, beginning to smile.

"I'm a brat sometimes, aren't I?"

"We always fight when we go somewhere new. That's nothing special."

"We've got to cut it out, huh?"

"Starting now," I said.

Again, she brushed her lips against my ear and then against my neck. "From now on we'll get along like a couple of canaries. Like twin puppy dogs."

I returned her kisses: one on the ear, one on the neck. "Or better still," I said, "we'll get along like Tommy and Antoinette. They never fight. We'll use their system: count to ten and do whatever I tell you to do."

"Absolutely," she said, deadpan. "It'll make life so much easier, so much simpler . . . especially," she added, "for me."

I was still smiling, lightening up. "Maybe we should start hanging out with these people more often."

"Right," she laughed. "Maybe we can come every Friday night. For noshes and Pictionary."

"And then stand around for a half an hour waiting to be offered a drink."

"And for Antoinette to put on her war paint."

"Once we get to know them better," I went on, continuing the joke, "we can start taking our vacations with them. Fly down to Aruba together, all four of us."

"And we'll spend the days taking pictures of Antoinette."

"When we get back," I said, falling into the rhythm of it, "we'll buy her some lingerie. At Foh's."

"And she can model it for us. That'd be a treat. You wouldn't be averse to that, would you, Mark?"

"And then, so Tommy doesn't feel left out, we'll buy him a ton of presents. All for him. Thirty-seven boxes of golf balls."

"And every Christmas," Liz added, enjoying the silliness, starting to laugh, "every Christmas, we'll all shave our, um, crotches for him." She closed her eyes and lifted her head, putting her lips together, waiting for my kiss. (This is a tradition of ours: she always gets a kiss when she makes a good joke.) Lightly I touched her lips with my own, a gentle kiss, and pulled her body close to mine.

"Listen," I said, "let's go. Let's just leave. Put on our coats and get out of here."

She opened her eyes; they were uncertain. "Just like that?" she asked, her voice a whisper. "Without saying goodbye?" Idly, she gazed through the window and watched the snowflakes falling, blowing with the wind. "And what happens next week? At work? When you bump into Tommy?"

"I never bump into him."

"What if he stops by your office?"

"He won't. But who cares if he does?"

"What if he calls you? Your extension?"

"I'll tell him that he's a pea brain."

She glanced across her shoulder, making sure that the two of us were still alone. She considered it a moment longer. *Just leave.* The thought seemed to intrigue her: no explanations; no apologies; no goodbyes. "How do we make it to the closet?" she asked. "For our coats? How do we get to the front door? Tiptoe? Make a dash for it?"

I pulled the car keys from my pocket, jingling them in my palm. "We'll saunter," I said. "Casually. All the way to the car. Leaving our tracks in the snow."

January, 1989

five
car trouble

"I HATE THIS." Laura stared at her watch as she tapped a foot against the pavement. "I really can't stand it."

We were waiting at the bus stop. Our car was in the repair shop: a transmission problem.

"Damn", she said and pulled a tissue from her purse. "I think my make-up's melting." She folded the tissue in half and then into quarters and dabbed slowly, delicately, at the perspiration beaded across her forehead. "Do I look okay?"

She looked fine; she always did. "Nothing's melting," I told her.

"How about my hair?"

I gave it a once over, regarded the thick auburn curls, shoulder length, cut and styled just last week at her favorite salon, *Coifs by Carmine*. "Your hair looks good, too."

"It's not frizzing? On top?"

"A little," I told her. "Not much."

The tissue dropped from her hand and fell to the pavement as she patted the hair. "I hate this so much," she let me know once again. "It's hot. And I'm bored." Casually she bent down, making an effort to retrieve the tissue from the sidewalk but the sanitation truck rolling past us, took the tissue with its waft of air.

She lifted her eyes toward me but I didn't respond to them. I was focusing on the doughnut shop across the street, the pay phone outside of it and considered, for a moment, phoning into my office and calling in sick.

"You know," she said, "I don't mean this as an insult but I really wish you knew how to fix cars."

"Well, thank you," I responded. "I appreciate that. And I wish you knew how to fix cars, too."

"You're the *man*, Robert. You're the one who's supposed to know."

I glanced across my shoulder. We were not alone. Several feet to our right, and slightly behind us, a guy in a dark blue suit was leaning against a mailbox. He was somewhere in his forties and he was wearing a pair of thick black sunglasses. His hair was black, too, and he appeared to be checking us out, or, more particularly, he appeared to be checking Laura out.

"My father," she went on, "knew how to fix cars. A lot of my old boyfriends could fix them, too. But I marry you and you don't know a thing about them."

This was true. I wasn't, however, about to admit it to her; not, at any rate, with a stranger listening in.

"You should take a course in mechanics," she said, "at a trade school or something. Or a continuing education program."

I set my briefcase onto the pavement, saying nothing, and loosened the knot of my necktie.

"It'd be good for you," she added. "In a lot of ways."

I nodded and coughed into my hand.

"You'd meet new people, make some friends. And it'd save us money, too. Instead of being at the mercy of—"

"Alright," I told her. "Let's drop it, huh?"

"Well, don't get defensive. I was making a suggestion. Most men know how to fix cars. You should learn, too."

"Fine," I said. "As soon as I get to work, I'll walk into Miller's office. I'll hand in my notice and tell him I'm enrolling in mechanic's school."

"Robert," she said, *"please . . ."*

"I'll quit and apply for a job at Sunoco. I'll become a wrench monkey."

She laughed. "The term is gas monkey, you dope."

Actually, the term was grease monkey but why mention it? "I'll start my life over again. Take a pay cut. Six bucks an hour. Whatever the going rate is for a thirty-five-year-old rookie mechanic."

"Robert," she groaned, "I didn't say I wanted to be *married* to a mechanic. I don't want you to become one. I'd just be happier if you knew how to fix cars. That's all."

"Well, you knew I couldn't fix them when we got married."

"What does that have to do with it? Really," she said, "you're over-reacting."

I unbuttoned my jacket and slid a hand into my pocket. "I'm not over-reacting."

"Fine, Robert. You're not overreacting. You're acting very mature." She looked at her watch again, leaned forward on her toes and stared in silence at the cars rolling past us. With a sigh, a shake of her head, she turned to the man standing behind us. "Excuse me," she said to him. "What time does the bus get here?"

The guy hunched his shoulders and hooked a thumb into his belt. "The bus?" he said. "I couldn't tell you." His voice was deep and self-assured.

"Have you been waiting here long?" she asked him.

"I'm not here for the bus."

She pointed to the curb. "But this *is* the bus stop, right?"

"I couldn't tell you," he said. "I'm not here for the bus."

"What are you here for, then?"

"Huh?"

"What are you here for?"

I let out a long blow of air. What did it matter what he was here for? What business was it of ours? Of *hers*?

"But since you've been here," she continued, "has the bus come by?"

He shrugged; palms lifted at his waist.

"You didn't see a bus, right? That's what you're telling me?"

"I didn't *notice* a bus is what I'm telling you."

"But you've been here for a while, yes?"

"A while," he answered, "yes." A trace of a smile crossed his lips. He seemed to be pleased with himself—with his thick black sunglasses and dark blue suit, his relaxed posture, his vagueness and his understate-ment. He was playing with her and he seemed to be enjoying it.

"Alright," Laura told him, "thanks anyway." She returned to me at the curb, running a hand along her thigh, smoothing down her skirt. "Now I'm not sure if we're even in the right place. Who knows if this is the bus stop or not."

I pointed to the sign beside us: it was red and white with a picture of a bus and, on top of the picture, two words, in large bold letters, saying, Bus Stop. "Of course this is the bus stop."

"That guy didn't think so."

"What does it matter what he thinks?" I glanced across my shoulder. He was leaning back against the mailbox, one ankle crossed over the other, his attention still on us. "Besides," I said softly, "he didn't say he didn't think *so*. He said he didn't know."

"It's the same thing, Robert."

"No, it's not."

She ignored this and shifted her attention towards the street and observed the cars rolling steadily by, perhaps wishing to herself how nice it would be if she and I were flowing along with them in our own car, if only her husband, like her father and old boyfriends, knew how to fix them.

"Not to get back on the subject of cars," she told me, "but I think it's about time we bought a second one."

In a way, somewhere in the recesses of my mind, I was waiting for this. "It was your decision not to," I reminded her. "It was your decision to hold off on a second car and put as much money as we could towards the house."

"Well, you shouldn't have listened to me. Most men would have insisted their wife have a car of her own. What's the use of having a house, anyway, if you can't have two cars?"

This was growing tiresome. I fiddled with my tie and took a look around. While the street was busy with traffic, the sidewalks were nearly empty. Other than the man beside us and the occasional customer walking in and out of the doughnut shop across the street, I hadn't spotted one pedestrian since arriving here. "Listen," I said, "let's stop fighting, alright? If you want a second car, we'll talk about it after work."

"Fine with me." She opened her purse, pulled out her wallet and poked around for change. "What does a bus cost these days, anyway?"

I wasn't sure. "To White Plains? About a dollar."

"*About*?" she asked me. "Or *exactly*?"

"About."

She turned to the guy behind us and took a step toward him. "Hi. It's me again. I know you're not waiting here for the bus but would you happen to know how much it costs to ride one?"

"A bus ride?" he said, tugging at the cuff of his suit coat. "It'll cost you ninety."

"Ninety," she repeated. "Thanks." She stepped back to the curb, nudged my elbow with her own. "How much change do you have?"

"Not ninety cents worth."

"Well, can you check?"

"I have singles," I told her. "They'll take a dollar."

"I've got singles, too," she informed me, "but bus drivers don't make change anymore." She picked out a few coins from her wallet. "I've got sixty cents. What do you have?"

I tapped my front pockets and drew out what I had: a quarter and two nickels. "Thirty-five."

She stuck out her hand and pushed it forward. "Good," she said. "Give them to me. I need thirty."

I looked at her hand: palm facing upwards, the fingers wiggling at me, beckoning for my coins. She moved her hand closer, fingers still moving. "Are you going to give them to me or not?" she asked. "Because I want at least one of us to have exact change."

I slid the quarter and the two nickels back into my pocket. "No," I told her. "You can't have them."

"Just give them to me."

"No."

"Then you take mine."

"I don't want yours."

"Oh, please, Robert. Stop being a baby. Just give them to me."

"No."

"And you're not going to take mine?"

"That's right. I'm not."

She shook her head. "This is great. I'm married to a jerk. You're such a—"

"*Lady*, how much do you need . . . ?" This was from the guy behind us. Laura turned to him quickly. So, did I. He was running a hand through his hair, straightening himself from the mailbox.

"A gentleman," Laura said. "Thank you." Her smile was warm, if a bit smug. She pulled a bill from her wallet. "Can you break a dollar?"

"Don't worry about the dollar." He stepped towards us, reaching into his pants pocket. "How much do you need?"

"Thirty cents," she said. "But it'd be great if you could just break the dollar."

"Forget about the dollar." Slowly he pulled some change from his pocket, making a show of it. "It's my treat."

"Oh, then, don't bother. I'll get it from Robert." She pointed a thumb in my direction. "He'll give it to me. He's just being a baby."

The guy smirked, touched the rim of his sunglasses. "No bother," he said. He picked a couple of coins from his palm. "It'll be worth it to me, okay? Just to see you two be friends again."

"Don't pay attention to Robert and me. We're just fighting. He's my husband."

"*Lucky Robert*." He stroked a finger along the length of his nose and gave me a nod. "You're a fortunate guy, Robert."

I looked him over: the broad jaw, the confident mouth. I felt like telling him to drop dead, to screw off. But I didn't; I said nothing.

"We were just bickering," Laura told him. "We aren't always like this. We're in rotten moods. Our car broke Saturday."

He nodded, uninterested, and offered her the coins. "You want them?"

"No, no. Like I said, my husband will give me his." She glanced my way. "Won't you, Robert?"

I didn't answer. Was she trying to put me on the spot or was she simply oblivious to my feelings? I attempted a grin but it was difficult.

"Listen," he said to her, "it doesn't look like Robert's going to give you his change. I'm offering." He touched his sunglasses again. "You can think of it," he said, "as my price for the entertainment."

I lifted my briefcase from the pavement and squeezed its handle tight. What was with this guy? I turned to Laura. "Come on," I said to her softly, "let's go."

But she was holding out her hand. "Well, thank you," she said to him. "And if I see you here tomorrow, I'll pay you back, okay?"

Slowly, one at a time, he placed the coins into her outstretched palm. "Actually," he said, "let's hope you're not here. For both our sakes."

She raised her eyes, a wrinkle of confusion across her brow. "Excuse me?"

"Let's hope your car is fixed. That's what I'm saying."

I touched her hand, the one holding the thirty cents. "Laura," I said, "give it back to him."

She turned to me, her eyes suddenly cheerful. "Why? *You're* going to give it to me?"

"Just return it."

She closed her hand, clenching it tight. "What for?"

"Because he's being a wiseass. He's insulting us."

She shook her head. "What are you talking about?"

"Come on, return it."

The guy stepped back a pace and squared his shoulders. "I'm not insulting anyone, pal."

I held Laura's gaze. "Just give it back, alright?"

She thought a moment, glancing at the change in her palm. "I don't see what you're getting so upset about, Robert. He's just trying to be nice."

"Forget it." I moved towards the guy and pulled the quarter and both nickels from my pocket. "Here," I told him. "Thanks a lot."

Casually, coolly, he accepted the coins and jingled them in his hand. "I wasn't insulting anybody, pal. "

"I must have misunderstood."

"When I insult someone, they know it."

"Is that right?"

He didn't respond, just played with his thick black sunglasses, the smile returning to his lips. An hour from now he'd forget I'd even existed.

Laura tapped a finger against my shoulder. "Robert," she said, peering into her purse and rummaging inside of it, "I think I forgot my keys. Check to make sure you have yours."

I patted the right pocket of my pants and felt the ring holding all of them together: the key to the front and back doors of our house, the key to my office at work and the spare key to our broken Buick parked somewhere in the lot of Manny's Auto Repair. "Got 'em," I answered, almost proudly, as she continued hunting inside of her purse.

The guy slid my coins into his pocket and returned to his spot at the mailbox. He veered his head to the left and pointed down the street, addressing my wife, "Lady," he called to her, "your bus is coming."

Laura stepped back toward the red and white Bus Stop sign and, just in case the driver didn't see her standing there, she raised an arm into the air and waved it back and forth, signaling for him to stop. Smoothly, the bus glided into its spot and, after the doors opened, Laura climbed its three stairs and deposited her ninety-cents of coins, one at a time, into the meter, telling the gray-haired driver, "Thank you, sir."

I followed and stuffed my dollar bill into the meter, expecting to hear the sound of the bus's doors close behind me. Instead, I heard another person climbing up the three steps and then the deep, self-assured voice of the guy in the dark blue suit and thick black sunglasses. "Happy Monday," he said to the driver. "How was your weekend, Charlie?"

August, 1989

a thief in her home

THIS IS TOO MUCH. She looks at him and then back at the report card, holding it with both of her hands. She can't believe it. After all of his promises. After all of their talking. She focuses on the grades. Algebra: D. English: C. History: Incomplete. "I can't believe this," she says. "After all of your promises. After all of our talking."

He is staring at his shoes, cigarette hanging from his lips. He says nothing.

"And what does the Incomplete mean? It's as good as an F, right?"

He shrugs; it's the I-dunno shrug.

She goes back to the report card, checks for a date. "And why are you showing it to me tonight?"

"What's wrong with tonight?"

"It's Saturday. When did they give it you? Monday?"

He grunts, no reply.

"Well, I'm not signing it."

He doesn't respond, the cigarette still stuck in his mouth.

"And forget about the movie. The movie is off." Not much of a punishment, but, for the moment, it's the best that she can come up with.

He plucks the card from her hands and folds it into quarters. He shoves it into his back pocket and walks toward the couch, slow, cool, a tough guy.

"So, what are you going to tell them? When they ask why I didn't sign it? Are they going to call me in? Or do I make an appointment on my own?"

He shrugs, his face slack, still refusing to look at her. "Do what you want. Tell them what you want." He picks up the remote and turns on the TV, flicking an ash into the ashtray on the coffee table and drops onto the couch.

"And put out that cigarette," she says, focusing her stare on him. Look at him: he's fifteen-years old; he looks ridiculous.

He lifts his feet onto the table and takes one last drag on the cigarette. Smooth, easy-like, he tosses it into the ashtray. His eyes are on the television; a rerun of *The Jeffersons.*

"New rule," she announces, holding up a finger. "If you're going to smoke, you'll do it outside. Never again in the apartment."

He doesn't look at her, just aims the remote at the TV, turning up the volume; a smart ass. He flips through the channels, letting the cigarette burn in the ashtray.

"I mean it," she says. "You're a kid. You look like a jerk."

"At least," he tells her, "I'm not smoking crack."

She shakes her head. *At least I'm not smoking crack.* It's a tired routine, half defending himself, half threatening her. If she catches him swiping money from her wallet, it's "At least I'm not out mugging old ladies." If he returns home after ten p.m., it's "At least I *come* home." Next, he'll be threatening her with the "*I'll-move-in-with-Dad*" bit.

She runs her palms down the sides of her skirt and pulls at the collar of her blouse. "And another thing," she tells him, "if you're going to smoke, stop stealing mine—my cigarettes. Buy your own. Or bum them from your hotshot friends."

"I do," he answers.

"Bum them? Buy them? Steal them?

"I buy them, bum them. I don't steal them."

"Yes, you do. You take them from my purse. Cut it out."

He turns her way, not quite looking at her. "I don't steal them," he says. "You smoke them yourself."

She touches her temple, rubs it. Maybe he doesn't steal them; maybe he does. "Well just make sure you don't," she says. "I won't put up with a thief in my home."

"I don't steal them. I don't steal nothing."

Double negative, she thinks. "*I don't steal nothing.*" Clever.

"I never stole from you."

"That's not true."

"Oh, yeah?" He stands from the couch. "What, then?"

"My money," she says. "A dollar here, a dollar there. It adds up."

"We've already been through that. A dozen times. You're going to keep beating me over the head with it?"

"I give you an allowance."

"I've apologized. How many times do I have to say I'm sorry?"

"You've never apologized. All you tell me is 'At least I'm not out mugging old ladies.' That's not an apology."

"Well, I'm sorry. But that doesn't make me a thief. You can't accuse someone of being a thief for a few bucks. That's not fair. It's not right."

He's always worrying about what's fair, she thinks, and what's right. She reaches to the floor and grabs an empty pretzel bag from beneath the table. She stands, examining the room: magazines are spread everywhere, record albums scattered in front of the stereo, an open can of Pepsi on top of the TV. "And listen," she says, "let's try to keep this apartment clean. Okay? It's always a mess."

"It's your mess, too."

"We'll both be cleaner."

"But it's me you're blaming. It's me that steals and me that—"

"You do steal."

"I don't," he says. "Tell me. What else do I steal?"

My life, she thinks. You're stealing my life. She doesn't, of course, say this. She lifts her hand, instead, the one holding the pretzel bag.

"You accuse me and you can't name one damn thing."

Should she mention the vodka? Yes, she probably should. "My vodka," she tells him. "You've been stealing my vodka. It's been going on for a month."

"Then why didn't you mention it a month ago?"

"Because I wasn't sure. Until now."

"It's you who drinks it. You drink it and you forget."

She shakes her head. "You water it down. I can tell. From its taste. Its smell."

He turns his face away, dropping back onto the couch. "You're crazy," he mutters. "You're paranoid. Dad was right about—"

"Shut your *stupid* mouth."

"You shut yours."

She crumples the pretzel bag and throws it at him. It drops, without sensation, to the floor. "I want you to start treating me with some respect."

"Then earn it." His voice is measured, indifferent, pleased with his remark, as if he had said something smart and original. "Anything else about me been bothering you?"

God, she'd like to . . . "Yes," she says. "Stop stealing my lotion."

This takes him by surprise. He shifts on the couch, a twitch of uneasiness in his eyes.

"You've been stealing my lotion. I know it. So, add that one to the list."

He lets go of a laugh, short, forced, and lifts up both hands as if in surrender. "Your *what*?" he asks. He makes a face of pain and stares at her like she's some kind of lunatic.

"You heard me. You've been taking it from the closet."

"Now I know you're paranoid. Is that how low you think I go? You think I'm stealing your crap and pawning it? Selling your goddamn lotion?"

"No," she says. "That's not what I think."

He looks back at the TV. "Then what?"

She doesn't answer. She crosses the room and stands before the open window. It's seven o'clock and there's still light in the sky. She closes her eyes and listens, for a moment, to the hum of the traffic from four stories below, the drone of cars rolling along the avenue, a large truck shifting gears, a horn blowing in the distance. Another car rolls by, its windows open, rock music booming behind it. She turns back to her son, leans against the windowsill. "I don't mean to embarrass you," she says, "but it's expensive stuff. I had two jars in the closet last week. Now there's only one."

"That's because you probably used it. Without realizing." He pulls a pillow from behind his back, eyes fixed on the TV, and lays the pillow onto his lap. "What would I steal your cream for?"

"You know what for."

She returns to the open window, focusing her attention on the street. It's a cool evening, the air fresh, and clean. It was unnecessary. Why did she bring it up? One jar every few months. Was it to hurt him? To win?

She lays her hands on the windowsill and lowers her gaze. Shops are starting to close; restaurants and taverns are beginning to come alive; a street lamp is flickering on and off, its orange glow growing dim. Across the street, a man and a woman are walking a small dog together, the man hanging onto its leash, allowing the dog to take the lead, the woman holding onto his arm with her own and laughing with him as he speaks. It's not long before they turn the corner and disappear from view.

She turns back and looks at her son sitting on the couch: his chin is tucked low, his body slouched, arms folded across his chest, eyes examining the floor and his shoes.

It's not right. It's not fair. She crosses the room and tucks in her blouse, smoothing it as she brushes the hair from her face. She's thirty-six years old, not bad looking, sort of fun. This isn't the way she planned it. Not at all.

April, 1989

mr. peters buys a handkerchief

I DIDN'T KNOW WHAT, exactly, to make of Rodney. He was a huckster probably, but, then, he might have been anything, too: a detective, a politician, a poll taker, a reformed alcoholic in search of a long-lost daughter. His clothes offered no clue: he was wearing a blue checkered jacket, yellow slacks and a pair of white loafers that shined almost as brightly as his smile. A Memorial Day poppy was pinned to the lapel of his jacket. He looked to be in his late fifties, early sixties, and very eager to enter my apartment.

"Well, hello," he had said. "I'm Rodney. Wife home?"

"What?"

"Wife. Is she at home? You do have one, don't you? A wife?"

As a matter of fact, no, I didn't have one. I married when I was twenty-four and my wife died before my thirtieth birthday. That was almost a decade ago. "Are you sure you have the right apartment, Rodney?"

He glanced at the T. PETERS plate on my apartment door and clucked his tongue against the roof of his mouth. "T. Peters, yes. I've come to see Mrs. Peters. We had an appointment. We agreed on noon but I got stuck in traffic."

"I'm sorry to hear that," I told him, "but, you see, Wife's not in right now." I didn't know what he was up to. Possibly it was an honest mistake: he had the wrong apartment, the wrong T. Peters. Probably, however, it was some hard-line sales technique: if a woman answers the door, fine, you sell her what you can; if the husband is the only one at home, better still, you push off every slow-moving item in your catalog.

"My luck," he said. "I must have missed her by half a sec, huh?"

"Right. She just stepped out."

He clucked his tongue again. "Idea when she'll return?"

"Wife?"

"Yes, Wife. We had that appointment, understand. Damn shame, too. Damn shame." He shook his head sadly. "She really wanted a look at my wares, you know."

"At your . . . ?"

"Wares. My merchandise. I sell things." He pointed to a suitcase behind him that was the size of a small refrigerator. Filled, it might have weighed a hundred pounds. "That's my office," he said with a slight groan.

"I'll bet it keeps you in shape."

He started to laugh but then thought better of it. "She left no message? No, uh, shopping list for you?"

"I'm afraid not, Rodney. Unless you sell cottage cheese."

"Pardon?"

"Cottage cheese. Or a Sunday newspaper. That's the list she left me."

His face dropped slowly and his posture began to sag. "I'm sorry, Mr. Peters. Strictly wares. That's all I sell. Hosiery. Lingerie. Creams, both facial and body. Household utensils. Items for the ladies mostly. Cloth napkins, doilies, monogrammed handkerchiefs. Many things, Mr. Peters, many things. All quality merchandise. All guaranteed." He sighed. "But no other list, eh? She didn't even mention our appointment?'

"Sorry, Rodney. No, she didn't."

He nodded sympathetically: he understood. "Mind if I sit?" Somewhere during our conversation he had worked himself into the living room, his enormous suitcase tagging behind him. "Maybe you, yourself, would like to make a purchase, Mr. Peters? A surprise gift for Wife, perhaps? She got a little birthday coming up? A little anniversary, perhaps? Christmas isn't too far off."

Christmas, actually, was very far off: seven months to be exact. But I offered him a chair nevertheless. Something about him, his sighing, his sad little poppy and his snazzy clothes . . . something made me feel sorry for him. Who knows? Maybe I was simply lonely.

"Open her up, Rodney. Let's have a look."

He beamed. The suitcase was already open. "Yes sir, Mr. Peters. Anything you say."

June, 1980

eight
boys night out

YOU SHOULD BE ashamed of yourself. You are too old for this type of thing, too responsible. Look at your watch: it is almost twelve o'clock, a Thursday night. You have to be at work tomorrow morning; a meeting to attend, a report to present. Even if you were to leave for home after this drink, which you have no intention of doing, you would still not make it to bed before one a.m.

You raise your head, fiddle with a cufflink and sip from your glass of bourbon. You are thirty-nine years old, you remind yourself, a married man with two children at home and a dog that needs to be walked. Yet here you are at Monique's Playtime Lounge, seated at the bar, center stool, eyes fixed on the stage as a bare-breasted brunette in silver stockings and matching G-string grinds against a mirrored wall. What, you ask yourself, are you doing here?

The question, of course, is rhetorical. You know very well what you're doing here. You had worked into the evening with two of your co-workers, preparing for tomorrow's meeting. Sometime around eight, with your reports finalized and your presentations outlined, the three of you drove to the Holiday Inn for a quick round of drinks before you would head for home. You talked shop for a while, traded office gossip. When your first round of drinks was finished, one of you ordered a second round and then another of you ordered a third. The alcohol took hold nicely, warming the stomach, relaxing the muscles. As your bodies went through their changes, you noticed, so did the atmosphere of the bar: the lights grew dimmer, the music louder. Over time, the patronage had changed, as well, with the after-work crowd giving way to a looser, evening crowd. Your conversation began to lighten. It grew boisterous. Soon enough, boys being boys and all, your party of three started to take notice of the females in the room: the long-legged redhead in the tight skirt, for instance, and the streaked blonde in the white sweater.

Topics changed rapidly then. For better or for worse, the ice had been broken between you three; you were beginning to know one another in a new way. Within minutes you were sharing stories about the *old days*, swapping tales about former girlfriends, frat-house parties and boys' nights out. Eventually the subject of strip clubs was introduced. One of you called out the name of a topless bar down in lower Westchester. Then another suggested the name of a similar bar up in Putnam County. One thing led to another and it wasn't long before the three of you were driving north in a convoy of three separate cars, heading for Monique's Playtime Lounge. "Exotic Dancing, 6 Girls Nightly, No Cover, No Minimum."

You loosen the knot of your necktie and swallow the remaining drops from your glass of bourbon. You scoop the quarters off the bar and shift your attention from the girl on stage to the nearest of your two co-workers. "Roger," you say, "I'm going to phone the wife again. I told her I'd be home by ten."

Keeping his eyes focused on the stage, Roger points to your empty glass. "Have another. For courage."

You like his attitude. You jingle the quarters in your palm and give his suggestion some consideration. Another drink would help. Not that you need another dose of courage, necessarily; you just need time to gather your thoughts. You are not prepared, at this moment, to speak again with your wife. You check your watch: midnight. She is probably sleeping anyway. Perhaps you'll skip phoning altogether. The previous call at nine o'clock is on your mind. You remember it as a dreary affair: "Why do you do this to me? I told you I'd be keeping your chicken warm and you don't call till now? Why are you sounding so different? I hate it when you drink. . . . You're telling the truth? Your boss is really with you? Alright. Ten o'clock. That's a definite, right . . . ? And don't risk driving. Take a taxi home."

No. Imagining an encore of that call leaves you without enthusiasm. You will have another drink, watch the dancers a while longer, and decide how to play it after that.

"Check it out. The babe's giving you the eye." The second of your co-workers, Andy, tugs at your jacket sleeve. He has wedged himself to a point halfway between Roger's bar stool and your own. He rests an arm on your shoulder, pointing forward. "She wants you, Chief. No time to be bashful."

You turn from Andy to the stage. The dancers have pulled a switch. While, as advertised, there are six of them in the club, you've noticed that they rotate their positions now and then, with three on the stage at any one time and three mingling among the patrons seated at the bar and surrounding tables. Right now, there is a new girl dancing before you. The former dancer, the one in the silver stockings and garter belt, has drifted to the far end of the bar. Her replacement looks to be somewhere in her twenties; she is on the short side, just over the five-foot mark with jet-black hair cut close to her head. She's wearing a leopard-print loincloth, high heels and nothing else. Her body is taut and lightly oiled and, indeed, as Andy had indicated, she is checking you out. She licks her lips slowly, giving you a foxy smile. There is a hungry cast to her eye, the *Take Me* look. She's a little too self-assured for your tastes, her expressions too practiced. She juts her hip to one side, shimmies her upper torso at you. "C'mon," the movement suggests, "get with it."

You meet her eye and attempt a smile. You hate this sort of thing: it's part of the game, you realize, but it leaves you feeling awkward just the same.

"*Uh, oh,*" Andy says. "She likes you, Chief. Go for it."

"Lighten up," you tell him.

"It's obvious, man. She wants your body."

You doubt this: a quick glance at your midsection confirms your skepticism. It's been years since you were in shape. You don't bother to diet. You don't work out. Lately, in fact, your sole exercise has been walking to the company cafeteria for your morning jelly doughnut. "Nobody," you tell Andy, "wants my body."

He retracts his arm from your shoulder. "She's got the hots for you, Chief. Pass her a buck. She'll join us later."

You shake your head. "If you want her to join us, Andy, you give her money."

"She's looking at you. Give her a buck, huh? The next round will be on me."

"Forget it," you tell him.

"She'll sit down and join us when she's through. And tell her to bring some friends. Maybe we'll get lucky."

"All this for a dollar?" you ask.

"Give her more if you want. Give her a twenty. I don't care."

What's with this guy? You turn to Roger, the more mature of your two co-workers, and exchange a look with him. Maybe the liquor has hit Andy the wrong way—perhaps it's the seedy atmosphere of this place—but he is acting stupid: you liked him better at the Holiday Inn. You tinker with the quarters in front of you, stacking them into a neat pile of six, waiting for the dancer to move on to another customer, someone more cooperative, more familiar with the game.

"You're letting her get away," Andy says. He pulls a bill from his wallet, inches his way between you and Roger, and stretches across the bar. A grin meant to charm is on his face as he leans toward the dancer, the bill extending from his fingertips, waving it at her. "Here you go, Sweetheart. All for you."

The dancer steps to the edge of the stage and accepts the bill. She folds it in half, sticks it into the waistband of her loincloth and mouths the words "Thank you."

"That's a five spot, Sexy. From the three of us."

Andy lays his left arm across your shoulders. He does the same to Roger with his right arm. "Stop by when you're through. We'll all have a drink."

The dancer lifts an eyebrow, mouths the word "Maybe." The same foxy smile and hungry look that she had given you just moments before she is now giving to Andy. Bending at the waist, hands behind her head, she rotates her hips as if working a hula hoop. The movement is slow, deliberate, intended to be suggestive.

"We're from Westchester," Andy calls out, as if someone had asked him the question, as if being from Westchester was somehow unique. "It's our first time here."

The dancer widens her eyes a bit and nods her head as if impressed. "Three lonely businessmen," Andy continues, "in need of female companionship."

She turns around, lifts the loincloth above her hips and does an exaggerated grind followed by a bump.

"Nice move," Andy calls. He pulls his arms from your and Roger's shoulders. "Have a drink with us. I'll buy you a Shirley Temple."

This is embarrassing. Andy is reminding you of a small-town conventioneer on his first trip to a big city: too eager, too friendly, a little arrogant and a little insecure. You glance towards Roger, nudge him with your elbow; he is more familiar with Andy than you are; maybe he can restrain him. "Talk to the man," you say. "He's going to get us bounced out of here."

Roger doesn't respond. He's hunched forward in his seat, chin resting on his fist, staring in close attention at the stage. "Bring a friend," he calls to the dancer. "I'm a lonely businessman, myself."

"*Two*," Andy pipes in. "Bring *two* friends. One for Chief here. I'll buy you all a Shirley Temple."

Roger, through his nose, allows half a laugh. "Big spender," he says to you, referring to Andy. When he receives no reply, he taps the back of your hand, examining your face. "What's the matter, Chief? Are you into this or what?"

No, you realize, you are not into this. It's not your scene. You would prefer to remain detached from the stage, to sit peacefully with your drink somewhere in the background, to leer at the naked ladies with a quiet dignity.

Andy returns his arm to your shoulders. "How about another

drink," he asks you. "That's what you need. Relax the old libido." He signals the barmaid and orders another round of drinks: bourbon for you, a couple of vodkas on ice for himself and Roger, and, predictably, "For our bodacious go-go girl up there, wiggling her hot, little fanny off —a Shirley Temple."

The barmaid gives a smile and shakes her head, no. "Gina likes champagne," she tells him. "That's the only thing she drinks."

"*Gina* . . . ?" Andy strokes his chin thoughtfully. "That's her name, huh? And she likes champagne." He pulls out his wallet, checks his cash. "That can be an expensive drink, champagne."

"Fifteen bucks a split," the barmaid tells him. "The bubbles tickle her nose."

"And what tickles *your* nose, Sweetie?"

"Champagne does the trick," she answers and leans an elbow on the bar, getting cozy ". . . among other things." She is an attractive woman, clean featured with large white teeth and confident green eyes. She has a full head of curly blonde hair and, unlike most of the girls, she looks to be somewhere in her thirties. What sets her even more apart from the others, however, is her clothing. She is wearing a plaid skirt and a turtle-neck sweater—street clothes—nothing fancy but it's a nice contrast to the G-strings and peek-a-boo negligees of the others.

"What's your name?" Andy asks her.

"Me? I'm Sharon."

Andy places a hand over his heart. "*Sharon*," he repeats. "That's a pretty name."

She lifts her elbow from the bar and claps her hands together. "So what's it going to be? Champagne for Gina or just the vodkas and the bourbon?"

"Champagne for Gina," Andy answers. "By all means. And one for yourself, Sharon. Tonight, I want to tickle as many noses as I can."

"You've got it," she says, and it isn't long before she returns with the two vodkas on ice, your bourbon and a pair of tall stemmed glasses, one for herself and one for the dancer. "When Gina breaks, I'll bring the champagne."

"Perfect," Andy says.

"That's forty-two, okay?" Sharon flashes a smile, pointing to the drinks on the bar. "Twelve for you guys. Thirty for the two champagnes."

Andy pulls three crisp twenties from his wallet, deals them, one at a time, into her palm, making a show of it. "And you'll be spending some time with us, too, right, Sharon?"

"On and off." She gestures around the bar. "There're other thirsty men I've got to look after." She rings up the drinks and spreads the change on the bar: a ten and several singles. "Enjoy," she tells you all. "Gina will be by in a bit."

You take a sip from your drink and lean back into your seat, more relaxed. You are still out of your element, of course, but you're beginning to adjust to the atmosphere. "Cheers," you say to Andy.

He touches your glass with his own. "Cheers, Chief." You don't touch glasses with Roger, just nod to him, exchanging a thin-lipped smile. You scan the girls dancing on stage and then turn past them to have a look around. There's a wide array of customers in the place: young, old, blue-collar, white-collar. A couple of IBM-types, in matching gray suits, watch the stage from a table in the rear; their interest in the dancing is keen; their posture, you notice, is impeccable. A few college kids are gathered at the far end, appearing both mesmerized and insecure. To the left of you, a silver-haired man is standing at the bar talking to a girl in a negligee who is absently shifting her feet; neither appear particularly interested in their conversation but they continue it nevertheless. Two biker-types, wearing sleeveless denim jackets, are seated at the table directly behind you; they're paying little attention to the dancers, or to each other or even to their drinks; they're just sitting in their chairs, a stoned, lazy cast to their faces. Eventually, one of them catches your eye, having spotted your surveillance, and you turn your gaze away, back towards the stage.

"Here comes Gina," Andy announces.

You look up. There is a new girl dancing in Gina's place. She rocks on her heels, getting into her routine, hands on hips, and thrusts her pelvis forward, wasting no time.

Andy nudges your arm and points with his head. "That way," he says.

Through the corner of your eye, you spot Gina approaching from the right. You take a sip from your drink and touch the knot of your tie.

"Over here, beautiful." Andy lifts one of the champagne glasses from the bar and hoists it into the air.

"I see you," Gina calls out. "Three lonely businessmen in need of some female companionship. You're a tough group to miss." She is wearing a black teddy, and, across her shoulders, a sheer black shawl. "I hope I was worth the wait."

"Worth the wait in gold," you hear yourself say aloud. It sounds stupid coming from your lips but you are glad to have said something; you've got to make an effort to rejoin this party.

"*Oh, great.*" Roger shakes his head and lets out a harsh laugh. "Chief's a comedian. Just what we need."

"Be nice," Gina tells him. "I like comedians."

You take another sip of your drink, then stand and squeeze past Andy, offering your seat to Gina. "Please . . ."

She smiles at your gesture, complimented. "A gentleman," she says, lifting herself onto the stool. "You knew my feet were killing me, right?"

"That Chief," Roger says. "What a prince."

You take your drink from the bar and step back a pace. Although the observation might be premature, you realize that you like Gina more than you had imagined you would; now that she has left her sultry temptress routine on stage, you feel almost comfortable with her. You spot Sharon behind the bar coming over with the two splits of champagne, both bottles open, oozing their contents slowly. Sharon fills Gina's glass, then her own. "Ready for some bubbly?" she asks her.

"Thanks," Gina tells her and then to Andy, "Just what I needed. You're a doll."

Softly, Andy clinks his glass with hers and then against Sharon's, a quiet toast. "It's our first time here," he tells them. "I had to talk these guys into coming with me. We've never seen breasts before."

Gina and Sharon laugh and, actually, so do you.

"Speak for yourself," Roger tells him. "I've seen my share. I'm a married man, remember."

Andy drops a hand onto Roger's shoulder. "You just blew it, pal."

He looks towards Sharon. "Roger's kidding, of course. He's not married. None of us are. We're three lonely businessmen."

"In need of some female companionship," Sharon says and exchanges a smile with Gina.

"That's right," you add. "Never married. Never in love." You clear your throat and tighten the knot of your necktie. You feel suddenly sophomoric, like a smart-ass, but you are enjoying yourself, too. "So your name is Gina . . ."

"And your name is Chief." She removes the high heels from her feet and sets them on the bar next to her split of champagne. With her bare right foot she touches your knee. "Why do these guys call you that? 'Chief'? You're their boss or something?"

At the moment, you can't recall exactly when they began referring to you as Chief. During your first drink at the Holiday Inn or, maybe, the second? Either way you wish they'd cut it out.

"He's not *my* boss," Roger tells Gina. "Chuck Kahn is my boss." His voice confuses you; it's curt, hostile, the voice of a disgruntled man. His face is unhappy, too, half a scowl.

"But Chief's next in line," Andy explains to her. "Chief's the senior member of our crew."

"Well, congratulations, Chief." Gina salutes you with her glass of champagne. "What do you guys do, exactly? Are you salesmen? Stock brokers?"

"Actually," you tell her, "we're secret agents. Double-O branch."

"Right," Andy says. "Licensed to cheat on our wives."

Gina wags a finger in the air. "*Only* if you're actually married."

"They're married," Roger grunts. "We're all married."

You say nothing, just sip at your bourbon. A silent gloom falls onto your party of five; it will last only a moment but it is as disruptive to the ambience as if someone had just farted.

Gina lowers her eyelids and traces a finger along her brow. "Who cares, anyway?" she says. "Me and Sharon don't. A lot of married men come in here. It doesn't make them bad people. A guy's got to sow his oats, married or not. There's nothing wrong with that."

"As long," Sharon says, "as he treats his wife right once he gets home to her. That's the important thing."

Gina nods her head profoundly. "Here, here," she says and lifts her bottle from the bar, adding a dash of champagne to her glass, creating a fresh head for herself. She and Sharon have been drinking slowly, no rush to move on. It's a surprise to you: you had expected them to belt down their drinks in a minute flat, affording you the opportunity to spring for another round of champagne or to watch them saunter over to the next paying customer.

"Tell me," Gina asks. "What do you guys really do? You're sort of corporate, right?"

You nod your head. "We're in finance."

"Finance," she repeats. "You do all right for yourselves. Money-wise. Not that I want to get personal or anything."

You smile. "Why? You want a job?"

"I don't know. I've been thinking about it. Not with your company, necessarily. But I want to get myself a legitimate job. Work at a big corporation someday. Benefits. Pension. All that."

"You mean hang up the old pasties," Andy calls out, "and join the real world?"

Gina turns toward him. "I worked in the *real world*, smart guy. In an office, too."

"As a secretary?" you ask.

"Worse. I was a typist."

"Didn't enjoy it?"

"What a degrading job," she tells you. If you think topless dancing is degrading, try typing. It's worse. And the pay stinks. Minimum wage plus a dime. . . . Not that I deserved any more. I was pitiful. They used to call me 'The Wite-Out Queen.' At our Christmas party, a week before getting fired, my supervisor gave me a six-pack of correction tape."

Andy flicks you on the shoulder. "Give her your card, Chief. Maybe Personnel can find her something."

"Give her *your* card," you answer.

"You've got more clout. Nobody cares about my recommendation."

You shake your head. It's a bad idea. You picture the scene: Friday afternoon, your boss, Chuck Kahn, will be returning from an extended lunch. And there, in the reception lobby will be Gina, decked out in a tube top and miniskirt and, on her feet, a pair of four-inch heels, explaining her situation to Ruth, your matronly receptionist. "Chief sent me. He told me I might get a job here. Something at decent pay. With benefits. And a pension . . ." "*Chief* who, dear?" "He's in Finance. Here's his card that he gave me." No. You'd prefer to avoid such a scenario. "What else," you ask Gina, "have you done? Career-wise?"

She sips her champagne, motioning for you to wait a second and places the glass back on the bar, touching a napkin to her lips. "I waitressed for a while," she answers, "worked at a clothes store, a lingerie shop, actually. That was alright. Last year a friend told me about exotic dancing, taught me some moves, introduced me around and here I am. Ta-da!" Her focus moves from you to the table directly behind you, the table where the two bikers in denim jackets are seated. She catches the eye of one and gives him a little wave. "Hi, Pinky. Where's Dennis tonight?" When she receives no reply, only a bored, glazed stare, she turns back to you. "So that's the story of my life, Chief. Interesting, huh?"

You polish off the last of your bourbon. You get Sharon's attention and show her your empty glass. "Anyone for another round?"

"I'm good," Gina says, pointing to her half-filled bottle.

"I'll take another," Andy says.

Roger slides his empty glass towards Sharon and wraps it on the bar. To Gina, he says, "You know those two guys? At the table?"

Again, Gina looks past you. "Those two? There's usually a third. A guy named Dennis. They stay for a drink—one drink, that's it—and then they split."

"They look like bikers," Andy says.

"They look like *jerks*," Roger says.

"Be nice," she tells them both. "Not that it's any of your business but, actually, they're musicians, not bikers. And they're pretty good, too."

You peer back towards them as your mind begins to wander, one blurred swoosh: how does Gina know that they're good musicians? Has she seen them perform in a club? Live on a stage?

"You know," she is saying to Roger, "you shouldn't insult people you've never even met."

"I made an observation," he tells her. "They look like jerks. Hair hanging down their backs. Tattoos smeared on their arms. They're disgusting."

"Ssshh," she says. "You're going to get yourself beat up."

Roger flexes his shoulders; his chest. "By who? Those two clowns?"

You see Sharon returning with your drinks: your bourbon and two vodkas. You lay a twenty on the bar. This, you decide, will be your final drink of the night. It's getting late, almost one o'clock, and Roger is starting to worry you. He's been a disappointment to you this evening; his behavior is far from what you had anticipated. If anyone's mood was to go south, you'd have assumed it'd be Andy's. You turn Roger's way; the muscles of his face are overly relaxed; his jaw hangs lower than it should; his eyes are small, a glassy red.

"If they try something," Roger is telling her, "don't worry about it. I can handle myself." He curls the fingers of his right hand, clenching it into a fist. "You ever hear of *Tiger Strokes? Death Blows?* I've got some moves."

Gina laughs. "Oh, please," she says. "Give me a break. If you're trying to impress me, this is not the . . ."

Roger isn't listening. "I did my hitch in the army," he tells her. "I learned some moves." From his seat, he performs a few of these moves into the air, striking, you suppose, at imaginary windpipes and solar plexus.

It is hard to know if he is being serious or not; you certainly hope he isn't. On the chance he'd actually win a fight against those two, the consequences he'd face could be severe. Police would get involved; there'd be a prosecutor and a judge to deal with. The media might pick up on it. You visualize the headline in tomorrow's newspaper, big bold letters: YUPPIE GOES BESERK IN TOPLESS BAR. You imagine your company's mailroom guy, Lonnie, making a hundred copies of the article and circulating them around your building. Roger's career would stagnate; conceivably he'd lose his job. His family would be humiliated, his marriage stressed. You flash onto an image of him a few years from now: he'd have deteriorated into a burned-out, self-loathing alcoholic, sitting all alone in some shabby studio apartment, a vodka in one hand, a baloney and cheese sandwich in the other, recalling with anger and remorse his night out with the boys, realizing, as if for the first time, how cruel and how significant consequences can be.

"What's your name again?" Gina is asking him. "I think I forgot it."

Through the corner of his mouth, he tells her.

"Well, Roger, I think you should start taking happy pills or something. You have a very negative attitude on life."

"What're *happy pills*? Is that a code word for cocaine?"

She turns her head from one side to the other. "No, Roger, it's not a code word for cocaine. *Happy pills* is an expression. It means, cheer up. Life's a ball. Do something to improve your—"

"You've got cocaine?" Andy butts in.

Gina raises her palms into the air. "I didn't say that."

"I thought you did," Andy says. "I heard you say cocaine."

"Why do you ask? You want to score some?" She lowers her hands, raises her champagne glass to her lips and takes a sip. "If you want some, tell me. It's not that hard to find."

"Do you like the stuff?"

"Maybe I do," she laughs "and maybe I don't. What's it to you?"

Andy turns to you. "You ever try it, Chief? Cocaine?"

You shake your head, no. You've had your opportunities over the years but you were never interested enough to actually try it.

Gina laughs. "No offense, you guys, but don't you think you're a little old to be taking up cocaine? I mean, if you want some I could probably find—"

"*Gina!*" Sharon, standing behind the bar, arms folded at her chest, is staring into Gina's eyes. Sharon's mouth is taut, one straight line. "Cool it, okay?" Her voice is controlled; its tone is significant. She glances at your drinks and then walks to the far end of the bar, tends to another customer.

Gina purses her lips. "*Bitch,*" she mutters. To Andy she says, "Let's forget it, okay? Forget we mentioned it?"

Andy says nothing but Roger straightens himself in his seat. "Why's that?" he asks her. "You think we're narcs?"

Gina laughs. It is a harsh, disparaging laugh directed straight at his face. "No," she says. "I don't think you're a narc. A prick, maybe, but I don't think you're a narc."

"You don't like me," Roger says.

Gina takes another swallow of champagne. "As a matter of fact, you're right. I don't like you. I don't dislike you, either. I don't feel one way or the other about you."

"But you like Andy, right? You like Chief."

"They're nice. They're fun. All I've seen you do is sit here and pout. The few things I've heard you say have been negative. Besides," she informs him, "you're drunk. Drunks bore me to tears."

"I've had some booze," Roger tells her. "But I'm okay. I'm not drunk.'

"Well, you look drunk."

"It's been a long day. I've been up since five-thirty."

You take a sip of your bourbon and fuss again with your necktie. It's funny, you realize, the way a man will spend good money and half of his evening in order to get himself drunk and then, once someone mentions that, indeed, he has succeeded in his task, his first reaction will be to deny it. No, you think: one should never point out to a drunk that he is drunk. It is one of those unmentioned rules of etiquette, like "Never compliment a man on his toupee," or, to pursue the thought a step further, "Never compliment a woman on the fit of her girdle." Your analogy, of course, is inappropriate and your observation is in need of refinement but it pleases you just the same: you will have to work it into conversation sometime.

"Hey, Chief. . . ." Gina is leaning toward you in her seat as she lays a gentle palm onto your thigh. "Help us out here. I say Roger's drunk. He's telling me he's just tired. Who's right?"

You think for a moment. You want to be careful before speaking. Gina appears to be having a decent time for herself. Perhaps she, also, is a little drunk.

"You're both right," you say. "Roger's had his share to drink but he's also had a difficult day. We both had a hard one. Andy, too."

She laughs and slaps the bar. "Three grown men sitting behind desks, working in finance all day. Sorry to hear it, guys. It sounds really rough."

"Look who's talking," Roger says. "You couldn't even cut it as a typist."

"Hey," she laughs, "watch it!"

"Then keep quiet about my work. You're ranking on it."

"That's right," Andy puts in. "You're calling it wimp's work."

"I'm not calling it that. It's just that it's not *demanding* work, in a physical sense."

Roger takes a swallow of his drink, saying nothing. His face, same as before, is unhappy, a look of anger stretched across it.

"My point," she continues, "is that I could understand being tired if you had a job where you worked with your hands or stood on your feet all day. Like a mechanic or an electrician or a carpenter."

Roger puts down his glass. "What do you know about it?"

"Why are you getting so upset?"

"You shake your tits for a living," he tells her. "And hustle champagne. You don't know a thing about—"

"You're out of line," she warns him.

"And you're almost out of champagne. So do us all a favor and take a walk, huh?"

Gina lifts her glass from the bar, cocks her arm as if ready to splash its contents into Roger's face. Something, however, holds her back. "You're a prick," she tells him.

"You already told me."

"Well, you are. You're a prick bastard."

"*Aww*," is Roger's answer.

"You're a drunk, too," she lets him know. "An insecure lush."

"It's better than what you are."

"Which is?"

"A slut, of course. A prick-bastard slut." Roger lets go of a laugh and reaches for his drink.

Andy laughs with Roger, moves a step forward to stand beside him and lays a hand onto his shoulder. "A coke-snorting slut," Andy says. "Don't forget coke snorting."

"Who shakes her tits for a living," Roger adds, "and hustles champagne."

This is too much. "Shut up," you tell them. "What the hell is wrong with you?"

Gina has heard enough, herself. She grabs her shoes from the top of the bar and slips them onto her feet. "Such clever boys." Her look, what you can see of it, is one of confusion, her eyes beginning to tear.

You don't know how to play this. You want to support her, calm her somehow, take her into your arms and hold her and tell her something wise and sincere. But you don't. You watch as she lowers herself from the stool, as she smooths the black teddy down her hips and tightens the lace shawl across her shoulders. Her movements are unhurried, measured and somewhat graceful.

"Listen," she says, squeezing her way between you and Andy, "I've got to get back on stage. It's been nice, huh?"

And with that, just as simply and abruptly as that, she is gone. She glances at the table behind you, sees that her two musician friends have left, and then she heads to the rear of the bar, disappearing behind a door marked No Admittance. She will not hear Roger as he calls after her, "It's been fun chatting with you, Gina." Nor will she hear Andy as he calls out, "Hey, sexy, what about my cocaine?"

They crack up at this, Andy and Roger. They give each other a nudge, a high-five, getting boisterous, feeling good about themselves: male bonding.

"Aww, look," Andy says, pointing at Gina's champagne bottle. "Too bad. She didn't finish her bubbly."

"She'll be back," Roger tells him. "I think she liked me."

And, again, they crack up and give another nudge of the elbows, another high-five.

You say nothing. You look at them both, first at Andy, then at Roger.

"What . . . ?" Roger stares back at you. "You're siding with her? You heard what she said. She was ranking on us, Chief. On you, too. If she says me and Andy do wimp's work, she's saying the same about you."

Your impulse is to smack them both across their stupid faces and tell them to shut their mean stupid mouths. But you do not: they are your co-workers; in a way, they are your friends. *One should never tell a drunk that he is drunk*," you hear yourself say. You pause a moment and think it over. "It's one of those unmentioned rules of etiquette. Like, never compliment a man on his toupee. Or a woman on the fit of her girdle."

Andy smiles, perplexed by your remark, but he appears happy just to know that you are speaking with him. "Good one, Chief."

You return his smile and step towards the bar. You move Gina's champagne glass to the side. It is with a disheartened spirit that you take your next swallow of bourbon and it is with reservation that you slide into the seat Gina has just vacated, still warm with the heat of her body. You have half a drink remaining: finish it and get out of here.

November, 1988

nine
golden gloves

SONNY JOINED us about four years ago. He was just a kid then and didn't know any more about boxing than, say, your typical schoolyard bully might. He looked to be about eighteen the first day he walked into the gym and by the way he talked you could tell this was the first boxing school he'd ever set foot in. "Who's managing here?" he asked me. "I'm Sonny."

I pointed to the second of our three rings. "Over there. Al Bonchick."

"Thanks, Champ. I'll remember you in my will. This'll be—"

I grabbed onto his shoulder and pulled him back. "Al's coaching now. Don't bother him."

"Why not?" Sonny jerked his shoulder free of me but he had the sense not to head for Al's ring. I would have had to stop him. Al runs one of the better gyms in New York and it stays that way more from his selectivity of boxing talent than from any exceptional training skills on his part. One of my jobs is to help him find the good boxers; another is to keep the bad ones away. Sonny didn't have what it takes. Period.

"Why?" he was asking me now. "Because I'm skinny? Well, I'm not. I'm skinny like a whippet's skinny, that's how I'm skinny. Lean but quick." He examined my arms and shoulders which are rather large and then, with something like disgust, he looked at my chest. "A body like yours, it's good for lugging a piano up a staircase. For real boxing you need speed, reflexes, street smarts. Those, champ, are my credentials."

He was talking kind of loud, his voice popping and breaking like a veteran choirboy's. By the time I had told him to quiet down it was too late. A pair of heavyweights had gathered around and a quick-fisted Dominican named Luis was already throwing finger pokes at his rib cage. "Hey, Speedy, catch this." Luis threw another poke to Sonny's ribs and then an open palm across his cheek.

Sonny's face turned red in a hurry and his eyes glazed over in a way that made me wonder if he'd go straight for Luis's throat or if, instead, he'd break down and cry. Luis wasn't going anywhere in a professional way (nor, for that matter, were either of the two heavyweights by his side) but, just the same, he'd have taken Sonny out in a minute.

I wasn't given the chance to be proven right or wrong, however. "Up yours," Sonny said to him and then he started towards the ring where Al was training one of our few ranked fighters, Jim Lacey, in a sparring match against a large southpaw named Streaker.

"Hey, Al," Sonny called. "Al Bonchick. Mister Fight Manager. I want to talk with you."

Al didn't even look up. Lacey's fight was set for Friday and he'd need all the sparring time he could get.

"Mister Bonchick, sir, I'm talking to you. I can wait, you know. But I won't be waiting for long." Despite the half dozen NO SMOKING signs lined across each of the gym's four walls, Sonny struck a safety match against the sole of his shoe and raised it to a short, skinny hand-rolled cigarette centered between his lips. After his first drag on the cigarette he appeared calmer. A faint smell of marijuana hit the air a moment later. "Listen," he said. "Give me a chance, will you, Al? I'm just another punk fighter, right? But you're wrong. In a couple of years I—"

Al had stopped Lacey's sparring almost as soon as Sonny had calmed himself with the cigarette. He stared gravely, disbelieving what he was looking at. "You are puffing," he said quietly, "marijuana in my gymnasium."

Sonny removed the cigarette from his lips but he made no effort to put it out.

"Why are you doing this, young man? Puffing marijuana and harassing people you don't even know?"

Sonny dropped the cigarette to the floor and ground it out with his heel. "Listen, Al . . . Mister Bonchick . . . I want to be a fighter. I've got speed, reflexes. I've got—"

"Street smarts," Luis called out.

"I do. All of it. But I need training. Professional training. Without it, I'm a bum. With it, I think I could be something."

Al sent Lacey over to the speed bags, keeping his eye on Sonny.

"Mister Bonchick . . . Al . . . I know I'm skinny and probably not so bright, right? But I still got something. I know I got something. I want to put it to work."

Al ducked through the ropes of the ring and moved towards Sonny. "Yeah, you're skinny," he told him. "And, yeah, you're not so bright, either. But, still, you want to be a prize fighter, huh?" Al stood a foot from Sonny's face, staring straight into his eyes. "It's hard work, Kid. Misery sometimes."

"I wasn't expecting no game of pinball, Mister Bonchick."

"Alright, good. I'll tell you what to do, then. You see that broom over by my office there?"

"I see it."

"Well, you get that broom, right? And you sweep up all your ashes here and your little marijuana cigarette and your safety match and then you sweep the whole damn floor. You got that?"

Sonny nodded that he had.

"Good. Because then I want you to find the mop and the pail, see? And real careful-like, real slow, I want you to mop up all the sweat from the floor. And I want you to scrub the blood from the mats and the spit and the puke from every corner in this whole stinking gym. And then, hey, what's your name, anyway?"

"Sonny."

"And then, Sonny, when you're done with all of that, then we'll talk about it. Then we'll talk about you becoming a prize fighter."

~

As I said, that was about four years ago. Life here has slowed since then. Last March our meal ticket, Jim Lacey, went into retirement after slithering down and finally off the ranks as a contender. Luis has also left us, as have the two heavyweights who made their brief appearance in the beginning of our story.

Sonny, however, has stayed with us ever since. And while he hasn't quite made it into the ring as yet, every night after the floors have been swept and mopped and the mats have been cleaned of the blood and the spit and the puke and all of the corners of this whole stinking gym have been scrubbed, every night after Sonny has finished, he and Al get together in the back office, their feet on the desk, mugs of hot black coffee in their hands, and they do talk about it. They really do.

February, 1980

girl talk: a mystery

IT WAS a few minutes past noon when the telephone rang. I was alone, holding down the office. "Cornelius," I answered.

There was silence on the other end of the line: no dial tone, no background noise; just silence.

"Cornelius," I said again. "Can I help you?"

"Is this Victor? Victor Cornelius?"

"*Speaking*," I responded, accenting the word, giving it the professional tone.

"Your wife needs you, Victor. She needs you immediately."

I stood from my chair and grabbed a pencil from the top of the desk. "Who is this? What's going on?"

"Your wife needs you, Vic. Pronto."

The voice belonged to a woman. Its pitch was low, unnaturally so, a false baritone. It was not unlike the voice of a child attempting to imitate an adult when making a funny phone call.

"Who am I speaking to? Is this Christine?" Something fishy was going on. I wondered if the caller might be a friend of my wife. She knew a few characters, my wife, particularly a woman she'd recently befriended named Christine. "Is this Christine?" I asked again. "If it is, I'd like to know what's going on."

Whoever it was had begun to laugh. "Your wife needs you, Vic. It's a matter of life and death."

The words were ominous but the voice they were delivered with was not. The tone was softer now; gone was that artificial depth, that phony baritone. "Listen," I said, "what's this about? Is something wrong with Beth?"

Christine laughed into her end of the line. I recognized the voice now; it was definitely hers. I'd met her only a few times face-to-face but, being that I was the one who customarily answered the telephone at home, I had spoken with her frequently. She was a pleasant sort, always cheerful, with a flair, it seemed, for keeping things light. It was difficult, therefore, to know how seriously to take her at the moment. "If this is Christine," I said, "and you're putting me on . . ."

"Alright, Victor. Fine. You got me." A certain merriment tickled the back of her throat. "It's me, Christine. My Boris Karloff didn't throw you off, huh?"

"Is that who you were doing? Boris Karloff?"

"It needs work," she admitted.

"I don't know. It threw me off a little. For a second anyway." What, I wondered, were we doing? Were we honestly critiquing her skills of mimicry when my wife was supposed to be in dire need of my assistance? I dropped my pencil onto the desk and sat back into my chair. "Could we," I said, "get to the point, Christine?"

"Something's going on here, Vic. But I can't tell you what it is over the phone." Again, she laughed. Was she drunk? Stoned? Or simply having some fun with me? "Cut it out, Christine. Put Beth on."

"Nope. Come to the house. My house. As soon as possible."

"Chris, I can't just leave the office. What's going—"
Click.

I found her number in my address book under the letter *B: Beth's Friends.* I called her back quickly but, not too surprisingly, she didn't answer. I held on for an even dozen rings and then I held for a dozen more. I hung up the phone and dialed again. This time, however, the line was busy. She was up to some sort of mischief, I realized. If Beth had been in any real need of my help, Christine would have surely phoned me back. Nevertheless, I dialed her number once more (what else could I do?) and received, for my trouble, the same sharp busy signal. The brat had taken her phone off the hook.

As much as I disliked the idea of slipping away from the office, I did just that, grabbing my pager from the top drawer of my desk and clipping it onto my belt. I jotted out a note of explanation and stuck it onto my door.

Family emergency. Might be back. Might not.

Vic

It was a half hour's drive to Christine's house. As I approached it, I found myself getting more and more annoyed, initially with myself for getting suckered into this, but then, even more so, with Christine for doing the suckering.

Too much of it didn't make sense. What, for instance, were the two of them doing at her house, anyway? She and Beth were supposed to be at a dance class this afternoon, or an aerobics class, or a cooking class; I couldn't remember which. It was hard, these days, keeping track of all their activities. Beth had lost her job last November when her company relocated down south. She was given a decent sum of money upon termination, offered extended benefits and such. So, rather than find a new job immediately, she decided to take some time off for herself, have fun and relax a little. After bumming around the house for a month or so, she decided that she needed a change. She enrolled in a modern dance class at the local college. It would be a good form of exercise, we agreed, and, perhaps, it would "broaden her horizons" a little.

For better or worse, there, at the dance class, was where she had met Christine. They took to one another quickly. She invited Christine over for dinner that first week they'd met; Christine had us both into her own home the following week. Pretty soon they were engaging themselves in a variety of activities, keeping their calendars full: dance and aerobics classes, a cooking class, an art appreciation course. They were both in their early thirties, shared a similar wit and several common interests, and, perhaps most important, they were both bored housewives, even if Beth was planning to be one only temporarily.

203

It was almost one o'clock when I pulled into Christine's driveway. Her snazzy white Camaro was the only car in it. I looked over my shoulder back towards the street, expecting to spot, as if I might have missed it, Beth's blue hatchback parked near the curb. It wasn't there, however. Other than a yellow station wagon parked halfway down the road, the street was bare of cars.

It was a warm April afternoon, sunshine everywhere. I left my jacket in the back seat and shut the door behind me. This was the first time I had been to Christine's house in daylight. I took a look around. It was a quiet neighborhood. Ranch and split-level homes lined the block. I walked the steps to her front door and gave the brass knocker a few sharp raps. There was a button to the side of the door that I might have rang in order to be more civil but I wasn't feeling pleasant at the moment, that rush of irritability striking me again. She had no right, I told myself, playing games like that on the telephone, especially while I was at work. I wanted her to feel my mood now. For the hell of it, I rapped out a few more beats on the knocker, as if sharing her sense of urgency. Then I banged out a rhythm to the tune of Shave and a Haircut.

"I'm coming," she called from behind the door. "Give me a minute."

I kept at it, however. Three short raps, three long. Then another Shave and a Haircut . . . two bits.

"Who is—?" Christine both unbolted and swung open the door in the same swift movement. When she saw that it was me, she rested a hand on her hip and offered a cool, bemused smile. "Brother," she said. "Break down my door, why don't you?" Slowly, her smile grew warmer, fuller, revealing a thin, rather endearing gap between her two front teeth. She was an attractive woman, probably the cutest of all Beth's friends. She had a plump lower lip, a pair of perfect green eyes and straight reddish-brown hair that just touched the top of her shoulders. Her face, at the moment, appeared flushed and somewhat heated.

"What's up?" I asked her, offering her a smile of my own. "Is Beth alright?"

"Beth?" she asked me back.

"Yes. My wife. There's trouble of sorts?"

"No. Not trouble. Not necessarily."

"A matter, however, of life and death?"

She shrugged. "I guess I have a tendency to exaggerate, huh?"

I lowered my focus from her face to her body. The outfit she was wearing surprised me: a two-piece suit, soft pink. Beneath the jacket she was wearing a white, silk blouse; on her feet she wore a pair of white heels: not the type of outfit that one would normally wear when going to a dance or aerobics class.

She followed my eyes, lowering her focus as well. "What are you looking at?"

"Your suit," I said. Then, almost word for word, I repeated my thought to her: "It's not the type of outfit that one would normally wear to a dance or aerobics class."

She raised her eyes from the suit to look at me. "What if," she responded, "one were to do some shopping first? Or if *one* were planning to have a late lunch afterwards?" She was enjoying herself, that cool, bemused smile returning to her lips.

"Is that what you were planning to do? Some shopping and lunch?"

"No," she said. "Not really."

"Was the dance class canceled, then? Or are you just playing hooky?"

"Today's Friday," she let me know. "Art Appreciation. But you're right. I'm playing hooky."

We had worked ourselves into the front hallway. I closed the door behind me. "Is Beth here? I didn't see her car out front."

"She's here. I was in your neighborhood this morning. So, I picked her up."

"That was kind of you," I said, a little suspicious. I poked my head into the living room. No Beth, however, just a roomful of clean white furniture: a white leather couch and overstuffed chairs, two shiny white tables and deep white carpeting. It was the type of room I'm never quite comfortable in. I turned back to Christine. "Where is she?" I asked. "What's going on?"

She touched my hand and gave it a friendly pat. "It's good seeing you again, Vic. When was it? The last time we saw each other? Around New Year's, right?"

"Sometime around there," I said. She liked the chitchat, I noticed; it seemed to comfort her. I decided to play along for the time being.

"You look good," she told me. "You lost some weight. Not to suggest, of course, that you were overweight before." We were in the dining room now. An empty magnum of wine was set on the long oak table. Two wine glasses, both stained with lipstick, were set beside the bottle. Beth never had a head for booze, nor a stomach for it. Maybe that was what happened to her: she got sick.

"So," I said to Christine, "you two had some wine, I see."

"Would you like some? I have more in the refrigerator."

"Not right now," I told her. Then, as nonchalantly as I could, I said, "Where is Beth?"

"Not in the dining room," she answered, deadpan. "But let me check." Still playing games, she bent at the waist and peered under the table. "Nope. Not in the dining room."

I offered her one of my sterner faces and stared, without amusement, into her perfect green eyes. She was a fun girl and all but, quite honestly, her routine was growing tiresome. "Christine," I said, "what's going on?"

Lightly she ran her palm along the waistband of her skirt. "Beth is upstairs," she told me. "She's lying down."

"What's wrong with her? Sick?"

"No, I wouldn't say sick, necessarily."

"Woozy? From the wine?"

"I wouldn't say woozy either."

"Then why is she lying down?" My speech was quickening, growing impatient.

If Christine was aware of this she didn't seem to care. She rested her butt against the edge of the table, leaning into it. "Maybe this wasn't such a good idea. I shouldn't have called you. I screwed up your day."

"It's not important."

"I feel bad now. Because, you see, really there's nothing wrong with her. I sort of made up the whole thing, about it being an emergency and all. I ruined your day for nothing."

"But Beth also wanted you to call me, yes? She had a hand in it?"

"True,"

"And she is, of course, here?"

"Yes. Of course." She pointed a finger toward the ceiling. "She's upstairs."

"Then let's go see her."

"Let's don't. Let's wait." She straightened herself from the table and took a step toward me and then another until barely a foot of space separated her face from my own. She circled a long slender finger before my chest. Her breath was warm and sweet. A glint of playfulness touched her eyes as she lowered the finger and traced it along my necktie. "This is pretty," she told me as her pink fingernail brushed across it. "I like the pattern. Where'd you get it?"

We were about to veer again, I realized, from our topic of conversation. Nevertheless, I answered the question that had been posed to me. "It was a gift from Beth."

"Herbert only wears solids. I bought him a tie just like this once. He wouldn't wear it, though. He said it made him look *unserious*."

Herbert was her husband. He was a quiet, conservative type, several years her senior. "How's he doing?" I asked, not really caring. The question, however, seemed appropriate.

"Stuffy Herbert? He's doing just dandy, thank you. I'll let him know that you asked." She picked up the wine glasses and moved towards the kitchen. I tagged along, one step behind. "He liked you," she added, "that time you and Beth were over for dinner. He said you're a regular kind of guy. Down to earth. I think so, too."

She flipped on the kitchen light. "How about you? What was your opinion of Herbert?"

"I liked him fine. He's an interesting person."

"*Interesting*?" She stopped and gave me a look across her shoulder.

"Well, maybe interesting isn't the word. *Intelligent* might be better."

"Okay, then, let's call him that—'intelligent.'" She rinsed the glasses in the sink and placed them upside down in the dish drain. "So," she said, drying her hands with a paper towel, "you wanted to see Beth, right . . . ?" With an underhanded throw she tossed the paper towel into an open wastebasket several feet away. "*Two points*," she said, leading us out of the kitchen. We walked in silence through the dining room, back into the front hallway and then up the staircase. Her movements were slow, almost languid, the palm of her left hand just brushing the banister, her hips rolling softly as we climbed the staircase together. When we reached the second floor, she stood still for a moment and tinkered with the top button of her jacket. She did a stretching movement then, arms shoulder-high, stomach tucked in, her chest and bottom pushed out. She had a well-proportioned body: nothing too big nor too small. I had the feeling that she was not unaware of this herself. "I've been thinking, Victor, maybe I should go in first. You know? Spend a minute with Beth alone." She pointed towards a half-opened door on the right side of the hall. "It might be better this way."

Her reasoning wasn't entirely clear to me but I didn't object. Somehow, we were still making progress.

She headed down the hallway and gave a little wave of the fingers, a bye-bye wave, and then disappeared into the room. "Hi," I heard her say cheerfully. "Vic's here."

The door closed behind her, clicking shut. I took a few steps forward and lingered just outside the room, hoping to hear their voices, sounds of movement, wanting to get a sense of what was going on. I heard nothing, however; nothing at all. Quietly, with hands in my pockets, I paced the hallway, glancing idly into the other rooms on the floor. There were six of them altogether: a bathroom, a study, an exercise room, two small bedrooms and the room she and Beth occupied now, probably the master bedroom. Although I had been inside this house before, this was my first time on the upper floor; I'd never been given the official tour.

"Vic?" Christine called from behind the closed door. "We're ready for you."

I turned as the door opened. She was no longer wearing her jacket. The shoes were gone from her feet. She wore only the pink skirt, stockings and the white silk blouse which, I noticed, had been opened a button or two since seeing her last.

"Do something for me," she said. "Close your eyes, okay? Before coming in?"

Her voice was firm but her face was playful. Once again it was tough knowing how serious she was being with me. I decided, however, to be a sport and go with her flow, closing my eyes and holding them shut.

"Okay, good." She worked her hand into mine and led me slowly into the bedroom. Her skin felt moist in my own, almost sticky. "Keep them closed," she instructed as we came to a halt. "No peeking."

I heard the rustling of sheets, a creaking of bedposts. A soft moan sounded; it was from Beth. "Damn it, Christine," I heard her say, low and muffled. "You really called him, didn't you? I don't believe this."

"Well," she said, releasing my hand, "that's what you wanted. You asked me to."

"I know I did," Beth told her. To me she said, "Vic? Do me a favor. Don't look over here please. Just leave the room without opening your eyes. Do that for me and I'll owe you for the rest—you bastard! Why'd you . . . ?"

I had, of course, opened my eyes. There was no chance of keeping them shut; no chance of simply walking out of the room.

"Stop smiling." Beth said. "It's not funny."

Was I smiling? If, indeed, this was true, it was more from confusion than from any degree of glee. There she was, Beth, my wife of eight years, lying face-down on a large brass bed, her wrists and feet tied to its brass bars with four separate scarves. A bottle of baby oil and a folded towel were lying close to her leg. She was wearing a black half-slip, a black bra and nothing more. I couldn't see her face; her long brown hair covered it from me, its length spreading halfway across the pillows. "Beth," I said, "what's going on?"

A groan of embarrassment was her only response.

"What are you two doing?"

She let out another groan and then a sigh. "It's not my fault," she told me, lifting her head to face me. "It's Christine's. She seduced me."

"It's true," Christine said, her voice rather matter-of-fact. She was standing to my left, still at the door. "I seduced her, Victor."

Beth lowered her head onto the pillow. "It started harmlessly . . . with *girl talk*." She emphasized the words with her hands, opening and closing her fingers, wrapping them around the bars of the bed.

"With girl talk," I repeated, not quite understanding.

"Yes," Christine put in. "Girl talk. You know how it is, Vic . . ."

I attempted a smile. "Like, *Those are pretty scarves, Christine. Would you mind tying me to the bed with them? Spread-eagled?*"

"Ha, ha," my wife said without humor.

"He thinks it's funny," Christine said.

"I know he does."

"You think it's funny," Christine told me.

I loosened my tie and undid the button of my collar. Actually, no, I didn't think it was funny, not in the least. I wasn't, however, ready to burst into a rage, either. Beth raised her head from the pillow, straining a bit at the effort. "Don't get upset, Vic. We haven't really done anything yet."

"No?"

Christine stepped toward me. "That's why I called you," she said, answering for my wife. "Beth wouldn't let it go any further. Not until you joined us."

"Any further?" I asked. To Beth I said, "I thought you said you hadn't done anything yet."

"Barely anything," Christine said.

From the bottom of her throat, Beth released another groan. "*Anything*, Chris. We didn't do *anything*."

Christine walked past me and sat at the edge of the bed next to the bottle of oil and the towel. She patted the back of Beth's thigh. "How about the massage, then? That's what I was talking about, Beth, when I said 'barely anything.'"

"Alright, that's true, Vic. She gave me a massage. I admit it."

I looked at the two of them: Beth, in her slip and bra, tied to the brass bars of the bed, her friend's palm resting against the back of her bare thigh. "And what about the bondage?" I asked. "The scarves?"

Christine laughed.

Beth tightened her grips on the bars. "It's not bondage," she told me. "*Jesus!*"

Christine patted her thigh once again. The gesture was soft, meant to comfort. "Listen, Victor, the scarves are easy to explain. While I was giving her the massage and touched her anywhere lower than her shoulders she started giggling and squirming around. She kept slapping my hands away, covering herself up."

I nodded, stone-faced. "So you tied her to the bars of the bed. Spread-eagled."

Beth let out another of her groans. "Stop saying that. *Spread-eagled.* It sounds perverted."

I ignored her, keeping my attention on Christine. "And after securing her to the bed, you continued with the massage. That was the extent of it?"

"Victor," Beth said, blowing again at her hair, "it's not like we were doing S and M together."

Christine leaned towards my wife and brushed the hair from her face. "But it did give us a kick," she told her. "Tying you up. You've got to admit that."

Beth raised her head, her blue-gray eyes looking as vulnerable as I'd ever seen them. To Christine she said, "Why are you doing this? Why are you trying to get me in trouble?"

Christine touched me with the sole of her foot, resting it against the top of my knee. Its warmth, its pressure, felt almost cozy. "She's not in trouble, is she, Vic?"

"Nothing happened," my wife said. "That's why we called y— ouch!"

Christine, with the full force of her hand, landed a sharp slap onto the center of my wife's ass. "Give it a break," she told her. "And stop lying to your husband. Stop sugar-coating everything for him."

"What if it was your husband that was here? Frumpy Herbert? And you—"

"*Stuffy* Herbert," Christine corrected.

"God," Beth said and pushed her face deeper into the pillow. "I feel so dumb." Her voice was low, muffled. She tugged again at the scarves holding her wrists and groaned into the pillow once more.

I moved to the head of the bed and examined the blue-and-white scarf that held her left hand. Its knot, in a way, didn't surprise me; it was a single knot tied loosely around the wrist, easy enough to escape if she cared to. I glanced at the scarves that held her feet at the other end of the bed; same thing: both scarves were single-knotted, both of their loops offering plenty of slack, a cinch to work free of.

She lifted her head to face me, that vulnerable look back in her eye. "What are you doing?"

My hand was on the knot of the blue and white scarf. "What did you want me to do, Beth? What did you have in mind for us?"

"I don't know. I thought I did."

"Tell him," Christine said.

"I feel so stupid."

"Tell him what we had planned, the reason we called him here." When Beth said nothing, Christine looked at me. "You know, Vic, it's your fault, too. I hope you realize that."

I held her look, offering no response.

"You corrupted her. Sort of."

"Corrupted," I repeated. "How's that?"

"Not that you meant to. But you did. With those movies you rent and bring home from the video store."

"Movies," I repeated, without emotion.

"She told me about how you watch them together. On Saturday nights."

I didn't respond, surprised a little that Beth would share with her anything as personal as that, as our watching the occasional porn movie together. To an extent, however, hearing it from her helped give me a clue as to how this might have all started. Once they arrived here at the house, they had opened the wine. It was still early, sometime, probably, around ten-thirty. The alcohol, therefore, would have affected them a little stronger than it might otherwise have; it would have reached their libidos a little more quickly. The conversation would have flowed more freely after that, bouncing from one topic to the next. Eventually the subject of sex would have been introduced. It might have started on Christine's end with a rundown, perhaps, on how straight and how predictable making love with Stuffy Herbert can often be. Beth, hopefully, would have countered with something like, "Things are pretty good with Victor and me. Vic's okay." And from there the conversation would have taken off: Have you ever done this? Have you ever done that? Yes, once. No, never that. How about *blank*? Or *blankety-blank*? No, but I've thought about it. . . . Really? You've honestly thought about doing it with another . . . ? Yes, I've seen it in movies, these X-rated ones Vic brings home on Saturday nights.

Again, of course, this is only guesswork on my part. I am one of those men who, quite honestly, haven't the vaguest idea of how women actually speak with one another when they're alone. In fact, I am always shocked when Beth relays to me a conversation about how one friend's sex life is nonexistent or how another friend got a urinary tract infection because she let some Romeo pour a jar of honey all over her private parts. Really? I think, semi-amazed. She told you that? Women actually talk about things other than clothes and shampoo and recipes?

I took a look around the bedroom. It was twice the size of Beth's and mine and had chalk-white walls, a couple of large white dressers and a rich brown vanity and, set in front of the vanity, a low back chair. Draped over the chair was Beth's green dress.

I pulled the car keys from my front pocket. It disturbed me more than a little spotting her dress over the chair like that. I jingled the keys in my palm and squeezed gently on the ring.

"What . . . ?" Christine's eyes flashed onto mine as if the sound of the keys had awakened her from a short snooze. "You aren't getting ready to leave, I hope." She was still on the bed, sitting cross-legged next to my wife. Her feet were drawn beneath her; her pink skirt hiked to a point just above mid-thigh. "You're not going to walk out on us like this, Victor. I hope you realize that."

Beth turned her head towards me. Her fingers were still wrapped around the bars of the bedpost. She took in a long breath of air and released it. "Listen, Vic, the reason Chris called you . . ."

"He knows why I called. He's not dumb." Christine said this with a smile but her voice was rather matter of fact. With the tip of her tongue, she moistened her lips. "You've figured it out, Vic. You don't have to play innocent."

I shifted my eyes from their faces to the bottle of baby oil lying on top of the folded towel.

"Victor," Christine said, "it's not like we did anything wrong. It's not like Beth was actually cheating on you."

"Definitely not," Beth told us both, sounding just a tad indignant.

"That's why we called you here," Christine said. "To get your permission, sort of. And to include you in it. If you felt like it."

"To include me," I repeated. "That was thoughtful."

"I thought so." She turned to Beth. "Don't you think it was?"

"I sure do," she replied.

Christine stood from the bed to face me. "Do you know how many men would kill for an opportunity like this? To make love to a couple of women like us?

"No," I said. "How many?"

"You find me attractive. I know you do. And I know, from what Beth tells me, that you have a pretty good imagination about these types of things."

I didn't answer her. Too much had been said already. I leaned across the bed and loosened the scarf holding Beth's left hand.

"Victor," she said, "stop it!" Beth kept her hand where it was, fingers wrapped around the brass bar as if she was still tied to it. She turned to Christine. "Maybe you should try seducing him like you did me."

Christine lowered her eyes and smiled. "Really? You think so?"

"He likes you. I can tell."

"And you're okay with it?"

"Do anything you want. Just make it quick. I'm starting to get stiff here."

With a certain assurance, a new attitude, Christine placed one foot carefully in front of the other. Softly, she bit her lower lip. "You're not going to brush me off now, are you, Vic?"

"Don't worry," Beth told her, lifting her head to observe us. "He won't."

"Because if you do, Victor, I'll be crushed. Devastated . . . I'll have to sic my cat on you."

I feigned a look of surprise. "You have a cat? I didn't know that."

"His name is Oscar. He'll be three next week. But let's stay focused, okay?" She traced a finger across my cheek. "Let's not fight each other. We'll have some fun. You and me and Beth."

I made no move towards her but I didn't back away, either. I felt the tips of her fingers dance across my shoulder and then the coolness of her palm as it settled onto the back of my neck. She ran her other hand behind me and took a half step closer, leaning forward that extra inch, and soon her breast was pressing against me, warming my chest. She brought her lips to my own. They were wet, a little sweet, tasting faintly of wine. "Mmm," she growled. "You see? This isn't so—"

"*Hey . . .*" Beth lifted her face from the pillow. "No kissing! Nobody said you could kiss."

Christine stared at her, astonished, her mouth a large O. "Are you serious?"

"Yes, I'm serious. He's my husband."

"So?"

"So, nothing. Seduce him like you did me."

"How? With a massage?"

"Yes. What's wrong with a massage?"

"He doesn't want his *back* rubbed, Beth." Christine looked at me, her lips parted into a grin. "Is that what you want, Victor? A back rub? Because, like we told you, that's the way me and your wife got started."

"What's *that* supposed to mean?" Beth asked.

Christine shook her head. "Jesus! Now what's wrong?"

"You said, 'That's how we got started.' Implying something more followed. That's *all* that got started, Chris. A back rub. That's *all* that we did."

"Come on. Vic doesn't want to hear that whole thing again."

"Well, it's the truth. That's all that took place. And then you left me for an hour, tied to this hard as a rock bed, waiting for him to get here."

"Brother," Christine muttered to me, "touchy, isn't she?" To Beth she said, "All right, I won't kiss him, okay? We'll do it without kissing."

"Fine," she said and returned her head to the pillow. "Thank you."

Christine moved closer to me. "Okay, Victor, we're going to try again. We're going to recover." She placed her hands on my shoulders, her fingers touching me lightly as I stood motionless before her. It was an awkward embrace, rather one-sided. Her eyes had a new cast to them: they were uncertain, hesitant. "So, Vic, what's up? Do you think one of my world-famous massages will do the trick? Put you in the mood?"

From the bed, Beth let out a short hoot. "Yeah, right. *World famous!*"

Christine turned from me to Beth. "What is your problem now? Why are you making this so difficult?"

"I'm sorry," Beth answered, blowing the hair from her face. "Please, go back to what you were doing. Seducing my husband. Don't mind me."

"If you want me to stop, just say so. We'll switch places. You can tie me to the bed and I'll bark out the orders."

"No, really. I beg your pardon. Just ignore me."

"I'll try," Christine told her, "but, come on, huh? No interrupting. I'm starting to lose my mojo here."

In spite of herself, through half-closed lips, Beth muttered the word mojo. And then, with a soft laugh, she repeated it again, "*Mojo.*"

This time Christine was able to block her out. She wrapped her arms back around me, wriggled herself in closer and pushed up on her toes. "Come on," she whispered softly, "snuggle me back."

I looked into the mirror on the vanity. Through its reflection I could see Beth observing us from that odd posture she continued to hold on the bed: her head lifted, her neck craned and her left hand, the one that I had untied just minutes before, still grasping the brass bar of the bed.

Christine nuzzled her face against my chest. Her hair smelled fresh and flowery, as did her body. Her weight shifted and so did mine until we were flush against one another. I raised my hands to the blades of her shoulders and then lowered them to the center of her back.

"There," she said, "that's better. I knew you'd come around."

I held her as tightly as she held me, lowered my mouth to her ear and gave its lobe a nip.

"Careful," she giggled. "The rules, Vic. Remember? No kissing."

Keeping my mouth close to Christine's ear, I said to Beth, "How about nibbling? Is nibbling allowed?"

Beth stirred on the bed and let out another of her moans as she coughed into the pillow.

Turning from right to left, I brushed Christine's nose with the tip of my own. "How about Eskimo kisses," I asked Beth. "They're allowed, aren't they?"

I could hear squeaks from the bed frame; Beth growing restless, agitated. "You know," she said, "I don't think I'm enjoying this as much as I thought I would." She let go of the brass bar and brought her free arm to her side. "Maybe we should forget it, okay? Forget the whole thing." With her left hand, she unknotted the scarf that held her right hand, slipping free of it in one easy move.

Christine separated herself from me. Her face lacked joy: it had the frown of a hostess whose party had fallen apart before dinner had even been served. She looked towards the bed. "Let's give it a while longer, Beth. Okay?"

My wife reached for the scarves that held her feet to the lower posts of the bed. She undid them casually, one at a time. "I'm sorry," she told Christine. "It's not working. I'm more jealous than I realized."

"But there's nothing to be jealous about."

"Don't get me wrong. It was a good idea at the time. With the wine and the talk . . . but I guess I'm not as sophisticated as I imagined. Or as secure." With that, my wife swung her legs over the side of the bed and stood up straight, smoothing down her short black slip and fussing with her bra.

I took a couple of paces towards her, grabbed the dress draped over the chair and handed it to her.

She stepped into it quickly, without fanfare. "Could you zip me?" she asked, pointing at the bare V of her back.

I moved forward to assist. "God," she said to us both, "I'm never going to live this one down."

"Don't say that," Christine told her. "You will. Eventually."

Beth shook her head. "Well, if you had seduced my husband properly, like we'd planned, maybe I wouldn't be feeling so dumb right now."

"Oh, so, it's my fault?"

"There wasn't much I could do to help, Chris. Thanks to you, I was tied up at the time. Spread-eagled."

Christine dismissed her with a wave of the hand. "My sister, Anna," she said, changing the subject, "had a threesome once. She told me it was a lot of fun. No regrets at all."

Beth perked up. "I didn't know you have a sister."

"We're not that close. She was mean to me a lot, especially when we were young. A couple of years ago she married a gym teacher named

Fred. It's kind of mellowed her out. They're planning on having a baby soon."

"I don't think I could ever marry someone named Fred."

Christine made a face. "It's not as bad as being married to someone named Herbert."

"Don't say that. Herbert's a nice name. *Herb . . . Herbie.*" Beth moved to the vanity and checked her face in the mirror, fluffing her hair with the tips of her fingers. "It's getting late. Do you guys feel like lunch?"

Christine looked into the mirror, too. "There's that Sushi place we're always talking about. But I'm okay with whatever you want."

"I read an article last week about raw fish. It was kind of scary."

I felt my pager start to vibrate against my hip. It was time to be heading back to the office. I glanced at my watch: one thirty-five. A week from now, while lying awake in bed at midnight, unable to sleep, I'd probably be looking back on this afternoon fondly, my imagination running freely with its possibilities. But, for now, as I leaned against the bedroom wall, all I could do was watch and listen as they talked about family and friends and food and restaurants. . . . They were a mystery to me, those two. Most girls are.

March, 1989

eleven
fillers

TIMMY? What'd I do? What happened?

He's dead, man. You killed him.

Charlie covers his face. He's sitting on the pavement, knees in the air. Don't shit me, man. . . . Shit.

She's losing it. She's bouncing off the walls. Screw it, she says. She crosses town, goes to her mother's place, rings the buzzer.

What do *you* want?

I got to talk to you, Mom.

Her mother lets her in, walks back to the kitchen, ignoring her, returning to her potatoes, cutting them up, pretending like she isn't there, waiting for her to talk.

Mom, she says, I need money. I'm starving. I haven't eaten in days.

I gave you twenty Saturday. You said that'd be it, never again.

I was robbed. Three men rob—

You're hungry? There's bread in the cabinet. Help yourself. I don't have any more money.

She stuffs a piece of bread into her mouth, the whole slice, make the bitch happy. Mom, you've got money. I know you got some.

Not for *you*. Get it? Now finish eating and leave or your mother is going to cry.

Time's right. She lays a hand on her mother's shoulder. Please, Mom. I've got to live. I've got nothing for myself. I've got . . .

She follows her mother into the living room and watches her reach under the couch for the purse.

Now this is all that I have, understand? It's eleven dollars. And I don't want you buying any crap with it.

No, Mom. I won't.

Good. Now take it and go. Before your boy gets home and sees you here.

This job sucks. He lowers the press, drills his hole and makes another widget.

I hear McCann's leaving next month. You should try out for his position. You'd have a good shot at it."

Are you joking? That's all I need: me . . . a supervisor. I've got enough problems working in this dump, as it is. You want me looking after twenty snot-nosed mopes, too?"

"How about Sales? They've got an opening in Bridgeport. The pay's pretty—"

"*Sales*? And what? Go home with an ulcer every night? No thank you."

"Administration's always got openings. Take a couple of night courses and try—"

"Be real, huh? Eight hours a day behind a friggin' desk? I'd go nuts." He lowers the press, drills his hole and makes another widget. "This job sucks."

Dad? Does God have a heinie?

I don't know. Ask your mother.

~

We received a report concerning a disturbance.

A disturbance, officer? No. Everything's fine.

Your name, sir?

My name? It's Johnny Philips, officer.

Why are you holding that hammer, Johnny?

This one? I was doing some hammering. I was hammering some nails.

Why is there blood on your hand, Johnny?

Blood? On *this* hand?

What's wrong with your friend, Johnny? Why's he lying on the floor? Is he feeling alright?

Who? Him? Yeah, he's feeling okay.

You got a lawyer, Johnny?

~

Tuckahoe—

A town where it is always raining
But no one carries an umbrella.

Tuckahoe—

A town where it is either too cold
Or too hot
But no one wears an overcoat
Or short pants.

It's good. I see what you're going for. But there's—I can't quite put my finger on it, exactly—but there's something . . . just . . . not . . . right.

~

STOP
    reading
    these so
    fast

They will
    lose
    their
    effect

~

3:47 *WABC radio*. You're on the air.

Bob Grant? This is Jerry from Lyndhurst.

What would you like to talk about, Jerry?

Well, Bob, I'd like to talk—how are you, by the way?

I'm fine, Jerry. What's on your mind?

Well, Bob, I'd like to talk about our public school system. I think it stinks.

I agree with you, Jerry. Is there—?

But, Bob, I think the system has some good and caring teachers in it, too. And some fine young students. God bless them, Bob—black, white, yellow and polka dot. Thank you. That's all I wanted to say.

5:14 *WFAN*. You're on the air.

Mike? This is Jerry from Lyndhurst. Thank you for taking my call. In their respective day, who do you think was the superior ballplayer? Willie Mays or Johnny Bench?

Willie Mays. No question about it.

6:23 *WNYK*. You're on the air.

Bruce? This is Jerry from Lyndhurst.

Hi, Jerry. What song would you like to hear?

I'd like to request *Sunshine Lollipops* by Leslie Gore.

Sorry, I don't think we have that one, Jerry.

Does that mean I win something?

7:12 *WABC Money Talk Radio.*

Bill Bresnan? This is Jerry from Lyndhurst. I was hoping to get your opinion on my financial situation.

Okay, Jerry. Shoot

Well, Bill, I've got ninety thousand dollars in CDs, forty thousand in mutual funds, a hundred and thirteen thousand in government-backed securities. I've got nine hundred shares of IBM and own four rental properties in Essex County that net me about three thousand a month apiece. Also I own my own home. It's valued at close to a quarter of a million.

Are you retired, Jerry?

Yes, I am, Bill. I collect eight hundred and thirty a month in Social Security. Another fourteen hundred from my pension. And, last time I checked, I've got close to three hundred thousand in IRAs.

You're in good shape, Jerry. Nothing to worry about.

Todd's a wiseass. I swear to God.

We're in his Volkswagen, smoking a joint, driving along that dirt road by the farm where the horse path comes out and we see these two middle-aged ladies, around fifty years old, riding on these two huge horses. The horses are trotting a little fast, but not too fast, and Todd rolls down his window and calls out, "Slow down, ladies . . . or you're going to break your hymens."

I cracked up. I couldn't help it.

～

Phil? This is Benny.

Hey, Benny. What's up?

I was at the White Owl last night. Down in Yonkers?

Sure. I know it.

And I saw your wife there . . . with this young dude. They were getting kind of friendly towards each other, if you know what I mean.

We've been having some problems lately, Benny.

I know. She told me about them. But you should have seen her. Her hands were all over the guy. It was a little out of place, you know? She was looking kind of loose.

Yeah, well, she gets like that sometimes, especially when she drinks. . . . Listen, Benny, thanks for the call, huh?

Sure, Phil. Any time.

～

I can't believe it. Kevin gave me a hickey. Right on the tit.

You're fooling around with Kevin?

Yeah. And now I got my date with Ronnie tonight. He's going see it. He's going to kill me.

Can't you cover it with makeup?

Look at it. It's huge. She lifts her shirt, pulls the tit from her bra and shows it to Donna. What am I going to do?

Donna looks at the tit, the purple brown hickey. I guess you'll have to keep your top on. If you screw Ronnie tonight, don't take off your shirt.

No way. Ronnie *loves* my tits.

Then cancel the date, Donna tells her. She takes a moment and thinks it over. Tell him you can't make it and that you'll see him next week.

You're right. I'll call him up and say I'm feeling sick or something.

Donna looks at her; she's still holding up her shirt, the tit still plopped out of her bra. What a dope.

Oops. You're writing another filler, aren't you? And I just walked in on it.

That's alright. Have a seat, I said.

What are these things, anyway? You call them fillers but aren't they more like outtakes? Like bloopers, sort of?

No, I said. Not really. Each one should stand complete on its own.

Like poems? Except punctuated? Is that what you're going for?

Not really. Think of them more as snapshots.

That sounds cool. Snapshots. Is that why you're putting them into your book? To be cool? Sort of hip?

It might be, I said. I haven't thought about it much.

And what about this one? Do you think you'll include this one in your book?

Possibly, I said. Unless I come up with something better.